"You know, John E  **careful, I could red** **having you aroun**

"Would that be a bad thing?"

She set the glass on the table, considering the question. "If you were going to stick around long-term, maybe not. But if you're just some stranger passing through—"

He didn't say anything, looking down at his plate of food. "I don't know what happens next," he admitted.

"Then maybe we should just keep things casual," she said, swallowing an unexpected rush of disappointment. "No strings, no expectations. No taking things too far."

He followed her to the door when she started to leave, catching her hand. "Does kissing count as taking things too far?"

STRANGER
IN COLD CREEK

PAULA GRAVES

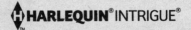

For my mom. Who still makes it possible to live my dreams.

ISBN-13: 978-0-373-69891-2

Stranger in Cold Creek

Copyright © 2016 by Paula Graves

The publisher acknowledges the copyright holder
of the additional work:

What Happens on the Ranch
Copyright © 2016 by Delores Fossen

Recycling programs
for this product may
not exist in your area.

HARLEQUIN®
www.Harlequin.com

Printed in U.S.A.

CONTENTS

Paula Graves, an Alabama native, wrote her first book at the age of six. A voracious reader, Paula loves books that pair tantalizing mystery with compelling romance. When she's not reading or writing, she works as a creative director for a Birmingham advertising agency and spends time with her family and friends. Paula invites readers to visit her website, paulagraves.com.

Books by Paula Graves

Harlequin Intrigue

The Gates: Most Wanted

Smoky Mountain Setup
Blue Ridge Ricochet
Stranger in Cold Creek

The Gates

Dead Man's Curve
Crybaby Falls
Boneyard Ridge
Deception Lake
Killshadow Road
Two Souls Hollow

Bitterwood P.D.

Murder in the Smokies
The Smoky Mountain Mist
Smoky Ridge Curse
Blood on Copperhead Trail
The Secret of Cherokee Cove
The Legend of Smuggler's Cave

Visit the Author Profile page at Harlequin.com for more titles.

STRANGER IN COLD CREEK

—

PAULA GRAVES

CAST OF CHARACTERS

John Blake—Lying low in a sleepy Texas town while recovering from gunshot wounds, the last thing the Gates agent needs is a brand-new mystery crashing into his life.

Miranda Duncan—Injured when her police cruiser is run off the road by an unknown assailant, the deputy finds herself turning to a mysterious stranger for help.

Delta McGraw—Miranda's prickly friend has a history of secrets. Could one of those secrets be the reason she's gone missing? And are Delta's secrets behind the attempt on Miranda's life?

Gil Duncan—Miranda's father has never been completely at peace about her decision to work in law enforcement.

Miles Randall—The Barstow County sheriff wants Miranda to steer clear of the Delta McGraw investigation, especially when there's a disturbing break in the case.

Coy Taylor—The sheriff's department desk sergeant took the call that lured Miranda into an ambush. Could he hold a clue to her assailant's identity?

Jasper Layton—The dead man's secrets may have been part of a blackmail scheme involving Delta.

Jarrod Whitmore—The son of a wealthy rancher may have committed a hit-and-run homicide—and Delta was blackmailing him to keep the secret. If he believes Miranda knows his secret, too, will he kill to keep it hidden?

Chapter One

The tinkle of the bell attached to the front door of Duncan's Hardware heralded the arrival of a new customer, though on this frigid March day in the Texas Panhandle, the gust of icy wind blowing through the entryway would have been plenty of warning by itself.

In the fasteners aisle, John Blake winced as the cold seeped under the collar of his jacket and seemed to attach itself to his mending collarbone. The gnawing pain stole his breath for a moment before settling into a bearable ache.

The new arrival was a woman. Tall and rangy, with hair the rusty color of Georgia clay and worn in a simple ponytail, she had alert eyes the color of the gunmetal sky outside. Her rawboned features, free of makeup, were more interesting than beautiful.

She nodded at Gil Duncan, the proprietor, and scanned the shop with those sharp gray eyes, her gaze settling on John and narrowing.

He looked away, feigning a lack of interest, though every nerve in his body tingled to attention.

He felt more than saw her approaching him, but he didn't look away from the boxes of screws he was studying.

"You're new in town."

John looked up at her, finding himself the object of those smoky eyes. Close up, her gaze was sharp, her expression intelligent and curious. She also gave off an air of authority, and he thought the word *cop* even before she flipped open her jacket to reveal the six-pointed star badge of the Barstow County Sheriff's Department.

"Yes, I am," he answered with a mild smile. He was barely an inch taller than she was, and in his current condition, he was fairly sure she could take him down without much trouble. Cooperation was by far the smarter option for him, especially since he wasn't looking to draw much attention to himself during his hopefully brief stay in Cold Creek, Texas.

"You're that fellow who's renting the Merriwether place on Route 7?"

"Yes, ma'am."

Her lips twitched a bit at his polite response. "You're from…North Carolina?"

Not a bad guess, he thought. "Tennessee."

She gave a nod. "How do you like Cold Creek so far?"

"It's quiet. Been chilly since I got here."

"That won't last," she warned with a friendly smile that displayed a set of straight, white teeth. She was prettier when she smiled, he decided. "If you're plannin' on stayin' long, that is."

Was that her way of asking whether he was going to stick around? "So I hear. Hopefully it's a little less humid than where I'm from."

The musical tone of her laugh caught him by surprise. "You can bank on that. But it's windy as all get out, so you need to take care with any open flames. Doesn't take long for a fire to get out of control in these parts."

"Hey, Miranda, I got those two-by-fours you ordered

in the back," the florid-cheeked man at the front counter called out. "Wanna meet me back there with your truck?"

"Be right there, Dad," she called before turning back to John. "I'm Miranda Duncan." She grinned before adding, "Of the hardware Duncans."

He laughed. "John Blake. Of the accounting Blakes," he said in return, wondering if she could tell he was speaking the truth.

It had been a while since he'd used his real name. But Quinn had suggested it, since the people who might want to do him harm knew him by other names. Nobody he'd crossed recently would connect him to some guy named John Blake who lived in Cold Creek, Texas.

Miranda cocked her head for the briefest moment before she smiled at him again. "Welcome to Cold Creek, John Blake. Hope you'll like it here." She headed back out the door, letting in another blast of icy wind that made his bones hurt.

Damn shame, he thought, that he rather liked the red-haired deputy, because the last thing he needed to do while he was recuperating in Cold Creek was to make friends with a local cop.

He was here to stay out of sight and let his bones and muscles mend.

In that order.

Gathering up the screws and bits he'd need to repair the wind-battered storm windows of the rental house, he paid at the front counter and headed out to the old Ford pickup Alexander Quinn had purchased for his time here in Texas. The plates were from Garza County, a couple of hours south, registered in the name of a construction company called Blanchard Building. It belonged to an old friend of Quinn's, who apparently owed the man a favor.

If anyone asked, John Blake's name was on the payroll as a carpenter, and the repair work he was doing on the rental house was all part of the cover.

Quinn was nothing if not thorough.

The wind was strong and icy, hinting there was snow hiding behind the flat gray clouds that hung low over the ridgeline to the east. To the west, there was nothing but scrubland and sky as far as the eye could see.

John tugged the collar of his jacket closed and hurried to climb into the truck, grimacing at the steady drumbeat of pain in his bones. Maybe he should have checked the weather report this morning before he planned a day of manual labor.

The last thing his aching bones needed was snow.

LOOKED LIKE THE weatherman was right, Miranda thought as she gazed at the lowering gray sky overhead. They were getting snow this afternoon.

She pulled the truck into the parking lot outside the Cold Creek Municipal Complex, suppressing a smile as usual when she read the building's name on the large sign out front. The single-story rectangular brick building housed a small courtroom, the mayor's tiny office and the four-room Barstow County Sheriff's Department. There wasn't anything complex about this little dot on the sprawling Texas map, and with more and more young people leaving for the bigger towns and cities, Cold Creek might not be a dot on the map much longer.

Sheer stubbornness was all that had kept Miranda in the panhandle, herself. Stubbornness and a marrow-deep love of the land of her birth. She knew everyone in Cold Creek like old friends.

Well, almost everybody.

It was rare for Cold Creek to have new folks in town. Maybe in a bigger city, like Dallas or Houston, John Blake would blend into the crowd. He had that kind of face—pleasant features but nothing that made him stand out. His hair was neither long nor short, neither dark nor fair, and his skin tone was medium. He wasn't short, but he wasn't tall, either—only an inch or two taller than she was. He wasn't heavy or thin, neither muscle-bound nor weak.

He was simply average.

But even average stood out in Cold Creek, Texas. Because he was a newcomer in a town that didn't attract newcomers.

Settling in at her desk in the sheriff's department, she checked her messages in hopes of a new case to distract her from her inconvenient curious streak. But there was nothing waiting for her. There rarely was.

She woke her computer and grabbed a notepad from the top desk drawer. *John Blake*, she wrote at the top of the pad. He was from Tennessee—east Tennessee, she added to the notepad as she searched her memory for everything he'd told her and a few things he hadn't. His accent had definitely held a hint of the mountains.

He'd been buying nails and screws, but nothing that pegged him as any sort of builder. And he'd told her he came from a family of accountants, hadn't he?

John Blake. Accountant. Eastern Tennessee.

That should be a place to start.

Ten minutes later, she knew a good bit more—and still, a whole lot of nothing. Jonathan Eric Blake, age thirty-six, six feet tall. Until just over a year ago, he'd worked at Blake and Blake, an accounting firm in Johnson City, Tennessee, owned by his father. Before that, he'd worked for a global marketing firm in Europe for about a year, fresh out of grad school.

His current address was just off Route 7, the main north-south highway through Barstow County. He also showed up on the payroll of a construction company called Blanchard Building, Inc., in Garza County.

Working as an off-site carpenter.

What was an accountant doing working as a carpenter?

As she reached for the computer keyboard again, the desk sergeant, Coy Taylor, stuck his head through the doorway. "Duncan, we've had a call. Anonymous. Someone thought he saw Delta McGraw hitchhiking down near the Bar W."

She stood and grabbed her jacket from the back of her chair. "Was he sure it was Delta?"

"Claimed it was. You've got pictures of her plastered all over the county." Taylor gave her a sympathetic look. "You might be about the only person left in these parts who gives a damn. That girl's burned a lot of bridges in this town."

Miranda couldn't argue otherwise, but Delta had lived a hard life and maybe she had earned some of the prickliness that set most people on edge. And while this wasn't the first time Delta had gone missing for a few days, this time just felt different. She'd been gone too long, with no word to anyone, at a time when she'd seemed closer than ever to putting down permanent roots in Cold Creek.

Miranda zipped up her jacket and headed out to the fleet parking lot. The small sheriff's department had jurisdiction for the whole county, but most of the crime, such as it was, happened near the county seat of Cold Creek or along Route 7.

She turned on the cruiser's light bar but left the siren silent as she sped down Route 7 toward the sprawling Bar W Ranch, one of the largest cattle spreads in the panhandle. Despite the chilly temperatures, the Bar W Ranch kept their cattle grazing year-round through a strategic plan utilizing both warm- and cold-growth grasses. Some patches of grass were already green, despite the frigid temperatures, and several dozen head of cattle had gathered there to graze.

She peered down the highway, looking for a hitchhiker. But with the threat of snow, even traffic on the highway was nearly nonexistent. Nor could she find any sign that a vehicle had pulled over on the dusty shoulder on either side to pick up anyone thumbing for a ride.

Had it been a false report?

She called it in. "Taylor, I'm seeing no sign of a hitchhiker on Route 7. Could the call have come from a hoaxer?"

"Could have, I suppose." Taylor's gusty sigh roared through the radio. "Sorry about that, Duncan. I know you were hoping hard for some sign of the girl."

"I think while I'm down this way, I'm going to check in on Lizzie Dillard. She swears someone's been stealing eggs from her henhouse."

"A lawman's work is never done," Taylor drawled, amusement thick in his gravelly voice.

The narrow one-lane dirt road that led to Lizzie Dillard's farm, well-rutted and hell on the cruiser's shocks, had been given the dubious name Glory Road. At one point, in the area's distant past, a charismatic preacher had turned this part of the panhandle into a series of peripatetic tent revivals, and Glory Road had come into being to accommodate wagons, horses and pedestrians traveling from revival to revival.

The revivals had ended after a spectacularly messy sex scandal involving the preacher and a half dozen of his pretty young acolytes, but the name of the road had lived on to the present.

By the time she pulled into the bare yard in front of Lizzie Dillard's farmhouse, a light snow had begun to fall, whipped into icy needles by the hard north wind. Miranda tugged up the collar of her jacket and hurried up the porch steps. She knocked on the sagging screen door. "Lizzie?"

Lizzie didn't answer, even after another knock, so Miranda headed around to the chicken coop out back. "Lizzie?"

Lizzie Dillard came out of the chicken coop and looked up in surprise. "Hey there, Miranda. What're you doin' out here? You want a piece of pecan pie? It's still warm from the oven, and I could put on a pot of coffee."

Miranda ignored the answering rumble of her stomach. "No, thank you, Lizzie. I just came by to talk to you about those stolen eggs."

"Aw, honey, I didn't tell your daddy about that so you'd come out here. It's probably some wily ol' gray fox." Lizzie handed Miranda the basket full of brown eggs and turned to secure the door latch on the coop.

"A fox got in the henhouse and just stole the eggs?" Miranda tried to temper her skepticism, but Lizzie shot her a knowing look.

"I reckon I raise tough hens." Lizzie laughed at her own joke. "Sometimes, they just want the eggs. It happens. You sure you don't want to come in and warm up?"

The snowfall had started to pick up, the flakes fatter

and denser than before. The ground temperature was still above freezing, but if the snow got much heavier, it wouldn't take long to start sticking, even on the roads.

"I'd better get on the move," Miranda said, not letting herself think about Lizzie's warm kitchen and hot pot of coffee. "Call us if anything else happens out here, okay?"

"Sure thing." Lizzie walked with her to the cruiser. "You be safe out there. My old bones are tellin' me this might be a big snow."

"I hope your bones are wrong," Miranda said with a smile.

Back in the cruiser, she checked in with the station. Bill Chambers was manning the front desk instead of Taylor, who'd taken a lunch break. She filled in Chambers on the call that had brought her out here. "No new calls about a hitchhiker?"

"Not a thing."

"I'm coming back in, then." At the end of Glory Road, she took a left onto Route 7, heading south toward town. Snow had limited the visibility to about fifty yards in all directions, forcing her to drive slower than she normally would. Fortunately, the snow seemed to have convinced most other drivers to stay off the road.

She was halfway to town before she saw another set of headlights in the rearview mirror, cutting through the snow fog behind her. A second glance revealed the headlights moving closer at a reckless rate of speed.

Miranda turned on the light bar and the siren, figuring that would be enough to make the car flying up behind her slow down.

She was wrong. The second vehicle whipped around the cruiser and pulled even in the passing lane. It was a Ford Taurus, she saw. Dark blue. She tried to get a look at the driver, but the dark-tinted windows, liberally frosted with a layer of snow crystals, hid the car's occupants from view.

She grabbed her radio and hit the bullhorn button. "Pull over," she commanded, easing off the gas.

The other car slowed with her but didn't pull over.

She pushed the call button and gave Chambers a description of the vehicle. "Don't know what this fellow's up to, but if there's a unit in the area, I could use backup."

"On its way," Chambers promised.

Snow was starting to dance across the road surface, collecting on the edges. If the precipitation didn't slow soon, the road would become hazardous.

"Pull over," she ordered again, but the driver of the Taurus didn't change speed at all.

What the hell was going on? Was this an ambush?

Why would someone ambush a Barstow County deputy?

With shocking suddenness, the Taurus fell back, catching Miranda off guard. She glanced in her side mirror, trying to figure out what he was doing.

The right front of the Taurus was even with the left rear panel of the cruiser. In the split second Miranda had to think, she realized the Taurus was in the perfect position for the classic police chase tactic known as the PIT maneuver.

Just as the thought flashed through her mind, the Taurus bumped the left rear panel of her car, sending the cruiser into a textbook spin.

If the road had been dry, she might have been able to recover from the PIT maneuver. But as the cruiser turned in a wild circle, the wheels hit a patch of accumulating snow and spun off the road, hitting a shallow arroyo that sent her into a roll.

Amid the shriek of crumpling metal and the blaze of fear rising in her chest, her head slammed into the side window and the whirlwind of sound and color faded into dark silence.

The squeal of tires and the crunch of ripping metal broke through the whisper of snow falling outside the rental house, rousing John from a light doze.

His nerves rattling, he froze for a moment, his pulse hammering inside his head as he listened for a repeat of the noise.

Had he dreamed it? His house was close to Route 7, the busiest highway in Cold Creek, though so far, he hadn't seen all that much traffic on the road, certainly nothing like the busy street in front of his apartment building back in Abingdon, Virginia.

Still, it was snowing outside, and cars and snow didn't mix that well, especially in an area where there wasn't a lot of snow over the course of an average winter. Maybe he'd heard a car's tires squealing outside and in his half-dream state, imagined the rest?

His shoulder ached as he donned hiking boots and shrugged on his heavy jacket, but he ignored the pain. Pain was good. It was a reminder he'd taken three bullets and lived to tell about it.

He headed out to the porch and peered into the fog of falling snow. About fifty yards down the road, a flash of color caught his eye. Strobing color, like the light bar on the top of a police vehicle.

Except the light wasn't coming from the road. It was coming from several yards off the highway.

Patting the back pocket of his jeans to make sure he still had his phone, he left the porch and headed into the snow shower, keeping his eye on the flashing light. Within a few yards, he could see the light was coming from the light bar on the roof of a Barstow County Sheriff's Department cruiser lying on its side in a patch of scrub grass. The roof was damaged, the front windshield shattered, but the light bar continued to flash.

As he neared the cruiser, movement on the highway caught his attention. A dark-colored sedan crept along the shoulder, as if rubbernecking the accident.

John waved at the slowly passing vehicle. "I need help here!"

The sedan kept going until it disappeared into the fog of snow.

Grimacing, John headed for the cruiser. A loud creak sent John backpedaling quickly. The cruiser started to shift positions until it landed on all four wheels. Two wheels were flat, John saw, and there was significant damage to the chassis. Clearly a rollover.

Once the cruiser settled, he hurried to the driver's door and looked through the open window. The first thing he noticed was blood on the steering wheel. Then hair the color of Georgia clay.

Damn it. Could it be the deputy from the hardware store?

"Deputy Duncan?"

She didn't answer. Looking closer, he realized the window wasn't actually open. Instead, the crash had wiped out the window, showering pebbled bits of glass all over the floorboard, the seats and the injured deputy.

It was definitely Miranda Duncan, though half of her face was obscured by a sticky sheen of blood that seemed to be coming from the vicinity of her hairline. Gusts of wind carried snow flurries into the cruiser's cab to settle on the deputy's bloody face and melt into the crimson flow.

John tried the door. It resisted his attempt to open it, so he let it go and leaned into the cruiser through the window. Swallowing a lump of dread, he touched his fingers to her throat, feeling for a pulse. It was there, fast but even. He started to draw back his hand, reaching for his phone.

With shocking speed, Miranda's left hand whipped up and clamped around his wrist, while her right hand snapped up, wrapped around a Smith & Wesson M&P 40, the barrel pointed between his eyes.

"Don't move an inch," she growled.

As John sucked in a deep breath, he heard the crack of gunfire. His pulse misfired, and he grabbed the side of the window frame, pebbled glass crunching against his palm.

"Get down!" Miranda shouted as a second shot thumped against the cruiser's back door.

Chapter Two

John Blake disappeared suddenly, leaving Miranda with an unobstructed view out the cruiser window. But she could still see nothing but falling snow—the storm had reached white-out proportions.

Pain throbbed in her head as she squinted in hopes of seeing her hidden assailant, but she couldn't even see the road now. She could hear an engine, however, growling somewhere out there in the white void.

Behind her, the car door opened, and she swung around to find John Blake gazing back at her, his expression urgent. "You're a sitting duck," he warned, stretching his hand toward her.

Gunfire rang outside, the bullet hitting the front panel of the cruiser with a loud *thwack*, ending her brief hesitation. She unlatched her seat belt and scrambled toward John, taking his outstretched hand.

He pulled her out of the cruiser and pushed her gently toward the front wheel, giving her an extra layer of protection against the shooter. The movement made her feel light-headed and nauseated, and she ended up on her backside, leaning her back against the wheel as she sucked in deep draughts of icy air.

"I can try returning fire," John suggested. "I'll need your weapon—"

"Wait," she said, forcing herself to focus. Was it her imagination or was the sound of the car motor moving away?

"I think whoever's out there is leaving." John had edged closer, near enough that she could feel the heat of his body blocking the icy wind. She leaned toward him, unable to stop herself.

"I think you're right." Her chattering teeth made it difficult to speak. "I called for backup but I think the radio got smashed in the wreck."

"You could be hurt worse than you think," he warned, crouching until his gaze leveled with hers. Up close, his hazel eyes were soft with concern.

"I d-don't think I have any broken limbs," she stuttered. "B-but I'm freezing."

"My house is about forty yards in that direction." He nodded toward his right. "Want to chance a run for it?"

She nodded, realizing she was too warmly dressed to be as cold as she felt, which meant she was probably going into some level of shock. She needed to get warm and dry. "Let's do it."

He stood first. Trying to draw fire, she realized, so they'd know if the shooter was still out there. She grabbed his hand, trying to draw him back down behind the cruiser, but he shook his head. "I think the shooter's gone."

He pulled her up, wrapping one arm around her waist to help her wobbling legs hold her upright.

She drew deep on her inner resources. Forty yards. She could run forty yards on a sprained ankle if she had to, and as far as she could tell, her only injury was the pain in her head. "Let's do it."

The first few steps felt as if she was running through mud, but with John's help, she picked up speed and strength. By the time the small farmhouse loomed up out of the white fog of snow, she was feeling steadier.

John half dragged her up to the porch and inside the door. Instantly, blessed heat washed over her, and she felt her legs wobble dangerously beneath her.

"Whoa, deputy. No face-planting on my nice clean floor." John wrapped his arms around her and eased her over to the sofa that was positioned in front of a crackling fire. He sat beside her, sliding her gloves from her half-numb fingers. "Sit right here. I'll get my first-aid kit."

She held her trembling hands out in front of the fire, soaking up the warmth. She heard a cabinet opening and closing, then footsteps as John returned to the front room holding a soft-sided first-aid kit.

"You holding up?" He sat beside her and unzipped the kit.

"No face-planting yet," she answered with a lopsided grin that made her face hurt. "I need to call the station. I guess my phone's probably somewhere on the cruiser's floorboard."

"Of course." He pulled a cell phone from his pocket. "What's the number?"

She gave it to him, and he dialed the number while she looked through the first-aid kit for antiseptic wipes. She found a sealed packet and ripped it open.

"Who should I talk to?" John asked.

"Just talk to the desk sergeant," she replied, touching the antiseptic pad to the sore spot just above her hairline. It stung, making her wince. "I'm not sure who's on the desk."

While John gave his address to whoever answered

the phone, Miranda went through a handful of antiseptic wipes trying to mop up the blood from her head. It seemed to be bleeding still, though not as heavily as before. Blood stained the front of her jacket and the uniform pants she wore, enough that she no longer wondered why she felt so light-headed.

"The sergeant said backup is already headed this way, but the snow's making it slow going." John leaned forward, examining her first-aid work. "How's your head feeling?"

"Like it just rammed into a brick wall."

John's lips curved slightly. "Noted."

"I don't remember exactly what happened," she admitted, trying not to let the blank spaces in her memory freak her out. She'd probably sustained a concussion in the accident. The memories might never return. Or, conversely, they'd come seeping back bits at a time.

She wasn't sure it mattered. It clearly hadn't been a simple accident.

Not if someone had started taking potshots at her immediately afterward.

"Do you know why you were out there in a snowstorm?" John asked.

That much she could remember. "We'd gotten a call from someone who said he'd seen a woman on our missing person's list out here on Route 7, hitchhiking. I came out to check on the report, but it didn't pan out. I stopped by to talk to another constituent about a possible theft, then I headed back toward town. That's the last thing I remember before I came to in the car just before you showed up."

"The sergeant said you'd called for backup a few minutes ago. You reported a vehicle following you too closely for comfort. You seemed to think the other driver was up to something."

"Did I give a description of the vehicle?" Surely she had.

"He didn't say."

She could remember nothing about another vehicle, but something had sent her rolling off the highway and she didn't think it was the snowstorm. The visibility wasn't great, but Route 7 was about as straight as a ruler all the way into town.

"You don't remember anything about it, do you?" John asked.

"I don't," she admitted, reaching for another antiseptic wipe packet.

John covered his hand with hers, stilling her movement.

Heat rolled up her arm from where his fingers touched hers. It settled in her chest like a hot coal, warming her insides.

"Let me grab a washcloth and see if we can get that bleeding stopped for good." He was back a minute later with a wet washcloth and pulled a chair up in front of her, gazing up at her hairline with a frown between his eyes. "This may hurt."

Bracing herself, she smelled a hint of soap as the cloth passed her face, then felt the sting as John pressed the hot cloth to her head wound. She sucked in a quick breath.

"Sorry," he murmured. "At least you've stopped shivering."

So she had, she realized. She felt steadier also, her vision less off-kilter. The mental fog was starting to lift, as well.

"I don't know if I'd have survived out there without

you," she admitted, the words strangely reluctant to pass her lips. She'd been self-sufficient since she was quite young, the result of losing her mother in childhood. Her father had worked long hours, keeping the hardware business running through good times and bad. She'd learned early how to take care of herself. Accepting help from others wasn't something she'd ever done easily.

But she owed John Blake her life, even if she still had questions about what he might be doing in town. He certainly hadn't been the person firing shots at her from the highway. He'd come perilously close to getting shot himself. She'd been looking right at him when the bullet hit the back door right beside him.

A few minutes later, he withdrew the bloody washcloth from her head.

She tried not to cringe at the thought of help arriving soon. Her practical side told her she needed medical attention, especially given her memory loss. She'd have told any other accident victim to let the paramedics do their job, wouldn't she?

But she sure as hell wasn't going to enjoy her colleagues poking and prodding her as if she was an ordinary civilian involved in an MVA. She was one of them, damn it.

And she wanted to be the one who investigated what had happened.

"They're not going to let you investigate your own case, you know." The knowing look in his eyes made her feel as if she'd been laid bare, all her secret thoughts on display.

How the hell could he do that? He didn't know her.

She grimaced. "I know that."

"And while I'm sharing unwanted news with you, you should do whatever the paramedics say you should do."

"I'm fine."

"You're not." He leaned closer. She couldn't stop herself from meeting his gaze. "I spent time in the hospital not long ago. I felt like a specimen under glass. People wandering into my room all hours, poking this and drawing that. Hated every minute of it. So I know how you're feeling."

She nodded, then regretted the movement as her head spun for a couple of seconds. "They're going to want to bus me to Plainview for observation."

"Maybe you should let them do that."

"No."

"That's a pretty good knock on your head."

"I probably have a slight concussion. But I'm clear-headed now."

"Closed head injuries can be unpredictable," he warned. "You have someone who can watch you? A husband?"

"My dad," she answered. "He's probably already closed up shop and headed home. I'll get one of the guys to take me there."

"So, no husband?"

She looked up at him, surprised by the interest in his voice. "No husband."

His gaze held hers. "I'm not exactly known for my good timing."

She couldn't stop a smile, though it made her head ache. "Clearly."

"So we should probably just forget I asked that question." He looked toward the front door. "Do you hear any sirens?"

"Not yet."

"Should we?"

Good question. "How long ago did you talk to the station?"

He looked at his watch. "Twenty minutes. He said backup was already on the way, so it might be a little longer than that."

It took about ten minutes to reach this part of Route 7 under good weather conditions. "The snow's probably slowed them up."

He gave a quick nod and fell silent, his expression hard to read. She wouldn't say he looked worried, exactly. Watchful, maybe.

Silence unspooled between them as they waited, the silence of forced proximity between strangers. Normally, Miranda preferred silence to pointless chatter, but the events of the afternoon had left her nerves raw.

So when John Blake's cell phone rang, it sent a shock wave rippling up her spine. He gave a slight start and pulled the phone from his pocket. "It's the station," he murmured. He lifted the phone to his ear. "John Blake."

He listened a second, then looked at Miranda. "She's right here." He handed the phone to her.

It was Bill Chambers on the other end. "How're you holding up, Duncan?"

"I'm okay. Head's a little sore, but I'll live."

"Good to hear, because we have a problem."

JOHN LEANED AGAINST the back of his chair and tried not to eavesdrop, though there was no way to avoid hearing Miranda's end of the call without leaving the room.

She picked up the washcloth he'd laid on the coffee

table beside her and pressed it to her head wound while she listened to the caller. "How many injuries?"

Whatever answer she received made her frown.

John stopped trying to pretend he wasn't listening and met her troubled gaze. She was still pale, but her hands had stopped shaking finally and her gray-eyed gaze was clear and sharp as it rose to meet John's.

"I'm fine. The cruiser's not going anywhere, and I'm not alone. Just stay in touch, okay?" She ended the call and handed John the phone. "There's been a pileup on Highway 287. Over a dozen vehicles. Every EMS service in three counties is responding. All the deputies are out on calls, too. I guess you're stuck with me a little longer."

He nodded, but something in his gut twisted a little at the realization they were alone and more or less stranded out in here in the middle of snowy nowhere for the next while.

He had a pistol packed away in the closet. His Virginia concealed-carry license was honored in Texas—he'd made sure before he headed west to finish his recuperation in relative anonymity. But if he retrieved it now, what would Deputy Duncan think?

"What are you thinking?" she asked, apparently reading his expression.

"That we're sort of isolated out here," he answered, not seeing the point of hiding his concern. Someone had run the deputy off the road and then taken shots at her.

Would they take a chance and try again?

"You think the person who was shooting at us may come back?" She laid down the washcloth and sat up straighter, her gaze moving toward the front door.

He hurried to the door and turned the dead bolt to the locked position before moving the curtain aside to check the road. The snow had slowed finally, visibility restored to a hundred yards or more, though the highway in front of the house was covered with at least a couple of inches of the white stuff. He could probably drive to town without incident, he thought. Get her to her dad's house, at least.

He looked over his shoulder at her. "The snow has slowed. I think I could drive you back to town."

"I don't want to leave the cruiser," she answered. "If you don't mind my staying here a while longer."

Did he mind? On one level, he didn't mind a bit. She was an interesting woman, and not bad to look at, even with her hair plastered to her head with sticky blood.

But she was also a cop, and while he technically had nothing to hide from the law, he didn't want anyone looking too closely at his life. In a way, Cold Creek, Texas, was a hideout. There were people back in Virginia who'd like to get their hands on him, and he was currently in no condition to hold his own.

Soon, though, he promised himself. He'd be back in fighting form soon. And then it wouldn't matter who knew where he was.

"I don't mind," he answered.

Her eyes narrowed a notch. "Took your time answering that question."

He smiled. "I'm a bit of a loner."

"Is that why you moved out here? To be alone?"

"I guess."

"You said you were in the hospital not long ago. Car accident?"

He shook his head but didn't elaborate.

"Assault?"

He should have known silence would only pique her

curiosity. But he was tired of lying. It seemed as if he'd been lying for years, first as a CIA agent pretending to be an international finance manager, then the decade he'd pretended that he found life as an accountant satisfying.

And then, there was the past year, working undercover for Alexander Quinn. Using an alias, pretending a career that didn't exist, acting as a go-between for Quinn and another undercover operative trying to infiltrate a dangerous militia group called the Blue Ridge Infantry—

What would Miranda Duncan think if he laid out his whole deception-riddled history for her examination?

She'd probably think he was crazy. Or lying.

Or both.

"I guess you could say I was in the wrong place at the wrong time," he said finally.

"That's…cryptic."

He smiled. "Yes."

To his surprise, her lips quirked in response, a faint half smile that dimpled her cheeks. He felt a drawing sensation low in his belly that caught him by surprise.

She was so not his type. Hell, he wasn't sure he even had a type.

But damned if he wasn't sitting here, wondering what she'd look like naked. In his bed.

Her smile faded suddenly, and her head turned toward the front door. "Do you hear that?"

Listening, he realized what she was hearing.

A car engine, idling somewhere outside the house.

He crossed to the window and parted the curtains an inch. The snow was picking up again, but not enough to obscure his view of the road, where a dark blue sedan sat idling on the shoulder, directly in front of the house.

"What is it?" Miranda asked, her voice closer than he

expected. Glancing to his right, he found her beside him, trying to see out the window.

"It's a dark blue sedan," he answered, easing the curtain closed and pulling her with him deeper into the cabin.

"Is it—?"

"I don't know," he admitted. He hadn't had a chance to get a good look at the vehicle earlier while dodging bullets and trying to get Miranda to safety. "It looks similar. And it's idling outside my house, about forty yards from your wrecked cruiser."

Miranda's face went paler. "Are all your doors locked?"

He met her troubled gaze. "I don't know."

Chapter Three

While John went around the house checking the locks, Miranda pulled the M&P 40 from the holster at her hip and crossed to the front window, taking a quick look outside. The sedan remained idling at the side of the road. The windows were tinted, obscuring the occupants from view.

What do you want? she wondered.

John's footsteps drew her gaze to him. He was carrying a pistol in his right hand, barrel down, his finger safely away from the trigger. But the sight still gave her a start.

What did she know about him, really? Did he even have a license to carry that pistol?

"I have a Virginia CCW," he answered as if she'd asked the question aloud. Was she that easily read?

Up close, she saw that the pistol was a Ruger SR45. Big and black, with a brushed stainless slide. If she were the type of cop who indulged in weapon envy, she'd be indulging in it big-time.

"We need to call for backup," she said, forcing her gaze away from the big gun and back to the sedan idling outside her house.

"Already done." He nudged her away from the window. "I told the guy who answered that we needed a unit out here if they had to pull it off the pileup."

"That could take a while."

"Better late than never, right?" He glanced toward the window, his brow furrowed. "I wonder why they're just sitting out there."

"Maybe it's an intimidation tactic."

"Or maybe they want one of us to come outside to see what's going on."

"If we did that, we'd be sitting ducks."

"So we wait."

She nodded. "Whoever's out there knows I'm armed. But they can't be sure whether or not you are."

John slanted a quick look at her. His expression was neutral, unreadable, but something in those hazel-green eyes set off warning bells in her head.

Did he know something about the car outside? She had the strangest feeling he was keeping something from her.

Something important.

"The doors are locked," he said. "The windows, too."

"The windows, too?" She looked in his direction again, took in his wary expression. He was definitely keeping something from her. But what?

She didn't think he wanted to hurt her. She was vulnerable from her injury—it wouldn't take much to get the drop on her. He could have done so at almost any point since he'd dragged her inside the house.

Hell, he could have killed her out in the car, or made it possible for the shooters to do so, if he'd wanted her dead.

So maybe what he was hiding wasn't about her.

"Accounting," she said.

His gaze cut toward her. "Accounting?"

"You said you were of the accounting Blakes. When I said I was from the hardware Duncans."

"Oh, right."

"Are you taking a sabbatical from that kind of work?"

A huff of laughter escaped his throat. "No. I did that kind of work for ten years. That was ten years too many."

"Are you unemployed?" She knew the answer to that question. She might not remember what happened to send her rolling off the highway, but she remembered her computer search earlier at the station.

Even then, John Blake had piqued her curiosity.

Seeing him armed and appearing both competent and dangerous, she knew she'd been right to wonder what he was doing in a sleepy backwater town like Cold Creek.

"I'm a carpenter," he said. "I work for a construction company. Blanchard Building."

"Down in Garza County?"

His eyes narrowed slightly, and she realized she'd made a mistake. What would a Barstow County deputy know about a construction company two counties to the south?

"Have you been investigating me?" His tone wasn't threatening, but his grip on the Ruger tightened enough to make her stomach turn a flip.

She decided honesty was her best option. "We don't get a lot of strangers in Cold Creek."

"So you did a background check?"

"Not quite that drastic. I just looked up your name in the computer. With a few search parameters."

"What did you find?"

"More questions than answers."

His lips quirked at her admission. "I'm an open book." He didn't even bother to pretend he was telling the truth.

She smiled. "If you were, you wouldn't be nearly as interesting."

One of his dark eyebrows lifted, but he didn't respond.

She was starting to feel shaky again, she realized. Some of the adrenaline that had kept her on her feet and moving had begun to seep away, and her injuries were making themselves known again.

She tried not to let it show, but John's sharp gaze missed nothing. "I think that car is trying to wait us out. So maybe we should do the same. We have backup coming. So let's go sit by the fire. It's cold in here."

She let him lead her back to the fireplace and gratefully sank onto the comfortable cushions of the sofa. The heat from the fireplace felt like a living thing, wrapping around her with tendrils of warmth until some of the shivers subsided.

"You're a Cold Creek native?" John asked a few minutes later, breaking the silence that had fallen between them.

"Born and bred."

"You like it out here?"

"I do," she said with a slight lift of her chin. She saw the hint of a smile curve his lips in response and felt a little childish, as if she'd stamped her foot and dared him to disagree.

"It's not quite what I expected." He didn't sound negative, just bemused, which was a good mark in her book. She knew few people who could appreciate the flat, wind-blown plains and endless isolation. But at least John Blake hadn't outright dismissed the possibility of its appeal.

"What did you expect?"

"More heat, for one thing."

"You came to the wrong part of Texas at the wrong time for that."

"So I've discovered."

"Where are you from originally?" she asked, even though she knew the answer.

He shot her a look. "Didn't your background check tell you that?"

"I didn't find your birth certificate or anything."

"Johnson City, Tennessee," he said.

Where his father's accounting firm was located. "You worked for an overseas company a while back, right?"

His lips quirked again. Not quite a smile, but close. "Yeah. For about a year."

"Didn't like global marketing?"

Her question made him smile. A knowing, secret-keeping smile that made her curious streak vibrate like a tuning fork in the pit of her stomach.

"I think it's more a matter of global marketing not liking me—" He stopped short, his head cocked. "Do you hear that?"

She listened, hearing nothing. "I don't hear anything."

"Exactly." He rose and edged his way back toward the window, staying clear of the glass panes as he checked outside. His back stiffened. "The car is gone."

Miranda joined him at the window. He was right. The car was no longer idling on the highway out front. "Do you think it's a way to lure us out of the house?"

He gave her a thoughtful look. "I don't know. But I don't hear its engine running anymore. Do you?"

"No." But she did hear something else, she realized. "Sirens."

They were only faintly audible. She supposed the walls of the house muffled the sound somewhat. But whoever had been sitting in that sedan outside might have heard them coming a good bit earlier.

"Maybe the sirens scared them away," John said, reading her thoughts.

Within a couple of minutes, a sheriff's department cruiser pulled up outside the house, and the sheriff himself, Miles Randall, emerged from the cruiser, along with one of the younger deputies, Tim Robertson.

John unlocked the door and opened it before the sheriff had a chance to knock. Randall stepped back in surprise, one hand dropping to the pistol holstered at his hip.

"It's okay," Miranda said quickly, showing herself.

Randall reacted with surprise at the sight of her. "Good God, Duncan, You look like hell."

"Thanks."

Randall gave John Blake a quick, curious glance, then looked at her again. "Want to tell me what happened?"

"That," she admitted, "is a very good question."

It TURNED OUT that the deputy Sheriff Randall had brought with him had previously been a volunteer fireman with some paramedic training. Tim Robertson looked ridiculously young to John, but he assessed Miranda's condition as if he knew what he was doing, working with a skillful efficiency that set John's mind at ease.

Sheriff Miles Randall was a tall, rangy man with a drawl as big as, well, Texas. He questioned John about what he'd witnessed, asking good questions and not overplaying his suspicions. But John could tell Randall wasn't ready to trust his word completely.

John couldn't blame the sheriff. He wasn't exactly a man without secrets.

"I think we need to get you at least to the clinic in town," Randall told Miranda after Tim Robertson finished his examination. "Tim's not a doctor, and your daddy would kill me if I didn't make sure you're not going to keel over the second I leave you alone."

Miranda smiled. "I promise, I won't. But shouldn't someone stay here and protect the crime scene?"

"That's what Tim's here for."

Miranda's gray-eyed gaze slanted toward John, as if looking for his input. He straightened his spine, surprised. What did she expect him to do, back her up? Tell the sheriff he wanted her to stay?

He did, he realized. He wanted her to stay. But that was a selfish impulse, fed by his hormones and his isolation out here.

"You should do what the sheriff says, Deputy Duncan," he said, keeping his tone impersonal. Formal.

Her brow wrinkled briefly at his words, but her expression shuttered quickly. "Thank you for your help, Mr. Blake."

"Glad I was here." As she started to turn to go, he said, "Wait."

She looked at him, her expression somewhere between curious and wary.

He reached into his back pocket and pulled out his wallet. Inside, he withdrew the card he'd picked up earlier that morning at the hardware store. Her father's name was on the front. He flipped it over. "Can I borrow a pen?" he asked the sheriff.

The sheriff pulled a pen from his front breast pocket and handed it over, his expression watchful.

John jotted his cell number on the back of the card and handed it to Miranda. "If you have any more questions."

She took the card and slid it in her pants pocket. "Thanks again for everything."

She walked out with the sheriff, her gait slow but her

spine straight. She didn't look back. He told himself he never expected her to.

"I'm going to guard the wreckage until the tow truck can get here." Robertson headed out the door.

John nodded, his gaze still fixed on Miranda. The sheriff opened the passenger door of the cruiser for her, and she settled in the seat, moving gingerly. The aches and pains of the car crash were starting to catch up with her, he realized.

She'd feel like hell warmed over in the morning.

But at least she was still alive. There had been a moment, as he'd approached that crashed cruiser, when he'd been afraid he was about to unbuckle a corpse.

His cell phone rang, loud enough to jangle his nerves. He checked the display. No name or number, just the word *unknown* across the smartphone's window.

He answered. "John Blake."

"You rang?" Alexander Quinn's voice was low and smooth on the other end of the line.

He had. After calling the Barstow County Sheriff's Department to ask for backup, he'd put in a call to his boss. Quinn hadn't answered, so John had left a message for a call back.

"There's been an incident here," he said, and briefly outlined the events of the afternoon.

"Any reason to think you were the target instead of the deputy?" Quinn asked.

"I'm not sure," John admitted. "The deputy doesn't remember the crash, and I only heard it when it happened. I don't know how the other vehicle ran her off the road, so I don't know whether the location of the crash was deliberate or happenstance."

"The tri-state task force has been rolling up the remainder of the Blue Ridge Infantry over the past few weeks. Lynette Colley's been talking to the investigators. She's given them a lot of names and dates they hope to use to bring all the key leaders of the BRI to justice." Quinn didn't bother to hide the satisfaction in his voice. Bringing down the Blue Ridge Infantry had been a personal mission for Quinn since he formed The Gates. While the security agency took on plenty of well-paying cases, Quinn always kept some agents working the BRI angle.

John had asked him once why taking down the BRI was so important to him. Quinn's answer had been simple. "They're destroying these mountains, one soul at a time."

"So what you're saying is, this incident might have nothing at all to do with the bounty the BRI put on my head?"

"It's not likely that it does."

"Even with that car idling outside the house?"

"Sounds like the deputy's the one who has an enemy there in Cold Creek. Any idea why?"

"No," John admitted, walking across the front room to the side window. He parted the curtains and saw that the snow had settled to a light but steady fall. From here, he could see the wreck of the cruiser and the lanky young deputy standing guard, bundled up against the cold.

Miranda Duncan seemed an unlikely target for murder. Small-town deputy in a place with maybe three hundred residents.

Who would want a woman like that dead?

"Just keep your eyes open," Quinn said. "We've made big progress, but there are still a few members of the BRI and their ragtag crew out there, looking for a win."

"And getting to me would be a win."

"Yeah."

"I'll keep my eyes open," John answered, his tone flat.

"You should be in bed." Gil Duncan's voice rumbled from the doorway behind her, drawing Miranda's attention from the computer screen.

"I'm fine, Dad. Dr. Bennett said the concussion was mild and probably wouldn't give me any more trouble." She met her father's worried gaze and smiled. "I promise. My head isn't even hurting anymore."

Not much, anyway. Just a little ache where the doctor had sewn a couple of stitches to close up the head wound.

"What are you working on?" he asked, nodding toward the computer.

"Just some web surfing. Nothing to worry about."

"Like I'm not going to worry about my daughter rolling her cruiser in a snowstorm." Gil Duncan sighed, looking as if he'd aged a decade in the past twenty-four hours.

Miranda rose and crossed to where he stood in the doorway, wrapping her arms around his waist. "I really am okay."

He gave her a swift, fierce hug, a show of affection that he rarely displayed. "Maybe you should get yourself a different career."

She pulled back to look at him. "Maybe join you at the hardware store?"

"You worked there for years."

"Which is why I know it's not for me." She smiled to soften her words. "You know I love being a deputy."

"Rebel," he muttered, but not without affection.

"Go watch your basketball game. I'll finish up what I'm doing and I'll join you for the second half."

She watched her father walk down the narrow hall before she returned to the laptop on her bed.

She was fairly sure the blue sedan parked outside John Blake's house had been a Ford Taurus. So she'd just run the description through the Texas Department of Motor Vehicles database.

No response yet from the DMV. They'd be looking at a five-county area around Cold Creek, so it was too early to expect an answer yet.

She slumped back against the bed pillows, her gaze wandering around the bedroom that had been hers growing up. The poster of the country band Lonestar taped to the closet door was dog-eared. Softball and junior-rodeo trophies covered the top of her dresser, along with a few blue ribbons from the county fair.

In this room, she felt sixteen again.

Not a good thing.

Sheriff Randall had retrieved her cell phone from the wrecked cruiser and returned it to her at the clinic. It had survived the crash without damage, which was more than she could say for herself. She pulled her cell phone from her pocket now and called the station. The night sergeant, Jack Logan, was manning the desk. "Things still crazy from the storm?" she asked when he answered.

"Duncan, aren't you supposed to be in bed recuperating?"

"I'm in bed," she said. "Just a little bored."

"Well, everything here's settled down, so it's not like you'd be any less bored if you were here," Logan told her in a tone that reminded her of her father. Jack Logan was a thirty-year veteran, winding down his time on the force on the night shift. "Snow's stopped and the temps should be above freezing by early morning."

"How about the pileup—how many casualties?"

"No deaths. Fifteen hospitalized but none of the injuries are life threatening. Looks like we dodged a bullet."

"Some of us literally," Miranda murmured.

"Ah, hell, Mandy. I wasn't even thinking."

"Has my cruiser been towed to Lubbock for examination?"

"Yeah. We got to it by late afternoon."

Maybe they'd get something from ballistics, Miranda thought.

"They've also taped off the area and will do a grid search for more evidence after the snow melts tomorrow," Logan added.

John Blake would love that, she thought. His privacy had been well and truly invaded today. "Is Robertson still there guarding the crime scene?"

"No. The sheriff figured it was okay to just tape it off and pick up in the morning."

Miranda frowned, but she supposed the sheriff had a point. The evidence, such as they'd find, was probably in the cruiser anyway. "I'll let you go, Jack. Leave the sheriff a note—I'll be in tomorrow for a debriefing." She said goodbye and hung up before Logan could protest.

So, the crime scene was sitting there, unprotected, about forty yards from the house rented by a stranger in town.

Hmm.

When she'd first seen John Blake at the hardware store, she almost hadn't noticed him. He was that kind of guy—aggressively average, at least at first glance.

Up close and in action, however, he was anything but average.

Her uniform pants were hanging over the chair in

front of her battered old work desk. She dug in the front pocket, pulling out the card John had given her.

She checked her watch. Nine o'clock. Was it too late to call?

Before she could talk herself out of it, she dialed the number.

John answered on the second ring. "John Blake."

"It's Miranda Duncan."

His tone softened. "Still alive and kicking?"

"So far, so good."

"The lab guys came and took your cruiser a few hours ago." She could hear him moving, the faint thud of his footsteps on the hardwood floor.

"So I heard."

"Any breaks in the case?"

"Not yet." A draft was seeping into the house through the window over her bed. She pulled up the blanket and snuggled a little deeper into the mattress. "Hopefully we'll know more after the lab finishes up with the cruiser."

"I thought they'd have a crime scene crew out here this afternoon, but nobody showed."

She tried not to feel defensive. "We're a small force to begin with, we're temporarily a deputy short and we're dealing with a snowstorm—"

"Enough said." John's footsteps stopped, and she thought she heard the soft swish of fabric.

Suddenly, he uttered a low profanity.

"What?" she asked, her nerves instantly on edge.

"There's someone wandering around your crime scene," he said.

Chapter Four

The figure creeping toward the taped-off patch of frosty grass was moving with slow, measured paces. Dressed in what looked like winter camouflage, he blended into the snow-flecked scrub, only his movement giving away his position.

"He's in camo," John murmured into the phone, wishing he had his binoculars to get a better look. But he was afraid to leave the window, afraid that if he took his eyes off the creeping intruder, he'd lose sight of him altogether.

"Is he inside the tape?" Over the phone, Miranda's Texas twang had a raspy touch, reminding him that she'd already suffered through a long, stressful day. Her head was probably one big ache by now, and she had to be bruised and battered from the rollover.

"Not yet."

"I can get a cruiser over there to look around, but it will take a little while," Miranda said.

Over the phone, John heard the creak of bedsprings. Was she in bed?

He wondered whether she was a pajamas or a nightgown girl. Or, God help him, was she a woman who slept in the buff? A delicious shiver jolted through him at the vivid image that thought evoked.

He drove his imaginings firmly to the back of his head. "So far, he's just circling the taped-off area. Maybe he's just a curious hunter?"

"Is he carrying a rifle?" Miranda asked. He heard the sound of fabric rustling over the phone—was she getting dressed?

"You're not thinking of driving out here yourself, are you?" he asked.

"That's my crime scene." Her tone was full of stubborn determination. "I can get there faster than I can round up a cruiser. I'm closer."

"That's crazy—you have a concussion—"

"I'll be there in ten minutes." She hung up before John could try to talk her out of it.

He tried calling her back, but the call went straight to voice mail. Maybe she was already on the line to her office, rounding up backup.

With a sigh, he shoved his phone in his pocket and turned off the lights in the front room, plunging the house into darkness. Maybe his camo-clad visitor had been waiting for him to go to bed before he made his move.

Ball's in your court, John thought, grabbing a pair of binoculars before returning to the window. He let his eyes adjust to the change in light until he spotted the intruder again. The man was still circling the yellow crime scene tape, staying outside the perimeter.

He lifted the binoculars to his eyes and focused the lenses on the man in camo. His visitor wore a snow camouflage balaclava covering his mouth, nose and most of his forehead, leaving only a narrow strip of brow, eyes and upper cheeks uncovered. A pair of binoculars hid his eyes from view. He appeared to be using the binoculars to search the ground inside the crime scene tape, sparing him from having to trespass beyond the perimeter.

Suddenly, the man turned his face toward the window, his binoculars seeming to focus directly on John.

John took a step back from the window, but it was too late. The man in camo turned and headed into a clump of bushes north of the house.

John shrugged on his jacket, grabbed a flashlight and took a second to check the magazine of his Ruger before he headed out the door in pursuit.

He'd barely reached the taped crime scene when he heard the sound of a car engine roar to life. A moment later, the taillights of a vehicle stained the night red as a car pulled away from the shoulder of the highway about fifty yards away, heading north. John trekked toward the shoulder of the highway, watching the taillights grow smaller and smaller. About a half mile down the road, the car took a left and disappeared from view, hidden by the overgrown shrubs that lined the crossroad.

John trudged back to the crime scene and flicked on his flashlight, moving the beam over the trampled snow just outside the tape. While there were footprints visible, they were shapeless and free of identifying marks. He searched his memory for details about the man he'd seen wandering about and realized he must have been wearing some sort of boot covers with a soft sole. No wonder he hadn't worried about tracking through the snow.

He followed the tracks, using his flashlight to illuminate the snow around the crash site. He wasn't sure what the intruder had been looking for, but he could see nothing of interest. He supposed a crime scene team might be able to glean more, especially once the snow started to melt off the next day.

As he was walking back to the house, he heard the motor of another vehicle. He turned to watch its approach, soon making out the front grill of a large Ford pickup truck. The truck slowed as it neared his house, pulling onto the shoulder in front of him. The headlights dimmed and the interior light came on as the driver cut the engine. John could just make out Miranda Duncan's tousled auburn hair.

She'd made good time. Great time, actually.

She stopped a few yards away from him, squinting as he lifted the flashlight toward her. "What are you doing out here?"

"The intruder left. I was trying to see where he went, but he had a car waiting." He aimed the flashlight beam toward the ground, leading her through the snow to where he stood.

She pulled up a foot away, tugging her jacket more tightly around her as a gust of frigid wind blew across the plains, ruffling her hair. "Any idea what sort of car?"

"Too far away to be sure. It seemed to be a sedan, though. Not a truck."

"Did you see which way he went?"

"He turned left about a half mile up the road."

She nodded toward the taped-off crime scene. "Did he get inside the perimeter?"

"Not that I saw. He stayed outside the tape, but he was looking around with a pair of binoculars."

Miranda's gaze dropped to the pair of binoculars hanging around his neck.

He smiled. "I thought I'd see what he was trying to see."

Miranda frowned. "You went to the crime scene? Did you trample over his footprints?"

"He didn't leave prints." He told her about the boot covers. "He did seem to be looking for something, though."

"Like what?"

"I have no idea. I looked around after he left, but I didn't see a damn thing. I'm hoping maybe tomorrow the crime scene unit will come across something after the snow starts to melt."

"Tire prints," she said suddenly, looking up at him. A spark of excitement glittered in her eyes, lighting up her weary face. "Didn't the crew who came to tow the cruiser make imprints of the tire prints on the road out front? They were supposed to."

"I think so." He'd watched them doing something on the road and had assumed they'd been pouring molds of the prints.

"Maybe there are tire prints up the road where you saw that vehicle pull out and head down the highway."

"The temperature is supposed to be rising overnight. Those tracks—"

"May not be there tomorrow," she said, already heading for her truck.

He caught her wrist, stopping her forward motion. She looked first at his hand around her wrist, then slowly lifted her gaze to his, her expression bemused.

"You're supposed to be home in bed, getting rest," he said. "Not traipsing through the snow in search of tire prints. Besides, isn't there a unit coming from the station?"

The look of frustration in her eyes was almost comical. "They might obliterate them coming here."

"Call and warn them."

"Another vehicle could drive through—"

She wasn't going to let it go, he saw. "I don't have any way to make a mold for the tracks, Deputy," he pointed out. "And neither do you."

"We could take photographs."

"Of tire prints in the snow. At night."

Her mouth pressed to a tight line of annoyance. It was a cute look for her. In fact, his first impression that her features were more interesting than beautiful seemed, if not wrong, at least incomplete. There was an unexpected elegance to her strong bone structure, like the rugged beauty of a mountain peak or a winter-bare tree. A stripped-down sort of beauty that was all substance, all nature's bounty.

"Why don't we go inside, warm up until they get here?" he asked to distract himself from a rush of heat rising from deep in his belly. He gave a backward nod of his head, coaxing her toward the fireplace.

She gave him a reluctant look but didn't resist. It wasn't long before she was settling on the sofa and leaning toward the heat.

"How long have you been a deputy?" he asked, taking a seat beside her.

Her forehead crinkled at the question. "Almost ten years. I joined right out of college."

"Where did you go to college?"

Her slate-colored eyes narrowed slightly. "Texas Tech. You?"

"That information didn't come up in your background search?"

Her gaze narrowed. "I got a call about a missing person's case, so I didn't get to finish stripping your background bare."

The tart tone of her reply made him smile. "My bachelor's degree was from Wake Forest. My master's was from the University of Alabama."

"And now you're a carpenter?"

"After all that time and money, I realized I really hated accounting."

"Unfortunate." Her lips curved at the corners but didn't quite manage a smile. "Did you feel pressure to go into the family business anyway?"

Her tone suggested she understood that sort of pressure. "Your dad wanted you to go into the nuts-and-bolts biz?"

"I'm it for his branch of the family tree. No other kids, no living siblings. He's not that far from retiring, and I know he'd love it if I quit the sheriff's department and joined him in the sale of hardware." She laid her head against the back of the sofa, closing her eyes as she relaxed into the comfortable cushions. "Don't get me wrong. I'm so grateful for the life my dad's business gave me growing up. But I love being a cop."

"Even in a little place like Cold Creek?"

"Especially in a little place like Cold Creek." Her smile was genuine. "These are my people. I grew up with most of them. They're here in Cold Creek not because there's nowhere else they could go, but because there's nowhere else in this big, wide world they want to be. This place is in their blood, like it's in mine." She slanted a quick, sheepish look at him. "That was a little hokey, wasn't it?"

"No," he disagreed, meaning it. He had left his Tennessee roots behind a long time ago, but the pull of the mountains had never gone away. He'd felt it, a tug in the soul, during the months he'd recently spent in the Blue Ridge Mountains of southern Virginia.

He wondered if he could feel the same sort of tug from another place, especially one as flat and desolate as this part of Texas seemed to be.

Then he wondered why he was even thinking about spending more time in Texas than it took to get himself back into fighting shape, in case law enforcement couldn't round up all the stragglers left in the moribund Blue Ridge Infantry.

The sound of a car motor approaching on the highway dragged his attention away from that worrisome thought. He rose quickly and edged to the window to take a quick peek through the curtains.

A Barstow County Sheriff's Department cruiser had pulled up outside, parking next to Miranda's truck. "It's your colleague," he murmured as a tall young man stepped out of the cruiser and made his way through the crusty snow to the porch. He was the deputy who'd accompanied the sheriff earlier that day. What was his name?

Miranda followed him to the door as he opened it to the deputy's knock. "Robertson," she said briskly, joining him on the front porch rather than letting him in. She filled him in on what John had told her about the intruder. "He was wearing boot covers, so we don't have any tracks around the wreck, but Mr. Blake believes he drove away from behind that small stand of shrubs down the highway." She waved in the direction John had indicated. "He doesn't think any other vehicles have come through since then, thanks to the snow, so I thought we could get tire impressions, at least, to compare to the vehicle that took potshots at me earlier today."

Robertson took in everything she told him quietly, jotting notes. Then he looked up at Miranda, his blue eyes gentle with concern. "I thought the sheriff told you to get some rest."

John didn't miss the look of not-so-professional interest in the deputy's expression, but if Miranda was aware that the deputy had a bit of a crush on her, she didn't show it as she shrugged and said, "I was on the phone with Mr. Blake when he saw the intruder. I was at my dad's place, so I was several minutes closer than a cruiser could be."

Robertson flicked his gaze up to meet John's eyes. "I see."

"Well?" Miranda asked. "Did you bring the casting material?"

"It's out in the cruiser."

Miranda went inside to grab her jacket, zipped it up and started out the door after Robertson.

John caught up with her on the porch. "Do you think this is a good idea? It's freezing out here, and you took an awfully hard knock to the head earlier today. I'm pretty sure the EMTs told you to take it easy."

"I feel fine," she insisted, starting down the steps. But she swayed as she reached the bottom, and John hurried to give her a bracing hand before she ended up facedown in the snow.

"Yeah, I can see how fine you are," he murmured, tightening his grip around her arm to keep her from following Robertson. "Robertson strikes me as a capable guy."

"He doesn't know where to look for the tire prints."

"Neither do you, really. Come on." He tugged her arm, gently leading her back up the stairs to the house. He stopped before they entered. "Deputy Robertson?"

The deputy turned to look at him. "Yes?"

"Hold up. I'll go with you to show you where I saw the car. Let me get Deputy Duncan settled." He nudged Miranda into the house.

"You're making me look like a slacker in front of my fellow deputy," she grumbled, but she didn't fight him as he led her back to the fire and urged her to sit. "Do you know how hard it can be for a female cop to be taken seriously?"

"I do," he assured her. "But working when you've been told you have a concussion and need to rest doesn't exactly shower you with glory. It just makes you look overeager."

Her eyes narrowed. "You've been waiting to hit me with that all night, haven't you?"

He smiled. "No, but you know I'm right. What would you be thinking right now if the shoe was on the other foot, and it was Robertson out there staggering and reeling against doctor's orders, trying to prove he's a hotshot investigator?"

"I'd think he was an idiot," she conceded gruffly.

"I'll be right back." John laid his hand on her shoulder for a brief moment, his thumb brushing over her clavicle. The skin there was unexpectedly silky and delicate, an intriguing contrast to her tough, no-nonsense exterior.

He forced himself to turn and head out into the cold again, where he found Robertson waiting for him impatiently. He waved John to the passenger side and slid his own lanky body behind the steering wheel.

Robertson cranked up the heat to high as he pulled out on the highway. "Stop me short of where you saw the vehicle enter the highway," the deputy said. "Don't want to mess up the tracks."

John told him to stop about twenty yards from the

stand of shrubs that had hidden the intruder's vehicle. "It should be about thirty yards up the road. I think he must've parked his vehicle behind those shrubs because they'd block my view of the car from the house."

Robertson parked on the shoulder and pulled a flashlight from the cruiser's glove compartment. "Stay behind me," he told John.

John could have given the young deputy a few lessons on evidence retrieval, but he wasn't a cop and this wasn't his town. Plus, nobody liked a know-it-all.

The tire treads in the snow weren't hard to spot, and to John's surprise, they were nearly pristine. Apparently no other vehicles had passed on this side of the highway since the intruder drove away.

Robertson handed John the flashlight. "Can you hold this on the tracks while I get the casting material?"

John directed the beam toward the tire impressions, bending for a closer look. The treads had a pretty distinctive pattern. If the tire impressions the deputies had made earlier in the day were clear at all, they should be able to tell whether or not their intruder tonight was driving the same car.

Robertson stopped beside John. "Those are the same treads."

John looked up. "Are you sure?"

"I'm the one who took the impressions this afternoon after the tow truck hauled the cruiser away. These look like fairly new tires. Firestones, I think. The lab in Lubbock will tell us for sure."

"So I may have seen the man who shot at us this afternoon."

"Looks like."

"And we have no idea who he is or where he's gone."

"That's right."

John looked down the highway behind him, barely able to see his house, sitting small and isolated nearly a mile down the road.

And he'd left Miranda in there, alone and vulnerable, with a target on her back.

Chapter Five

She should be the one out there with Robertson. She was a deputy, damn it. A good one. And John Blake was a civilian.

Everybody was treating her as if she was made of glass, something delicate that needed to be wrapped in cotton batting and hidden away for her own protection.

She pushed to her feet, ignoring the aches and twinges in her muscles and bones, and crossed to the side window that looked out across the snowy plain between the house and the stand of shrubs where John had seen the mystery vehicle enter the highway.

The lights of Robertson's cruiser gleamed in the darkness down the road, and she could make out their silhouettes in the beams of the cruiser's headlights.

Tamping down frustration, she moved her gaze to the taped-off crime scene, wondering what the intruder had been looking for. The cruiser was already at the lab in Lubbock by now, set for examination. An attempted murder of a Texas lawman would put the case high on the list of priorities, she knew. At the very least, ballistics should give them some idea of what kind of weapon the assailant had used.

She couldn't remember how many shots had been

fired. Two had hit the cruiser for sure. And there'd been at least one other shot, hadn't there?

Could the intruder have been looking for a bullet that hadn't hit the cruiser? But why? It's not like they could keep the lab guys from finding the two slugs embedded in the cruiser.

She rubbed her aching head, wincing as her fingers brushed against the bandage covering the gash in her head. Nothing was making any sense. She wasn't likely to be on anyone's hit list. Most of the cases she investigated were minor-league domestic disturbances, drunk-and-disorderly calls and property theft, usually of animals or farming tools.

Could it have been mistaken identity?

But how could someone make a mistake about a well-marked Barstow County Sheriff's Department cruiser?

The cold night air seeped through the seams of the window, making her shiver and intensifying the ache in her battered body. She headed back to the warmth of the crackling fireplace but made herself stay on her feet. Sitting and wallowing in weariness and aching misery was not something she was going to allow herself to do.

She was young and strong. And, she reminded herself, she was all by herself in the house of a mysterious, intriguing stranger who'd just wandered into her town.

What were the odds, really, that she'd end up rolling her cruiser off the road just yards away from John Blake's house on the very day she ran into him at her father's hardware store?

Was it possible that her accident, and the subsequent assault on the two of them, was actually more about John than it was about her?

All very good questions, she had to admit. And she

might never have a better chance to take a look around John Blake's residence than right now.

The living room sprawled across the full width of the house, but there was little in it that gave her any clue about its occupant. No artwork on the walls, no personal photos on the mantel or the side tables. The lamps were simple and inexpensive, the kind she could find in any discount department store. The furniture was equally free of personality.

Average, she thought, squelching a smile. Like the man.

Except she was beginning to understand that John Blake was about as far from average as a man could get.

The bathroom revealed a few details. He liked his toothbrushes medium and his razors single bladed. He used soap, not bath gel. His medicine cabinet was stocked with both acetaminophen and ibuprofen, along with a prescription for a stronger painkiller from a pharmacy in Abingdon, Virginia. The prescription had been filled a month ago, but based on the pill count on the bottle, he hadn't taken any since the prescription had been filled.

He'd told her he'd spent some time in the hospital recently. He'd said it wasn't an accident.

Then what?

As she was heading from the bathroom toward the bedroom, she heard the rattle of keys in the door and detoured quickly toward the living room, making it to the fireplace before the door opened and John walked inside.

"Did you find anything?" she asked, trying not to sound out of breath, even though her pulse was pounding like a drum in her ears.

"Robertson is taking impressions of the tire treads."

John locked the door behind him and crossed to where she stood. "You look flushed. Feeling okay?"

"I'm fine," she assured him, swallowing her guilt. She was a cop, and John Blake was a stranger in town who had been conveniently nearby when someone tried to kill her. He wasn't at the top of her suspect list, since he'd been in the line of fire himself, but she'd be stupid not to at least take a look around and make sure he wasn't hiding some deep, dark secret.

Wouldn't she?

"Did Robertson say anything about the tire prints?" she asked as he dropped onto the sofa and stretched his hands toward the fire.

"Can't be sure until the lab takes a look, but Robertson thinks the tires are the same as the car we saw parked out front earlier today."

"But was that the car that took shots at us?"

"I think it almost had to be. Don't you?"

She frowned at the fire, wishing she could remember more about the events that had sent her and the cruiser careening off the highway. "The doctor at the clinic in town said I might never remember exactly what happened today."

"Or, in a day or two, you might remember everything." John put his hand on hers, his touch gentle. Undemanding.

But a ripple of animal awareness darted through her from the place his hand touched hers.

She didn't know whether she was relieved or disappointed when he drew his hand away and turned back to the fire. The fact that she didn't know made what she was about to say that much more difficult to utter.

"I think I should stay here tonight."

John's head snapped toward hers, a quizzical expression in his dark eyes. "I really don't know how to respond to that."

"I'm not supposed to sleep much tonight anyway," she said with what she hoped was a reassuring smile. "Because of the concussion. So I thought I could stay up, keep watch on the crime scene until morning."

"Or you could get someone from the station who hasn't been in a rollover car crash to stand watch outside," he suggested. "You should be resting, not playing cop."

"First off, I don't play cop. I am a cop."

"You know what I meant."

"Second, maybe things are different where you come from, but here in Cold Creek, we don't have many officers to spare. I'm here. I'm awake and I'm way too wired to go to sleep tonight. I can pull up a chair to that window, bundle up and keep an eye out for anybody else who might wander into the crime scene. You won't even know I'm here."

He gave a soft huff of laughter. "Believe me, Deputy, I'll know you're here."

She shot him a challenging look. "Is there some other reason you don't want me here? Do you have something to hide?"

"If I did, it's within my constitutional rights to do so, Deputy." He spoke with a firmness that tweaked her curiosity.

So he did have something to hide.

But what?

"Stay," he said after a long pause. "If that's what you want to do. I'll stay up with you. Keep you company."

"That's not necessary—"

"That's my condition for your staying in my house overnight," he said firmly. "Take it or leave it."

She looked at him through narrowed eyes, debating her options. He was right—if he had secrets, keeping them was his right unless she could prove they broke any laws within her jurisdiction. And if she wanted to stay at his house, she would simply have to abide by his rules.

No matter how much inconvenience—or temptation—they might pose.

THERE WERE THREE WOUNDS, *he saw as he assessed the damage quickly from his hiding place behind a rocky outcropping near the top of the ridge. Dallas Cole and Nicki Jamison had gotten away, along with the woman and the boy they'd rescued from the cabin, but the woman's husband and his henchmen were out here in the woods somewhere, looking for him.*

It was dark, so there was a chance they wouldn't be able to follow the track of blood he'd left as he ran, but if the good guys didn't show up before morning, John was going to be in a hell of a lot of trouble.

Who was he kidding? He was already in trouble. The wound in his shoulder had, at the very least, cracked his collarbone, the slightest movement of his left arm sending agony racing through his body. There was also a through-and-through wound just above his hip—that one seemed to have missed the bone, though his jeans were now soaked with blood from the wound.

The one he was worried about was the bullet in his side. It was still in there somewhere. John wasn't sure what it might have hit on its way in.

And he was starting to feel very, very woozy. Too woozy to keep his eyes open any longer.

"John?" The voice was low. Female. Faintly familiar. It seemed far away at first, then louder. "John, wake up..."

He snapped his eyes open, bracing for the pain. It was there, in his shoulder most strongly, but still little more than a twinge. He wasn't in the woods, he realized, as early morning sunlight angling through the window in front of him made him squint.

The voice belonged to the bleary-eyed redhead curled up in an armchair next to his, gazing at him with a faint smile on her pale lips. "You told me if you fell asleep to wake you by six."

Right. The stakeout. The deputy with the head injury had managed to stay awake, but he'd drifted off like an old man.

He stretched, grimacing at the ache in his bones. "I take it nobody wandered into your crime scene?"

She slanted a sheepish look at him. "I might have dozed off an hour or so just before dawn."

"I don't think he planned to come back. He didn't spot whatever he was looking for, so he left."

"You don't think it's because he spotted you watching him?"

"I don't think he could have seen me." John stretched carefully, all too cognizant of the limitations of his recovery. The collarbone fracture had mended, but too violent an arm or shoulder movement could still make his nerves jangle. The other injuries to his side and the muscles over his hip were going to be painful for a while, but it was a dull ache that usually went away after the muscles warmed up.

"What kind of injuries did you have?" Miranda had turned in the armchair until she faced him, her long limbs tucked up under her and the blanket wrapped warmly around her. In the rosy light of morning, her sleepy face looked soft and young, giving her a delicate beauty he wouldn't have associated with her if he hadn't seen it for himself.

"Fractured clavicle and some muscle damage in my side," he answered vaguely.

"You said it wasn't an accident."

"No."

Her auburn eyebrows notched upward. "Okay."

Great. He'd just made her more curious, not less. "Actually, a hunting injury." And it was true, in a way.

"Deer?"

"No."

This time, her lips quirked with amused frustration. "I never could manage to enjoy hunting. I mean, I get the point of it from a conservation standpoint, and I like venison stew as much as the next person—"

He had to put her out of her misery. "Actually, I wasn't the one doing the hunting."

Her brow crinkled, but before she could say anything, her phone rang. She dug it from the pocket of her jeans and grimaced before answering. "Hi, Dad. Yes, I'm still here." She slanted a quick look at John. "I know, but—"

John walked away to give her a little privacy, but the room wasn't big enough to avoid hearing her end of what was clearly a paternal lecture. With a heavy sigh she sank deeper into the chair where she'd passed the night and settled in to listen.

John headed for the kitchen to start a pot of coffee. While he was waiting for the coffeemaker to finish, he searched his refrigerator for something that might pass for breakfast. He usually made do with coffee alone, but he'd bought a dozen eggs earlier in the week. He could make omelets. Every guy with any self-respect could make an omelet, right?

He had the eggs sizzling nicely in a skillet by the time Miranda wandered into the kitchen. "Hungry?"

She gave him an odd look but admitted she was. "May I help myself to the coffee?"

He waved his hand at the pot, and she poured a cup, stirring in a packet of sweetener from a jar sitting next to the pot. "Want a cup?" she asked as she stirred her own and gave it a sip.

"Black. One sweetener." He glanced at her over his shoulder. "What do you know? The way you like yours."

She smiled and made him a matching cup of coffee. "You didn't have to go to the trouble."

"I was hungry," he said and decided it wasn't exactly a lie. He *was* hungry, and she didn't need to know that if she wasn't there, he wouldn't have bothered cooking. "Your dad wasn't happy about your disobeying doctor's orders?"

"Not even a little. He wanted to take my keys away last night, but I threatened to arrest him." She grinned. "He didn't believe me, but at least he stopped grabbing at my keys. And he's even going to go by my house this morning on his way to work to feed my cats."

"You have cats?"

She slanted a narrow-eyed look his way. "Two. You have a problem with cats?"

"No. I like cats, actually. I just haven't been in a position to have pets in a while. What kind of cats do you have?"

"One's a silver tabby—Rex. And the other is a tortoiseshell named Ruthie." Over the cup of coffee, her eyes smiled, soft with affection. "They were litter mates I found while I was out on a call a couple of years ago. The mama cat had been hit by a car, and that had led to a drunken brawl over who had done it and—" She waved her hands. "Anyway, there were two little kittens nobody wanted, so I took 'em. And don't worry, they're neutered and spayed so I won't be having any surprise kittens."

"Good for you," he said, meaning it. Growing up, he'd seen his share of feral cats and kittens out fending for themselves and usually ending up as roadkill or coyote bait. "Nice of your dad to go feed them for you."

"I think it was his apology for being such a bear last night about my driving over here."

"He has a point, though. Beyond your very recent head injury, I mean. You're the victim. That's a pretty good reason why you really shouldn't be part of this investigation."

"I don't know if you've noticed, but this is a small town."

"No, really?"

She smiled at his tone. "We have fifteen deputies covering this whole county. And while that may seem like a lot, given the small population, we have a lot of miles to cover. I was a witness to what happened to me, even if some of the details are a little fuzzy. Who better to investigate it?"

"You still don't remember how the wreck happened?"

She shook her head. "I was out on a call—I remember that much. I talked to the sheriff, and he confirmed it. We'd gotten an anonymous call about a woman we've been trying to locate—a woman who seems to be missing."

"Seems to be?"

"Well, she's gone off without telling anyone before. She doesn't hold a steady job, so it's not like anyone's waiting for her to show up for her shift or anything. And she doesn't really have any family to keep an eye out for her anymore."

"Maybe she just moved without telling anyone."

"Except all her stuff is still at her trailer. I mean, there might be some things missing, but a lot of her clothes and all of her furniture is still there."

John could tell from the concern in Miranda's eyes that she was personally worried about the missing woman. "How long has she been missing?"

"The last anyone remembers seeing her was three weeks ago. Until yesterday, when that call came in. Someone claimed to see Delta—that's her name, Delta McGraw. Anyway, someone called and left a tip with the desk sergeant that he saw Delta hitchhiking on Route 7."

"So that's why you were out here yesterday?"

She nodded. "I drove past the place where she was supposed to have been spotted, but I didn't see anyone. I made one more stop to check on a farmer who's been complaining about someone or something stealing her eggs, then it started to snow, so I decided I'd better head back to the station before I got stuck out here."

"What happened next?"

"I don't know. I don't remember anything after I made the turn onto Route 7 heading back to town." She poked at the remainder of her omelet. "It's very strange, having this big blank place in my memory. I know something happened. I remember the aftermath. But what happened before—"

"That's not uncommon with concussions."

"That's what the doctor said. Knowing that doesn't

really help, though. I need to remember what happened. Why it happened. My roof lights were on—and apparently I made a call to the station to tell them what was happening."

"Right. I talked to the desk sergeant when I called for help. He said you'd said someone was following you."

"I don't remember that at all. But obviously, someone was. Chambers—that was the sergeant at the desk when I called it in—said I gave a description of the vehicle. Dark blue Ford Taurus."

"Same as the car we saw parked out on the highway. And apparently the car that was driving around here last night, too."

"I must not have gotten the plate number, though. Someone would have told me." She started to say something else, but the trill of her cell phone lying on the table beside her interrupted. She frowned at the display and picked up the phone, meeting John's gaze with an upward flick of her eyebrows. "Hi, Dad."

Her mild amusement disappeared almost immediately, her gray eyes darkening with anger. "How bad?"

Her father's answer made her jaw clench tightly. "Stay put, I'm on my way. I'll call the station." She hung up the phone and pushed to her feet, already halfway out of the kitchen.

"What's going on?" John asked as he caught up with her in the living room.

She grabbed her jacket and shrugged it on, turning to look at him, her eyes ablaze with fury. "Somebody tossed my house last night."

Chapter Six

Miranda came to a stop in the middle of the living room, her head aching and her stomach in knots at the sight of the mess intruders had made of her normally tidy living room. Sofa cushions had been removed from the frame and ripped apart, despite having zippered covers that could have been easily taken off. Books had been pulled from the built-in bookshelves that flanked the fireplace and left scattered on the floor beneath.

In the kitchen, the cabinets had been emptied and any open containers had been poured into the sink, creating a mess that would be a nightmare to clean up. She'd probably have to have a plumber in to clean out the pipes.

Her mattress had been stripped and cut open, just like the cushions from the sofa, and her closets emptied, the clothes left scattered on the gutted mattress and floor. The sheer level of cleanup that lay ahead of Miranda was enough to make her want to curl up in a corner and cry. Instead, she finished her circuit of the vandalized house and returned to the living room.

"What the hell were they looking for?" she asked, lifting her gaze to meet the troubled eyes of her father.

"I don't know." He made a helpless openhanded gesture toward her, and she crossed to where he stood, letting him wrap her up in a bear hug that made her feel both small and safe at the same time.

Boots on the front porch announced the return of Miles Randall, giving her time to extricate herself from her father's embrace and face the sheriff with her chin held high. Coy Taylor, who'd come on the call with the sheriff, gave her a sympathetic nod as he entered and closed out the cold behind him.

"The shed out back has been tossed, too," Randall told her, his dark eyes apologetic. "Can you tell if anything's been taken?"

She shook her head. "Anything worth any money is still here—TV, stereo equipment, appliances. I don't own any valuable jewelry, and my laptop was in my truck, locked in the chest. Was the lawn mower still in the shed? And the generator?"

Taylor nodded.

"Then they didn't take anything worth anything out of there, either."

"We can dust the place for prints," Taylor said, "but I doubt we'll get much, and all it'll do is make a bigger mess for you to clean up."

She couldn't argue with that. The destruction of property might end up being a misdemeanor, but she couldn't see that anything had been stolen. Probably a couple of kids, doped up or, hell, maybe just bored and looking for something to do. "I called my insurance man, but he's out on some weather-related calls, so he said he'd trust me to just take some photos of the destruction. Although he's not sure off the top of his head how much will be covered by my homeowner's policy."

"Have you found the cats yet?" a quiet voice asked from the corner of the room.

Miranda looked past the sheriff to lock gazes with John Blake, who'd insisted on following her to her place earlier. He'd settled there in the corner, keeping out of the way while Miranda, the sheriff and Coy Taylor had taken a look around the house.

"They're hiding under the bed," she said, blinking back hot tears that burned behind her eyes. "Once everything settles down, they'll come out."

"Honey, if you need me, I can call Mary to cover the shop—"

Miranda put her hand on her father's arm. "I'm fine. It's just a matter of cleaning everything up, and I can handle that on my own."

"I'll help," John said.

Miranda's father looked at the man in the corner, his eyes narrowed in mild speculation. Miranda tugged at his arm, drawing his attention back to her. "Go open the shop. If you leave now, you won't be late."

Gil gave her a kiss on the uninjured side of her forehead. "Don't overdo. And when you tire out, your bed's still waiting at the house." With a nod to the sheriff and Coy Taylor, he left the house, his boot thuds heavy on the wooden front porch.

Sheriff Randall gave her a thoughtful look. "I could call some of the guys off duty to come give you some help—"

She nearly recoiled at the thought. It was hard enough to be seen as an equal without having to turn to the boys for help. "I've got it covered, sir. But thanks for the offer."

"Let me know if you change your mind." Randall nodded for Coy Taylor to follow him out. The desk sergeant turned and flashed a sympathetic smile at Miranda before he left, closing the door behind him.

She let go of a deep sigh and looked at John. "You don't have to stay and help. It would be asking too much."

"You didn't ask. I offered."

"You know what I mean."

He stepped out of the corner and met her in the middle of the ravaged room. "You should be resting, but you won't. So I'm going to stick around and make sure you don't undo all my first-aid work from yesterday."

Her lips curved at his dry words. "Your work, huh?"

He just let the corners of his mouth twitch upward as he nodded at the sofa. "I think that's a loss."

"My bed, too." She quelled the urge to cry. "Just the mattress and box springs, though. I think the frame is still fine. I guess I need to make a trip to Plainview to pick up a new set." Her savings could handle replacing what she'd lost, though it would make a pretty big dent in her nest egg.

"I'm not sure you should drive to Plainview by yourself while you're still concussed, especially with the roads still messy for the next few hours. Why don't you take up your dad on his offer of a place to sleep tonight? Tomorrow, if you're feeling better, you can drive to Plainview and pick up a new mattress set."

"You have no idea how easy—" She clamped her mouth shut, appalled by how much personal information she'd almost revealed to a virtual stranger. Her relationship with her father was loving but complicated, and admitting just how complicated would make her much more vulnerable than she intended to be with anyone, especially someone she'd met only a day ago. "I just—I just need to stand on my own two feet."

"Okay." He nodded slowly. "But it's just a bed for one more night."

"There's a thrift store in Cold Creek. They might have a sofa I could buy to replace this one. I could sleep on the sofa until I have time to get a new mattress set."

His eyes narrowed as he looked at her for a long moment. "How about this? We clean up as much as we can, then I drive you to town to go sofa shopping. That way, I can help you load it in the truck and you don't have to drive while concussed. And you can sleep in your own house tonight. If that's what you want."

An odd tone to his voice gave her pause. "If it's what I want?"

He was quiet a moment, as if considering what he wanted to say. Finally, he walked over to the bookcases and started picking up books. When he spoke, his voice was deceptively casual. "Do you have any enemies?"

"Not that I know of."

"Not even someone you've arrested?"

She set another book in the bookcase next to the one he'd just restored. "Don't overestimate the number of people I've actually arrested. In a county this small, most police work is about keeping order and not much more."

He waved his arm around at the mess. "This looks personal."

Spoken like a man who knew what it was like to be a target, she realized. A dozen questions rolled through her aching head, but she had a feeling asking them outright, especially now, might send him running. If she wanted to know any of John Blake's secrets, she was going to have to be patient. Let him get used to her, feel secure enough to let down his guard.

"Well, look there," John murmured, his gaze slanting to his right.

Miranda followed his gaze and saw Ruthie creeping

slowly into the living room, her eyes wide with alarm as she scanned the room for threats.

"Hey, sweet girl," she crooned to the spooked cat.

Ruthie's ears pricked at the familiar sound of her voice, but her green-eyed gaze darted warily toward John. He ignored her, straightening the books they'd returned to the shelf with small, economical movements.

So he did understand cats, she thought.

The longer John ignored Ruthie, the bolder she became, moving slowly across the room. Her tail rose finally in a question mark, and she looked up at Miranda, her mouth forming a voiceless meow.

Miranda bent and gave Ruthie's ears a scratch. "You hungry, sweet cakes?"

"Does she usually answer you?" John asked softly without turning his head, his voice tinted with humor.

"In her own way." She led Ruthie into the kitchen, where she found that the canister of dry cat food had been dumped into the sink along with most of the other open containers.

The urge to cry overwhelmed her, and she sank into the only chair that hadn't been overturned. Ruthie jumped in her lap and rubbed her head against Miranda's chin, eliciting the tears she'd been trying to resist.

She pressed her hot face against the cat's tricolor fur. "Oh, sweetie, we're going to have to go get you some food, aren't we?"

"Your dad's shop carries pet food, doesn't it?" John's voice was a soft rumble from the doorway.

She looked up, blinking back her tears. "Yes."

"I'll run get a bag."

"He knows the brand they like." She flashed him a grateful smile. "Tell him to put it on my tab."

John gave a nod. "You sure you'll be okay here by yourself?"

She managed not to bristle at the question. "I'm armed. I'll keep cleaning up while you're gone."

He disappeared down the hall. A moment later, she heard the door open and close.

Releasing a deep sigh, she eased Ruthie from her lap and started picking up the overturned chairs around the breakfast table.

"THOSE BASTARDS." GIL DUNCAN'S voice was a deep rumble of anger as he heaved the bag of cat food over the counter and handed it to John. "She worked damn hard to make a nice home for herself. I tell you what, it was like a gut punch seein' what they'd done to her things. A real gut punch."

"Do you have any idea who'd do such a thing to Miranda?" John tucked the bag under his good arm. "I don't know her well, but everyone I've talked to seems to think the world of her."

Gil's smile was genuinely proud. "She's a good woman, like her mama was. Smart girl, too. It had to be kids, don't you think? All those hormones and restless energy just wantin' to bust out all over, but nowhere in this little town to let it rip. And these days, folks don't teach their young'uns to respect other people's things. Hell, they probably recorded what they did and put it up on YouFace or whatever you call it." Gil grinned sheepishly. "Lord, I'm soundin' just like my granddaddy, ain't I?"

John grinned back at him, deciding he liked Miranda's father. "Miranda mentioned something about a case she'd been working—a missing woman?"

"Yeah. Delta McGraw." Gil shook his head. "That

girl's had a hell of a life, and I don't reckon anybody'd blame her if she'd just picked up and left town for good. But Miranda seems to think she should've been back in town by now."

"Is she a young woman?"

"A little younger than my Mandy—maybe a couple of years younger. But in some ways, she seems a lot older. Life's been harder on her. Her mama ran off when she was real little, so it was left to that daddy of hers to raise her. All he knew how to do was make her his accomplice."

"He's a criminal?"

"Was. Con man, mainly. Small cons, get-rich-quick schemes. You know the sort. People liked him anyway, because he was that kind of fellow. Made you laugh even when he was fleecing you blind." Gil shrugged. "I reckon folks tended to give him a lot of leeway, too, because his wife ran off when his little girl was so young and he was left to take care of her."

"Is he dead or incarcerated?"

Gil gave him an odd look. "Dead. Big rig versus pickup truck. Big rig wins."

John grimaced. "So you don't think this missing girl has anything to do with your daughter's problems?"

Gill gave him a narrow-eyed look. "You seem awfully interested for someone who just met her."

"She nearly died in my side yard. We both ended up dodging bullets. I guess that makes me feel like I have a stake in her well-being," he answered truthfully.

"You a cop or something?"

"I'm a carpenter," John replied.

"Hmm." Gil didn't say anything more, turning to greet

another customer entering the store. John took the cat food and headed back to his truck.

The snow had melted off by midmorning, leaving the roads wet but clear, and traffic on the highway was starting to pick up. After John slid behind the steering wheel of his truck and buckled up, he called Miranda.

She answered on the second ring. "Checking up on me?" she asked.

"Just making sure you and the cats were still okay. Did the other one ever come out?"

"He did, and he's not very patient when he's hungry."

"I'll be there in a few minutes." He hung up and started the truck, but on second thought, he turned it off again and picked up his phone. He dialed another number and waited for the answer.

A moment later, Quinn's voice came over the line. "Marbury Motors twenty-four-hour hotline."

"It's me," John said. "Several things have happened since I talked to you last, and I guess you need to know."

Quinn was silent while John gave him a succinct but thorough recap of all that had happened since their last phone call. "Everybody swears there's no reason for anyone to target her, but—"

"But you're wondering if it has anything to do with the BRI."

"Del McClintock's still at large. He nearly killed me once—"

"He doesn't know your real identity."

"That we know of. If I've brought that mess here to Texas—"

"I really don't believe you have. But if you do something to start drawing attention to yourself there, you might."

"Fine." He made himself relax, even though he could

still feel prickles of unease running up and down the skin of his neck. "They're not after me."

"You don't sound as if you believe it."

"I don't think dropping my guard will help anyone."

"If it's not you, then it's the deputy. Are you sure there's no reason someone might want her out of the way?"

He thought about what Gil Duncan had told him about the missing person case Miranda had been investigating. "Maybe," he admitted. "And maybe you can help. Can you see if you can find me some info on a woman named Delta McGraw?"

JOHN ARRIVED WITH the cat food within ten minutes, and soon Ruthie and Rex were happily crunching their kibble while John took in the improvements she'd managed to accomplish while he was gone.

The sink was still a disaster area, but she'd picked up all the chairs and swept up the mess on the floor. In the living room, she'd finished putting the books in the shelves and piled the ripped-up cushions onto the sagging frame of the sofa.

"You've made some headway," he said, sounding impressed. But the look he shot her way made it clear that he could see right through her attempt at pretending she wasn't feeling like hell. "Why don't you rest a bit and let me catch up?"

"I'm fine."

"As fine as a concussed, sleep-deprived person could be," he agreed. "But if we're going sofa shopping in town a little later, you should rest up."

She leaned against the door frame that led into the hall

and crossed her arms, looking at him through narrowed eyes. "Why are you doing all this for me?"

"You mean helping you buy a sofa?"

She nodded. "Yeah, that. And everything else you've done to help me."

"I need another badge for my Boy Scout uniform."

She smiled. "There's a furniture-moving badge?"

"You sound skeptical."

He wasn't nearly as average as she'd originally thought, she was beginning to see. His eyes might be a muddy sort of hazel green, but they twinkled brightly when he was amused, like sunlight sparkling on a murky stream. His ordinary features seemed to come to life when he smiled, carving interesting lines in his normally unremarkable face. He wasn't ripped like a bodybuilder, but his body was well-proportioned, his muscles lean and well-defined beneath his long-sleeved T-shirt when he bent to pick up a picture frame she hadn't gotten to yet.

He looked at the photograph in the broken frame, a smile curving his lips. "Is this you and your mom?"

She pushed away from the door frame and crossed to where he stood, looking at the photo. "Yes. I was six. First day of school. My dad took that photo as Mama was walking me out the door to the bus." She'd been crying a little, the tears still sparkling on her cheeks in the photo. "She said I'd love it if I just gave it a chance."

"Was she right?"

She looked into his curious gaze. "She always was."

"She's not still around, is she." He didn't phrase it as a question.

"No. She died when I was still a kid. Hit head-on by a drunk driver over in Plainview. She was a nurse at the hospital there."

"I'm sorry."

She studied the photograph, relieved to find it hadn't been scratched by the broken glass of the frame. "Some of the photos are irreplaceable. Why would someone trash the place like this? What on earth could they have been looking for?"

John reached out for her, and to her surprise, she let him pull her into a comforting hug, feeling further evidence of his lean muscularity. He smelled good, too, she realized, despite a long night sleeping in a chair. He must have showered before she'd shown up at his place the night before.

She, however, hadn't showered since the previous morning. God only knew what she must smell like about now. With a blush, she extricated herself from his arms and flashed a sheepish smile. "Why don't we just get the sofa shopping over with now?" she suggested. "So I'll have somewhere to pass out when I finally hit the wall."

To her relief, he agreed, and she grabbed her jacket and followed him out to the truck.

John Blake was proving to be a surprising temptation, one she wasn't used to having to struggle against. Yes, she was finding him attractive, but if that had been the extent of it, she'd have been able to resist quite easily. It wasn't that she was immune to physical attraction— she'd had her share of boyfriends over the years, enjoyed their company and more—but she'd always found it easy enough to walk away when the time came for a relationship to end.

There was something about the mysterious newcomer with his murky eyes and murkier intentions that were proving to be damn near irresistible on a whole other level.

If there was anything she couldn't walk away from, it was a mystery.

And John Blake was nothing if not a mystery.

Chapter Seven

Miranda had hit the wall, as she called it, around three that afternoon, after they'd managed to clean up and bag up most of the trash in her house. It had taken a little longer than John had expected, mostly because Miranda had insisted on sifting through everything they picked up in search of trace evidence.

"Do you really think you're going to find any?" John had asked, dutifully holding the trash bag for her while she dumped a load of fiberfill stuffing from the shredded sofa.

"Probably not," she'd admitted with a grimace of a smile. "But I wouldn't be a good cop if I didn't check."

He'd talked her into leaving the bedroom for later, and she'd settled, finally, on the thrift store sofa she'd purchased in town earlier.

"It's in better shape than the original," she'd drawled upon seeing it in the previously bare spot in the middle of her living room. She'd tested it out for napping comfort and promptly fell asleep, leaving John on his own for the next couple of hours.

He was tempted to head back home to see if the crime scene unit had finished processing the scene of the wreck, but he didn't want to leave Miranda alone, asleep and vulnerable, in a house that had been ransacked in the past twenty-four hours. He settled, instead, in the only chair in the living room that hadn't been relieved of its stuffing— a wooden rocking chair that had no stuffing at all, only a slightly sagging woven cane seat that creaked a bit as he sat down.

It was solidly made, the handiwork painstaking and careful. An antique, he thought, not one of those mass-produced, overpriced jobs you could buy in almost any chain store.

He had trained as an accountant, a job he hated. He'd worked twice as an undercover agent, a job he loved, but now, as it had the first time, fate and circumstances had forced him out again, leaving his future in flux.

But carpentry was the skill he was actually good at. His grandfather on his mother's side had been a true artist with wood, and John had been the only grandchild who'd been interested enough to sit for hours at his side, watching him work and learning all the skills and tricks of the trade.

Blanchard Building was a real company that employed real craftsmen from time to time, and his cover for being in Cold Creek was a real job, using his carpentry skills to renovate the home where he was living for the next couple of months.

It was also a way to recover some of his physical strength and stamina, because carpentry could be a physically taxing skill, as he'd learned over the past week, when his rusty joints and muscles had been forced into work after almost a week in the hospital and another three weeks of physical therapy.

As he quietly rocked, the two cats wandered into the living room from somewhere in the back of the house.

They crept cautiously around the new sofa, sniffing the upholstery from end to end before they decided it was no threat. One after the other, Ruthie first, then Rex, jumped gracefully onto the sofa and settled side by side behind the crook of Miranda's knees. Ruthie gave John a wide-eyed stare for a couple of moments before she closed her eyes to nap.

John watched Miranda sleep for a little while, enjoying the view of her face soft with sleep. Awake, she was almost militantly competent, a woman of substance and power, but asleep, he saw a hint of girlish softness he suspected she tried to hide. He'd worked with female agents at The Gates, though largely from a distance, and he'd seen a similar sort of dichotomy in each of them, as well. Strength before softness, almost always. It was the only way they knew to survive in a world where men outnumbered women by a substantial degree.

He admired Miranda's strength. But it was that hint of softness that intrigued him the most, made him wonder what other secrets she hid behind that tough-girl exterior.

For one thing, despite her rangy build, she had delicious curves. He'd felt them beneath her clothes when she'd let him give her a comforting hug. Firm, round breasts and delectably flaring hips that would tempt a eunuch to let his hands wander. She'd pulled away from his embrace just in time, because John Blake was a lot of things, but a eunuch wasn't one of them.

With his mind drifting to dangerous places once more, he pushed to his feet and wandered around the house, looking for a distraction.

He found it in the back of the house.

He hadn't really noticed that the kitchen took up only half of the back part of the house. To the left of the kitchen, there was another room that hadn't been touched by the intruders, as far as John could tell. That was probably because it was nothing but a frame of a room, with no drywall or flooring. Not an addition, he decided as he took in the handiwork. Part of the framework was obviously older, the wood darkened and worn with age.

Repair work?

"Tornado damage." Miranda's voice behind him made him jump.

He turned and found her watching him with sleepy eyes the color of a stormy sky. The cats wound in complicated patterns around her legs and each other.

He remembered the order of two-by-fours she'd picked up at the hardware store the day he met her. "Are you rebuilding it yourself?"

"Slowly," she said with a rueful smile. "I wanted to do it myself. To see if I could."

"It's complicated work. Do you know what you're doing?"

"I've helped with other building jobs," she answered, not appearing to take his skeptical question personally. "My dad owns a hardware store, you know. I've grown up around builders and saved for college by working summers on building crews." She pushed her sleep-tousled hair away from her face. "I've just never been my own foreman before."

"When did the tornado hit?"

"Last November. Late in the season. I was lucky. It was a small twister and the wind only caught the edge of the house. I was working. Got home after a long day of dealing with multiple tornadoes to find the back corner of my house gone."

"How'd the cats handle that experience?"

"About like they did this time with the intruder. Hid under the bed for hours until they were convinced the freight train that hit the house was gone." She stifled a yawn.

"You should go back to sleep."

"So you can snoop around my house in peace?"

"I wasn't." He stopped before he told the easy lie. "Okay, I was snooping, a little."

"Sadly, my life is an open book." She stepped past him into the room, then turned suddenly to look at him. "Why do I get the feeling you can't say the same thing?"

Because he couldn't, he thought. His life hadn't really been an open book since his college graduation, over fifteen years earlier, when a man named Alexander Quinn had introduced himself by another name altogether and asked him to take a drive.

His CIA career had ended almost before it began, but the things he'd seen and done during that short time had changed the way he approached life. There had been no such thing as a normal life for him, even when he'd been working for his father at the accounting firm. There'd certainly been nothing ordinary about his life as Alexander Quinn's undercover operative in southern Virginia.

"Your name is John Blake. I'm pretty sure about that." She stepped closer to him, taking full advantage of her height to crowd his space. "Although you seemed to disappear for a while between your time at your family accounting firm and showing up on the payroll of Blanchard Building."

"I was finding myself."

She laughed, a deep belly laugh that made him want to laugh with her. "You know what? I'm not sure I want to know what you were doing. I have a feeling the truth wouldn't be nearly as interesting as what I'm imagining."

Damn, he wanted to kiss her. It would be so easy; she was standing there, near enough that he could reach out and pull her to him, close the space between their bodies. He remembered how her body had felt pressed to his all too briefly.

The air between them electrified, and her laughter faded until she was gazing up at him, her eyes luminous and her lips trembling apart.

So very easy to kiss her...

He pulled back, trying to remember why he was in Texas in the first place. He was here to lie low, not start an affair with a Barstow County sheriff's deputy. She was already curious about his background. She was smart and she had the resources at her command that could unravel a lot of his secrets.

He needed distance from her, not closeness.

Except someone wanted her dead. And protecting people was his business these days.

As she took a step back as well, her eyes narrowing, he said the first thing that came to mind. "Tell me about Delta McGraw."

She took another step back. "Who told you about Delta?"

"You did."

"I didn't mention her name."

"Your father told me her name."

Her brow furrowed, her eyes darkening to thunderclouds. "You talked to my dad about one of my cases?" She pushed past him and stalked down the hallway, her shoulders squared with anger.

He followed her into the living room. "Someone tried

to kill you. And me, in case you forgot. That same person came back to my house looking for God knows what. And someone also tossed this place and left no stone, canister or sofa cushion unturned."

She turned to face him. "That could have been kids."

He arched an eyebrow at her, and she sighed.

"Fine. It was probably related. But what do you think any of it has to do with Delta?"

"You said yourself it's the only real case you're investigating. And didn't you say that the call that sent you out to Route 7 in the first place was about Delta? Someone had seen her hitchhiking or something?"

"Right. But I didn't see her anywhere."

"Maybe you weren't supposed to."

Her eyes narrowed. "You mean that call was to lure me out there?"

"The weathermen were predicting snow. Hardly anyone was out on the roads by that hour because of the dire reports."

"But someone would have to know I was the one who took the call."

"It was your case. You would have been the first person the call would have gone to, right?"

She nodded, looking thoughtful. "But that still doesn't answer the question of why someone would run me off the road and try to shoot me. That's pretty drastic for a missing persons case."

"Unless she's not just missing."

"You think someone killed her." Her expression remained mostly neutral, but there was a flicker of pain in her eyes.

"How close were you and Delta?"

"Not real close. But I guess about as close as she'd let

anyone get." There was a hint of hesitation in her voice. "I tried to help her a few times. Adjusting to life without her dad was really strange for her. They had a...difficult relationship."

"Because he was a con artist?"

She frowned. "Did my dad tell you that, too?"

Busted. "I asked about her. He didn't know he was spilling state secrets or anything."

"Why didn't you just ask me?"

"Because you'd probably pull that whole police-business thing and keep it to yourself."

She shot him a look of consternation that told him his words had hit the mark. He was right and she knew it. "It *is* police business," she said weakly.

"And you weren't the only one who nearly got killed yesterday." He stepped closer to her, willing her not to back away. He needed her to understand that he had a stake in this mystery, too, because there was no way in hell he was going to let her whip out her badge and try to shut him out.

Her eyes went wide and unexpectedly soft. "I know. But you were only involved because of me."

He knew she was probably right. But there was that little sliver of possibility that he'd been the one who was the real target, wasn't there? Quinn didn't think anyone from the BRI had tracked him down to Texas, but despite his downright mythical reputation, Quinn didn't really know everything. He could be wrong.

And all it took to get a man killed was to drop his guard just once in the wrong place at the wrong time.

"You're not just a carpenter, are you?"

He snapped his focus back to her. She was looking at him with sudden understanding.

"I don't know what—"

"A year overseas working for a global marketing firm. But you're an accountant. Or a carpenter. Why doesn't that compute?"

"Miranda—"

"And there's a whole year missing more recently, until you show up a couple of weeks ago on the payroll of Blanchard Building in Garza County. But as far as I can tell, the entire time you've been on their payroll, you've been living here in Cold Creek."

"So?"

"You don't react to things like a civilian."

"I'm not a cop."

"No, you don't have that vibe," she agreed. "But I'm betting you've done some sort of intelligence work. No record of time in the military, so I'm guessing CIA or NSA. Maybe Homeland Security."

He decided to play it for a joke. "I'd tell you, but then I'd have—"

"To kill me. Right." She shook her head. "Don't worry. I'm not going to ask any more questions. Promise."

Good, he thought, though he wasn't sure it was a promise she'd be able to keep. Curiosity glittered in her eyes like diamonds, even now. How long would she be able to keep that desire to know at bay?

MIRANDA HAD MANAGED to find a bottle of bath gel that hadn't been dumped down the bathroom sink and took a long, hot soak while John went to the barbecue joint a half mile down the road to pick up takeout. By seven that evening, she was full and growing sleepy, but he showed no signs of leaving.

"You're not planning on leaving, are you?" she asked, stifling a yawn.

John met her gaze. "I'd rather not."

She leaned toward him. "Why, Mr. Blake, is that a proposition?"

He leaned toward her, as well. "Well, that depends."

"On what?"

"On whether you're being facetious or serious."

Good question. She sat back slowly. "Facetious." Sort of.

He smacked his hand against his heart, feigning pain. "Ouch. I still want to stay, though."

"You do realize I'm a well-trained law enforcement officer."

"I do."

"But you still think I need a bodyguard."

"Even a well-trained law enforcement officer sometimes needs backup."

She waved her hand toward the newly bare room. "I just have the one sofa."

"I can sleep on the floor."

"But you're still recuperating from a hunting accident."

His eyes narrowed, not missing the hint of skepticism in her voice. "Yes, but you made it plain you don't intend to share the sofa."

Before she could think up a decent comeback, headlights flashed across the front windows and she heard the rumble of a car engine rattle to a stop. Adrenaline flooded her system in a couple of heartbeats, and she reached for the holstered M&P 40 on the side table next to the sofa.

John was on her heels as she crossed to the window and looked out. "Who is it?"

She nearly crumpled with relief when she recognized her father's old Silverado. "It's my dad." She peered at the truck bed. "And I think that's a mattress set in the back of his truck.

GIL DUNCAN'S EARLIER friendliness had faded into a suspicious sort of watchfulness, John noticed as Miranda's father finished helping him position the mattress and box springs into the existing bed frame. "You're still here?"

John stifled a smile. "I am."

"Hmm." He glanced toward the open doorway, as if keeping an eye out for Miranda, who was still in the living room, checking in with the sheriff's department to see if there had been any word yet from the lab. "Any particular reason why?"

"Just keeping an eye out for her," John answered. It was mostly the truth. Even if he weren't attracted to Miranda, he'd still feel the need to be here to watch her back. The attraction was just a bonus.

"You plannin' on staying all night?"

"Dad." Miranda's firm voice from the doorway made her father close his eyes in frustration.

"Anything from the lab yet?" John asked, trying to distract Miranda from her father's nosy question.

"Not yet. I knew it would be too soon, though Bill Chambers promised me they've put a rush on it, since it was an attack on a cop."

"You need me to stick around tonight?" Gil asked. "I could sleep on that new sofa of yours."

Miranda glanced at John. He twitched his eyebrows upward, wondering how she'd answer.

"No, Daddy, I'm good. John's going to stick around a while. It'll be fine."

Gil angled a narrow-eyed look at John. "All right, then. I'll head on home, I guess."

Miranda gave him a quick hug at the front door. "Thanks for bringing the mattress set."

"It's not like you were plannin' on coming home to stay tonight," he grumbled. "So I figured you might as well have the mattress and box springs off your old bed." He gave John another speculative look and headed down the front porch step and out to his truck.

Miranda watched until his truck turned out of the driveway, then came back into the house and closed the door behind her. She looked at John. "He's overprotective sometimes."

"The best dads are."

She smiled at that. "Well, at least that solves the sleeping arrangements. You can have the sofa. Dad brought all the pillows from my old bed, so I should have plenty to spare."

"So you're not going to kick me out, then?"

"Not at the moment." She crossed to the fireplace, picked up the poker and pushed around the logs inside to stir the flames. John couldn't stop himself from moving closer, drawn by the heat.

She looked up at him, the flickering flames burnishing her skin to a soft gold and igniting the red glints in her hair. He wasn't aware of taking a step toward her, but he must have, because suddenly they were only a few inches apart, her breath mingling with his.

She was so warm, so alive. So very, very close.

All he had to do was bend his head and his mouth would cover hers.

She moved suddenly, backing away. "I'll find you those pillows."

John watched her hurry from the room, aching with frustration.

Chapter Eight

Miranda woke with the sun just after six, getting as far as the shower before she realized that, one, she wasn't expected back at the station until tomorrow, and two, she had a man sleeping in her living room, and it probably hadn't been a good idea to shed her nightclothes as she crossed the hall to the bathroom.

Wrapping herself in a towel, she tiptoed out to pick up her clothes, keeping an eye on the door to the living room.

"Hey, Miranda, I was looking at this room—"

She froze at the sound of John's voice coming from behind her.

Oh God, she thought, *please let this towel be covering everything*.

"Sorry."

She stood quickly and turned to face him, clutching the towel closed in front of her. "I thought you were still on the sofa."

"I woke early and couldn't go back to sleep, so I was looking at that room back there." He pointed his thumb toward the back of the house. "I can help you out with the repairs if you want."

"I thought you were working on your own place for your employers," she answered, acutely aware that the towel she'd chosen was entirely too short for a long conversation with a man in her hallway.

"I am, but I should be able to accomplish both in the time I have. You'll be going back to work tomorrow, right?"

She nodded.

"Then I could come over here while you're at work and start getting some of the frame repairs done, at least. And I could help you put up the drywall and lay the new floor. Those are two-person jobs."

"My dad was planning to help in the evenings."

"So there'd be three of us working. It would get done three times as quickly. What do you say?"

"I'd have to know your rates."

"I'm not talking about doing it for pay."

She cocked her head. "But we barely know each other."

He took a couple of steps closer to her, making her knees tremble. "We've spent two nights together now, haven't we? Surely that qualifies us as friends."

She tightened her grip on the edges of the towel. "You just want to keep an eye on me. You think I'm still someone's target."

"Don't you?" he asked.

She supposed she should. Someone had come close to killing her only two days ago. And someone had thoroughly searched her house with ruthless abandon—possibly the same person.

If they hadn't found what they were looking for—and how would she know, since she had no idea what that was—they might keep coming back.

So having her own personal bodyguard wasn't the dumbest idea she'd ever heard, she supposed.

"Tell you what. I'll give it some thought in the shower."

She darted back into the bathroom and closed the door, leaning against it for a moment to calm her twitchy nerves.

If being around John Blake left her this shaky after two days, what condition would she be in if he stuck around longer?

But maybe she should stop considering the question as a woman and start thinking about it with the instincts of a cop. John Blake was one big walking enigma who'd come into her life shortly before someone attempted to end it. Maybe that was a coincidence.

But what if it wasn't?

She pondered the thought while she showered, coming to the conclusion by the time she stepped out of the shower that John couldn't be the person who wanted to do her harm. She was pretty sure the accident happening in front of his house had been pure happenstance. And while there was a window of time when he could have tossed her house, it was a very narrow window.

He'd have had to rush over to her house as soon as Miles Randall drove her to the clinic for treatment, because the mess in her house hadn't been created in a short period of time.

She checked that the hallway was empty before scooting across to her bedroom, wrapped in the now-damp towel. After dressing quickly, she headed into the living room, where she found John folding up the bedding she'd provided for him the night before.

He looked up and flashed a smile that made her stomach turn a little flip. "Hey. Did you give my proposition any thought while you were in the shower?"

It was all she'd thought about. She'd spent the whole

time under the hot spray weighing the pros and cons of taking him up on his offer.

So what if he was still a bit of a mystery? He'd been nothing but helpful to her so far, and she had no reason to think that whatever he might be hiding was any danger to her. On the upside, he was apparently a good enough carpenter to get a job with a company as big as Blanchard Building. He was also pretty good to have around in a crisis.

And did it matter if she found him attractive and intriguing? She was single. So was he, according to the background check she'd run. And if she went forward without any illusions about some sort of romantic happily-everafter, who would get hurt?

"I could use the help," she said.

His grin spread wider. "Great. So why don't we go take a look and let me catch up on what you want done?"

"Slow down, tiger. How about we go find breakfast first?" Her kitchen was a useless mess, but the plumber she'd called the previous afternoon had told her he couldn't come until this afternoon. "There's a diner in town that serves an old-fashioned country breakfast, if that's your thing."

"It's my thing," he said with a smile. "Now and then, anyway."

SHE SHOULD HAVE known better than to try to dine in at Creekside Diner, because everybody there had heard not only about her wreck, but also about the mess an intruder had made of her house. Between the hushed questions from the wide-eyed waitress and the incessant whispers of the less brave diner patrons, Miranda felt as if she was having breakfast in a fish tank, with everyone watching the show.

"Small towns," John said with a shrug when she apologized later in the truck, speaking as if from experience.

"We should probably stop by the hardware store," she said as he started to turn back toward Route 7. "To tell my dad you're going to be helping out with the repairs."

She felt more than saw John tense up. "Is that going to be an issue for him or something?"

"No." Her father wouldn't have an issue with John helping out, really. But he might find it a matter of curiosity, and that was why she needed to tell him sooner rather than later and explain it in a way that wouldn't make him run right home and start cleaning his gun.

"That doesn't sound like a very confident *no*."

She laughed. "My dad is protective of our relationship. It's been just the two of us since I was pretty young, and my dad tends to be a little overprotective."

"Too overprotective?"

"Not really—"

"I just wondered, because of something you said the other night, about wanting to stand on your own two feet." He paused a little longer than necessary at the four-way stop at Temple and Main, slanting a curious look her way. "Is your dad being overprotective what you were talking about?"

"Sort of," she admitted. She nodded toward the intersection, indicating he should keep going. The hardware store was halfway down the next block. The sooner they got this over with, the better. "I'll tell you more about it when we get back to the house."

Her father took the news better than she'd anticipated,

though the curiosity she'd seen in his eyes earlier was back. At least he didn't say anything embarrassing.

"I've got my card game tonight, but I'll be sure to come help tomorrow night," he told her with a tight smile, his gaze darting toward John, who was wandering through the power tools aisle.

"I know you will." She touched her father's hand, and his smile loosened up, growing warm.

"You sure you can trust that fella?"

"He seems to check out," she answered carefully.

"You don't think it's odd you meet him the same day someone tried to shoot you?"

"They tried to shoot him, too."

Gil looked at John, who looked up at that moment. John gave a friendly nod and went back to examining the electric sander he was holding.

"You think I'm a nosy old man."

She reached across the counter and gave his work-roughened hand a squeeze. "I think you're a hardheaded, softhearted daddy who's still having a little trouble lettin' go of his baby girl."

"You'd think after all this time I'd have it down." He put his hand over the back of hers. "Call me if you need me."

"Always do."

John approached the checkout counter with the power sander and an electronic level. "I didn't remember seeing these things among your tools." As she brought out her debit card, he shook his head. "I might need them before I'm done at my place as well, so they're on me."

As he was paying for the tools, the bell rang over the front door and Miranda turned to see Rose McAllen enter, her thin hand closed around the plump little fist of her three-year-old granddaughter. She lifted sad eyes to meet Miranda's gaze, managed a brief, unconvincing smile and headed toward the back of the store.

"Still nothing on that case?" Gil asked quietly.

Miranda shook her head. "No witnesses, no trace evidence on the body—everything seems to be a dead end."

"A murder right here in Cold Creek?" John murmured as he handed over a credit card for the purchase. "I thought this place hadn't seen a murder in years."

"Technically, it's not a murder," she explained as her father rang up John's purchase. "It was a hit-and-run accident. Rose McAllen, the lady who just walked in, lost her daughter a couple of years ago. Lindy was a teen mom, always a little on the wild side, and she'd sneaked out of the house one night to meet friends. Apparently she tried to cross the highway and misjudged the distance between her and an approaching vehicle."

"And the vehicle didn't stick around to see if she was still alive?" John frowned.

"The coroner said she was probably dead on impact. She went under the wheels and her neck snapped."

John grimaced. "Surely the driver knew he'd hit her."

"Depends. If he was drunk or high—"

"Right." John glanced behind her and lowered his voice. "She's heading this way."

"Dad, I'll call you later." Miranda turned to smile at Rose again, and crouched to look at the little girl by her side, ignoring the ache in her legs and back, remnants of her rollover crash. "Hey there, Cassie. Did you get to play in the snow the other day?"

Cassie nodded and managed a little smile.

"She helped me make a snowman," Rose McAllen said. "A little one."

Miranda stood. "She's growing up so fast."

Rose's eyes darkened with pain. "She reminds me so much of her mama."

Miranda put her hand on Rose's arm. "Mrs. McAllen, we've gone through every bit of trace evidence and put out calls for information, but nobody seems to have seen or heard anything that night. But I promise, we haven't stopped looking. If we come up with any new leads, I'll let you know."

Rose just stared at her a moment, as if she wanted to say something, but finally she just gave a nod and moved on.

"Poor woman," John murmured as they got into the truck.

Miranda buckled her seat belt. "Sometimes I wonder if that's what happened to Delta. Wherever she disappeared to, she didn't take her car, because it's parked in the yard behind her trailer with two flat tires. Which means she either got a ride or took off on foot."

"And you think she might have been hit by a car?"

"It's a possibility, but nobody's found a body. And Cold Creek isn't the kind of place where it's easy to hide a body. You can see for miles wherever you look. Even if she were hit and knocked into an arroyo, someone would have found her by now." She grimaced. "They could just follow the buzzards."

"You said she lives in a trailer."

"Not much of one. She used to live in a pretty big double-wide, but the tornado took it out last year. She stayed with me a little while, until she could sell what was left of her old trailer for scrap and scrimp together enough money to buy a smaller used trailer."

"Where did she work?"

"Here and there. She never kept a job long, although from what I hear from people, she was a pretty hard worker and she was the one who'd walk away from the job, rather than doing something to get fired."

They reached her house and entered with caution, but if there'd been an intruder while they were gone, he'd been as unobtrusive as a mouse. While John carried the new tools to the unfinished room, Miranda checked to see if anyone had left messages on her landline. There were none.

"Where did she sleep?" John asked when he returned to the living room.

It took a second to remember what they'd been talking about. "Delta? On the sofa."

"Interesting that she turned to you for a place to stay. You said you weren't that close."

"I don't think that Delta was really close to anyone, thanks to her father." She sat on the sofa and patted the cushion beside her, inviting him to sit.

He sat next to her, close enough that his comforting warmth spread over her like a cozy sweater. "Con artists don't make many friends in the long run. I guess that probably limited her options for friends."

"Hal McGraw was a charming bastard, but by the time Delta was old enough to know what was going on, he'd pretty much worn out his welcome in Cold Creek. Delta told me he'd leave town for days and weeks at a time, going to other places to pull his scams, leaving her alone to fend for herself. And I'm talking about when she was as young as twelve or thirteen."

He muttered a low profanity. "Nobody intervened?"

"From what I've heard, nobody knew. It wasn't like they mingled with a lot of other people, and Delta always got herself to school somehow, at least once she was old enough to do it. She'd learned early how to take care of herself without his help. That's why she claimed emancipated minor status as soon as she was old enough. She still lived with her dad when he was in town, but she was her own person."

"Tough girl."

"You'd think so."

"But you didn't?"

Miranda sighed, resting her head against the sofa cushion. "She was tough in a lot of ways. I guess she can thank Hal for that. But she was also sort of frozen in time. There was part of her that was still that scared little girl whose mama ran out on her when she was little and had to figure out how to keep living without any real help from her dad. That little girl didn't trust anybody. Not even me. So there was always this wall between us. I could never get over it. And she never tried."

"She must have trusted you a little, if she came to you for help after the tornado."

"She didn't come to me. I offered, and she accepted. But she got out of here as soon as she could. She liked being alone."

"Do you?" His tone was curious. "Like being alone, I mean."

"I don't know that I like it so much as I don't mind it." She turned her head to find him studying her with a thoughtful expression. "I like standing on my own two feet."

"Yeah, that reminds me, you were going to tell me why you're so determined not to stay with your dad." He arched his dark eyebrows at her.

"Right." She looked up at the ceiling, wondering

where to start. "It's nothing that big, really. You've met my dad. You know he's great."

"Seems that way, yeah."

"I love him like crazy. And he loves me the same. But...you have to know what is was like when my mom died. If you think my dad is crazy about me, you should have seen how much he loved my mom." She could smile now at the memory, though it had been years before she could remember her parents' love for each other without wanting to cry at the loss. "When she died, he was so lost. He tried to be my rock, but he was more like a sand castle, crumbling beneath each crashing wave of grief."

"And you had to be his rock."

"For a while. Until he was strong enough to be mine."

"That must have been hard. How old were you when your mom died?"

"Twelve." She wrapped her arms around herself, suddenly cold, despite the mild March temperatures outside. "I think maybe that's why Delta and I ended up being friends of a sort. Because we both knew what it was like to raise ourselves in a way."

"You're not comparing Gil to Delta's con-man father?"

"No, of course not. But he worked hard to keep us going in good economies and bad ones, and there were lots of times when I had to take care of myself. I knew he wasn't going to remarry. He still thinks of my mother as his wife. I guess he always will."

"Romantic."

She smiled. "Who knew he had it in him?"

They fell quiet for a while, but it was a comfortable silence that left her feeling drowsy and safe.

When he spoke a few moments later, his soft voice still made her nerves jangle. "Miranda?"

She opened her eyes to look at him. "Yeah?"

"Do you think it's possible the attack on you had anything to do with Delta's disappearance?"

John's question caught her by surprise. "Why would Delta's case have anything to do with the ambush?"

"You told me the other day that you were out on Route 7 that day because of a tip about Delta, right?"

"Right." She sat upright, her gaze moving suddenly around the room. "We've sort of been assuming the wreck and what happened here were connected in some way, but…"

"But what?"

She pushed to her feet and paced around her living room, looking at each empty space in the room through narrowed eyes, picturing what had been there. At first glance, the destruction had seemed almost malicious. But thinking back, the things that had been destroyed were pieces of furniture or bric-a-brac that could have hidden something else inside it. Even the mess in the kitchen had been caused by someone searching inside containers and canisters.

"Miranda?"

She turned to look at John. "If the whole point of running me off the road was to keep me away from my house long enough to search it, what exactly are they searching for?"

Chapter Nine

Before John could answer, a pounding knock on the door rattled the house and made Miranda jump. With a sheepish smile, she checked out the front window before opening the door. "The plumber," she said.

A burly man with dark skin and black hair entered, grinning at Miranda like an old friend. "Hey there, Mandy. Heard you got a mess on your hands."

"I do, Garrett. I really do."

Garrett entered and stopped briefly as if surprised to see John in the living room. "Oh, hey."

"Garrett, this is John Blake. John, this is Garrett Navarre, plumber extraordinaire."

Garrett grinned as he gripped John's hand with his massive paw. "My wife would say I'm very ordinaire indeed. Nice to meet you."

"If you can fix that mess in the kitchen, you'll go straight to the top of my superhero list," Miranda said with a laugh. "I'll show Garrett what we're up against. John, could you get a fire going? I think it's supposed to be cold again tonight."

So was she expecting him to stay again tonight? he wondered as he added kindling to the logs in the hearth.

There wasn't much reason to stoke a fire otherwise, was there?

Or was he assuming too much?

"Garrett seems to think he can fix things without forcing me to take out a second mortgage." Miranda came back into the living room as he was touching a match to the kindling.

"Good." He rose to face her and blurted out what was really on his mind. "I think I need to stay here a while longer."

Her eyes widened slightly at the abrupt change of subject, but she gave a nod. "I think maybe you should, too, actually. Because I go back to work tomorrow, and I don't want to have to clean this place up again anytime soon. Having you here might, at least, discourage someone breaking in again."

"I don't remember anyone saying—were there tool marks on either of your doors? To tell how the intruders got inside. I don't remember seeing any broken windows."

"Nobody said." Her look of consternation suggested she hadn't thought to ask. She pulled her cell phone from her pocket. "I can find out."

While she made a call to the station, John crossed to the front door and examined the lock and door handles. There were no telltale marks of anyone trying to jimmy the lock, but some locks could be conquered easily enough without leaving much sign of what had happened.

"They checked all the doors and windows. All the windows were locked, and there weren't any signs of a break-in on the front or the back doors. The shed lock had been forced, though," Miranda told him after she'd finished her call.

"Could someone have a key to your front door?"

"Obviously my dad does."

"What about Delta? You said she stayed with you a while. Did you give her a key?"

Miranda pressed her fingers to her lips briefly. "She did have a key to the house. Not the shed, though. She didn't have a reason to need one."

"Did you get it back from her?"

She looked up at him. "Are you suggesting Delta did this?"

He almost wished it was what he was suggesting. "Actually, I was thinking about the fact that she's gone missing."

Miranda's face went pale.

Garrett came into the living room, carrying a large plastic bag. "Here's the stuff from the sink and drain. Can I just dispose of it, or is there any reason you'd need to keep it?"

Miranda glanced at John. "Could be trace evidence, I guess."

He grimaced. "I'm not volunteering to go through it."

A smile touched the corners of her mouth but got no farther. "Put it on the front porch," she told Garrett. "I'll take care of disposing of it."

Garrett complied with a cheerful nod and returned to the kitchen.

Miranda stepped closer to John, keeping her voice low. "You think maybe whoever trashed this place got the key from Delta, don't you?"

"It's possible, isn't it?"

"Probable, even." Using her fingers as a comb, she pushed her hair away from her face, wincing when her fingertips brushed against the bandage on her forehead.

"I don't think she'd have given the key to someone willingly."

"Your dad made her sound a little on the flaky side."

"Flaky doesn't mean traitorous."

"I know. But could she have been duped into doing it?"

Miranda appeared to give the question a moment's thought before shaking her head. "No. She was really savvy. Really cynical, I guess. She wouldn't have fallen for it. If someone else has the key I gave her, I think they took it against her will."

She didn't finish that thought, but the conclusion was hard to miss. If someone took the key from Delta by force, what else had they done by force?

"You think she may be dead, don't you?" Miranda's pained question broke the silence.

"It's been a possibility from the beginning, hasn't it?"

"A possibility, yes. But she's gone off before."

"You said this was the longest time she's been away."

Miranda sighed and paced over to the fire, gazing into the flames. The firelight seemed to deepen the sadness in her expression, giving her a tragic sort of beauty. "I wanted this case to have a happy ending. I wanted to see Delta come wandering back to town, surprised by all the fuss."

"It might still happen."

She turned her back to the fire and looked at him. "I don't think it will this time. I can't shake the feeling that something bad has happened to her."

"Did Delta have any enemies?"

"I don't know. I was probably the closest thing she had to a friend, but even I didn't know much about her life beyond what little bit she decided to share with me." She crossed to the sofa and sat beside him again, a little closer this time, her warmth washing over him. She smelled good, he thought, a fresh earthy scent like garden herbs warming in the sunshine.

"Could Delta be the one who broke in?"

She shook her head. "I thought about that, but why would she? She knows I'd let her in. And she'd know there's nothing hidden in this house that she'd have to rip things apart to find."

"So maybe it's someone looking for something Delta left here."

"I don't think she left anything, though."

Garrett came out of the kitchen again, carrying his tool bag. "All done, Mandy. You paying with cash or credit today?"

"I'll give you a check." Miranda pushed to her feet and grabbed her purse from the shelf by the door. She followed Garrett outside.

John pulled his phone from the pocket of his jeans and called Quinn to catch him up on the events of the past day.

"So, you've moved in with this woman?" Quinn couldn't quite keep the amusement out of his voice.

"Just for a while, until we can figure out what's going on and who might be gunning for her."

"Well, I have an update on someone who might be gunning for you," Quinn said. "The FBI thinks Del McClintock may have headed west to hide out with family in Oklahoma."

Too close, John thought. "What part of Oklahoma?"

"His cousins live in Altus. Not that far from Cold Creek, really. A little over two hours by car."

Damn it. "You think that's a coincidence? Or do you think he has a bead on my location?"

"It's hard to say. The FBI isn't a hundred percent sure he's in Oklahoma at all. It's just a place to look. But I think it's best if you keep your eyes open. Have you told anyone there why you're in Texas?"

"Of course not."

"Do you trust the deputy?"

He thought about it. "I think so. I think she's one of the good guys. But I'm not sure I want to tell anyone about John Bartholomew and what he was doing for the past year in Virginia." He heard footsteps on the porch outside. "I've got to go. I'll be in touch."

He pocketed the phone just before the door opened and Miranda came back in, holding a yellow receipt, looking exasperated. "Whoever made this mess in my place has cost me an arm and a leg. Most of the damage isn't going to be covered by my homeowner's policy, and now I have to worry about getting new furniture and canisters and—" She flung her hands wide. "I don't even know how much I'm going to have to replace."

"Well, your sink is working again, at least. Maybe we can make a grocery run and replace some of the stuff that got dumped down the drain."

"Probably going to have to wait until I get paid again now." She waved the yellow receipt at him. "Know what I need? Something to take my mind off my troubles. Why don't we go take a look at the back room and see what needs to be done next?"

John followed Miranda to the unfinished room and listened to her description of what she wanted to accomplish. "This was originally a second bedroom, and I don't want to lose that function, but I'd also like for it to be a little more versatile than just another bedroom. It's large enough that I think I could fit a desk in here as well, and maybe build in some shelves for books and file boxes. The sheriff's department is willing to pay my tuition for some continuing education courses and seminars in law enforcement, and I want to have a place to keep my books and notes from those courses."

He could picture it. The room was situated in the back corner of the house, with four windows offering a vista of the plains that seemed to stretch into infinity. A different sort of beauty than the hills and valleys of his Tennessee home, but beautiful nonetheless. She could work here, surrounded by the place she loved, improving her skills at protecting the community she served. It was a very Miranda thing to want.

At least, he thought it was. How much could he really know about a woman he'd met only three days before?

"I love this room. It's a little smaller than my bedroom, but I was considering changing rooms just for this view. And then the tornado hit and practically demolished it." Her eyes darkened with remembered pain. "It took out half of each corner wall and the rain ruined the floor and the other walls. We had to strip up the floors and take down all the drywall and the ceiling."

He looked up at the exposed wood of the frame. "You and your dad did the reframing?"

"Yeah, and we got the siding put up on the outside to protect it from the elements. But I haven't had a ton of time to get the interior fixed up the way I want it. I've had to do it a little at a time during my off-hours."

"I can help speed that up while you're at work. Looks like you're ready to put the walls in next."

She nodded at the sheets of drywall lined up on one side of the room. "I thought I'd try to tackle that when I got home from work tomorrow."

"I can get it started for you first thing in the morning. Do you have a basic floor plan for the room? Where you want the various elements to go?"

"Do I ever." With a grin, she motioned for him to follow her.

They made a quick stop in her bedroom for her to grab a notebook from the bedside table, then settled on the sofa in the living room, spreading the notebook open on the coffee table in front of them.

"I'm looking at a couple of different plans. I just can't decide which way I want to go." She pointed to the first page, where in neat pen strokes, she'd sketched out a simple floor plan featuring a bed, a single piece of furniture she'd labeled "highboy" and a desk against one wall between two windows. "This is the more traditional route," she said. "The bed is against one wall, the desk at its foot. Shelves would go on the wall opposite the bed, ending at the closet door."

He pointed to the opposite page. "And this?"

"I'd have to go with a daybed in this scenario, because more focus is on the corner desk and the shelves. This layout makes the room more of a study with a sleeping area. The other one is more a bedroom with a desk and bookshelves."

"What do you anticipate using the room for?"

"A study," she said.

"I think you've made your choice, then."

The smile she flashed at him made his whole body go hot. "My dad thinks it's crazy. He thinks I should be adding bedrooms to the house, not converting one to a study."

"Adding bedrooms?"

She rolled her eyes. "You know, for when I get married and start having babies. He keeps sending me clippings from the newspaper whenever one of my friends from high school gets married or has a baby."

"And, of course, this being a small town, those events all get big write-ups in the local weekly."

"Exactly." She laughed. "I make it sound like he's a terrible nag. He's not. I think he just worries that I'm alone here with no husband or babies in sight."

"Wants to get you settled so he can stop worrying."

She shot him a narrow-eyed look. "This sound familiar to you, too?"

"A little. My father wanted me to join the family business from the time I graduated college. I just—" He shook his head. "I wanted something more than a corner office in a Johnson City accounting firm."

"So you joined the Foreign Legion?"

What would it hurt to tell her about his work with the CIA? He hadn't lasted long, and everything he'd been dealing with had ended up being declassified or scrapped in the end. "I worked as a CIA liaison in Athens, Greece, for a year after college."

Her eyes widened. "I know I joked about that, but—"

"It wasn't nearly as interesting as it sounds. And I sort of blew my one and only assignment, so—"

"How'd you blow it? Or is that classified information?"

"Not classified. Just embarrassing." He rose and crossed to the fireplace, gazing into the flickering flames. "Athens was always volatile politically. Lots of protests— antiglobalization, anarchists, black bloc, you name it. About a week earlier, Athens cops had killed an unarmed teenager and things were really hot in the city. I was living in a hotel that offered long-term rentals, and that morning, I apparently walked right out of the hotel into the middle of a violent protest. I took a chunk of concrete to the head and woke up three weeks later in an Athens hospital with no memory of the event."

"My God."

"Needless to say, everything I had on me that might be considered sensitive information was gone. My hotel room had been searched and cleaned out. My cover was more or less blown and I wasn't any use to the CIA any longer."

"So they fired you? Because you got hurt?"

"Because I was compromised. It wasn't personal." He shrugged. He'd known the stakes, known how easily a career in the CIA could end. "At least I'm still alive. I've been told it was touch and go for several days."

"So then you went back to Johnson City and spent some time in that corner office?"

He laughed. "Not exactly. By then, my cousin Pete had earned the corner office. I had to start at the bottom. I figure I got maybe midway in ten years, at which point I realized being a decent accountant wasn't the same as wanting to be an accountant."

"So what did you do between the time you left the accounting firm and the time you showed up on the Blanchard Building payroll?"

"I worked for a company called The Gates. Ever heard of it?"

She shook her head. "No. Strange name."

"It's a security agency. Based in a little town called Purgatory, Tennessee, down in the Smokies. The boss is a guy named Alexander Quinn. Former CIA—legendary at the company, but most of what he's done in his life is so classified I'm not sure even the presidents he served knew some of it." John poked at the waning fire, stirring up embers. "Seems that Quinn came from money, and when he came in to a big inheritance, he left the CIA and started his own agency."

"What kind of security work?"

"All kinds, really. Some investigation, some body-guard work, some security analysis and threat assessment."

"In an agency working out of a little town in the Smokies?"

"That's the base. But he has people working for him all over the place. If you talked to the agents currently working for Quinn at the main office in Purgatory, they probably wouldn't recognize my name. I was working for him out of Abingdon, Virginia."

"Doing what?"

"Well, I was officially a freelance security consultant. I did some jobs consulting with companies in Abingdon that were looking to improve all areas of their security. But what I was really doing was helping an undercover agent Quinn had in place in a little town called River's End, in the Blue Ridge Mountains not far from Abingdon. She was trying to infiltrate a militia group—"

"The Blue Ridge Infantry," Miranda interrupted, her brow furrowed. "I've heard of them. But didn't I read that the FBI had finally had a big break in the case that's allowing them to round up everyone involved?"

"It wasn't the FBI who made that break happen. It was a tough lady named Nicki Jamison. I might have helped a little, too."

Miranda crossed to where he stood, meeting his gaze. "You weren't hurt in a hunting accident, were you?"

"No. I mean, I was being hunted, but—"

She closed her eyes. "Is that why you're here? Recuperating?"

"That, and lying low."

"So John Blake isn't really your name."

"No, it really is my name. But nobody in Abingdon—or River's End—ever knew it. I was known as John Bartholomew there."

"But you said you're lying low."

"I am. Just because John Blake isn't the name I used doesn't mean that someone with some computer savvy couldn't eventually figure it out. And the BRI had some pretty nasty hackers working for them."

"So maybe I need to be watching *your* back."

"Maybe you should. Because the FBI believes one of the guys who might be looking for me is somewhere in Altus, Oklahoma."

Her eyes widened even more. "That close?"

"They're not sure he's there. But he has family in Altus."

Before Miranda could respond, her cell phone trilled. "Hold that thought," she said before she answered. "Duncan."

As she listened, her gaze snapped up to his, her eyes looking huge and dark in her suddenly pale face. "When?"

Whatever she was hearing on the other end of the call, it was bad news, he saw. Her free hand rose to her mouth as she listened with increasing distress. "And she's sure?"

The other caller must have answered in the affirmative, for Miranda gave a brief nod and said, "I'm on my way."

"What is it?" he asked as she put her phone away and looked around for her jacket, spotting it on the back of the chair by the door.

She shrugged the jacket on. "A woman who lives off

Route 7 had some chickens escape their coop this afternoon. When she chased them down, she stumbled on the body of a woman." She lifted her troubled gaze to John. "They think it's Delta McGraw."

Chapter Ten

The dead woman lying in the shallow arroyo behind Lizzie Dillard's chicken coop was definitely Delta McGraw. And she'd been dead for at least a couple of days.

The sight of her friend's body, cold and mottled with cyanosis and in the early stages of decomposition, seemed unreal somehow. She knew the full emotional impact would hit her soon enough. But right now, she had to be a cop first.

"She definitely wasn't out here the day of my wreck," Miranda told Sheriff Randall as they stood looking down at Delta's cold body. "I was out here and I had a pretty good look around."

"She's been dead longer than that," Randall said. He looked toward the road, where John Blake sat in his truck, watching them work. "I see you brought your new friend."

"He's watching my back."

"You think we don't?" The sheriff's voice held an oddly defensive tone she hadn't expected.

"No, of course not. But we're a small agency. If John Blake has the time and wants to watch my back—"

"Didn't you say he's a carpenter or something?"

"He has some law enforcement training in his past."

"A wannabe." His tone was dismissive.

"No, more like a once was." She glanced at the truck, not wanting to reveal too much to the sheriff, even though she'd trust Randall with her life. If John was telling the truth, and she had no reason at this point to believe he wasn't, his life was in as much danger as hers. She was watching his back, as well. "He's nice and he saved me the other day. If he wants to use his off time to make sure I don't get ambushed alone again, I'm not going to complain."

"Fair enough." He looked down at Delta's body. "Poor girl. She had one hell of a rough life."

"I had such a sick feeling this time when she disappeared. She was finally starting to put down roots, I thought." Tears stung her eyes, but she blinked them away. Not now. She couldn't fall apart now.

Randall caught Miranda's arm and pulled her back as two more deputies arrived, armed with crime scene kits to gather trace evidence and secure the scene. "Putting down roots?"

Miranda nodded. "I put it in my first report on the case. When we asked people around town if anyone had seen her, Luis Gomez from High Plains Realty contacted me, said that he'd been talking to Delta about looking for a house to buy."

"She had that kind of money?"

"I didn't think so, but honestly, there's a lot about Delta I didn't know."

The sheriff was silent for a moment, then tilted his head toward the house. "You need to talk to Lizzie, see if she saw or heard anything. She was too rattled earlier for Jenkins to get anything out of her."

With a nod, Miranda headed across the yard to where

Lizzie sat on the top step of her front porch, her head down and her shoulders hunched. When she looked up at Miranda's approach, her normally ruddy face was sickly pale, and her eyes were red rimmed and puffy.

"I gave up smokin' ten years ago. I've never regretted it until now." Lizzie held her shaking hands out in front of her. "I'd sell this whole damn farm for a cigarette right about now."

Miranda sat on the step next to her. "It must've been a real shock to find her out there like that."

"I'm a farm girl. I see death all the time. It's part of raisin' animals for the market, you know? But that poor girl—" Lizzie buried her face in her hands. "I know she wasn't here yesterday evening when I went out to feed the chickens, because I walked out to the road to talk to Coy when he drove by on his way home and I went right by that arroyo."

Miranda made a mental note to check with the desk sergeant. Maybe he'd seen something on his drive home that might be helpful. "You don't remember hearing anything last night?"

"Not a thing." Lizzie scraped her graying hair away from her weathered face. "I work hard and I sleep hard. You know what it's like. Now, if old Rocket was still alive, he'd have barked his head off if there was anybody out there, but I had to have him put down last month, and I haven't had the heart to get me a new dog. Though Coy said his neighbor's hound mix just had puppies. Said he'd probably be happy to save one out of the litter for me."

So anyone could have come along this road and dumped Delta's body out during the night, Miranda thought, without anyone seeing it happen.

But who would know that?

Almost anyone, she supposed, when she thought about it. She herself knew about Lizzie having to have old Rocket put to sleep the previous month. She'd heard it from Tina Shire, who worked at the vet clinic in town. And anyone who'd ever driven down Glory Road would know there wasn't another house within almost two miles of Lizzie's farm.

In some ways, it was the ideal place to dump a body, as long as you didn't care if it was found sooner rather than later.

"Lizzie, if you think of anything you might have seen or heard last night, even if it seems unimportant, you'll let us know, right?"

"Of course." Lizzie patted Miranda's hand. "You must be sick about it. I know you two girls were friends."

"I'm not sure Delta ever felt as if she had any friends," Miranda said sadly, looking across the farmyard to where Sheriff Randall and the rest of the deputies had started processing the crime scene. Despite the warm sunlight beating down on the scene, Miranda still felt a bleak chill in the air.

Maybe it was coming from inside her.

"That's the fellow who moved into the old Merriwether place out on Route 7, ain't it?" Lizzie nodded toward John, who was watching Miranda rather than the deputies at the scene. "Hear tell he saved your life the other day durin' the snowstorm."

"He did," Miranda admitted. The cause of the crash was being kept secret at the sheriff's department, for now, but the crash itself was all over the town grapevine. Neighbors had been calling her father's store for a couple of days, asking if she needed anything and offering to bring food to her house.

If her place hadn't been trashed by the intruder search, she might have taken a few of them up on the offer.

"Heard he's some sort of builder or something," Lizzie said.

"Something like that. He's actually going to be helping me finish repairing the tornado damage on my place."

"Mighty kind of him."

"Yes." Miranda pushed to her feet, ignoring a symphony of aches and pains. The knocks and dings from the rollover wreck, combined with the strain of all the bending, lifting and carrying she'd done cleaning up her trashed house, had taken a toll on her body.

But you're still alive, she reminded herself as she headed back to where the coroner's truck had arrived to pick up Delta's body. Things could have been so much worse.

She could have been zipped up in a body bag just like Delta.

"Mandy, go home," Sheriff Randall told her.

"What? This is my case."

"You're still on medical leave until tomorrow. And even then, I saw the way you looked at Delta's body. You're too close to the case. We've got other people who can investigate. Take the rest of the week off and get your head straight. Then we'll talk."

"Damn it, sir, that's not fair."

"You still believe life is fair?" Randall's expression was set in stone. There would be no changing his mind, Miranda knew.

"Fine. Will you at least let me call in for updates on the case?"

Randall's expression softened just a notch. "Sure. But I'm serious about taking the rest of the week off. You could easily have been killed in that wreck the other day, and I can see you're still sore. Take these days to get some rest and clear your head." He nodded toward the coroner assistants, who were placing the body bag on a gurney to slide it in the back of a truck. "Since Delta didn't have any family left, she needs someone to handle her funeral. I don't know if she had any money stashed away anywhere or any sort of burial policy, but..."

Miranda doubted it. She hadn't been able to find any sort of bank account for Delta when she'd first taken on the missing person case, so it wasn't likely she had bothered with anything like life insurance. "Can I at least be the one to take another look at her place? I knew her better than anyone else on the force. There might be something there that'll mean more to me than another investigator."

Randall looked as if he wanted to say no, but finally he gave a gruff nod. "I'll want another deputy with you."

She bit back a protest and nodded. "Tell me when to be there."

"I'll get with Robertson and give you a call."

"Thanks." She returned to the truck and climbed into the passenger seat. John watched her in silence, waiting for her to speak.

"It was Delta."

He let out a slow breath. "I'm sorry. Are you okay?"

She buckled her seat belt and leaned her head against the backrest. "I don't know. I feel kind of like I'm in limbo. Waiting for it to hit me."

He reached across the cab and put his hand over hers where it lay on the seat beside her. "What happens next?"

"I have to look into a few things. See if she had any sort of will or plans for what would happen in the case of her death." She shook her head. "She was twenty-seven years old. Who plans their own funeral at that age?"

"Is there anything you can do right now?"

She looked across the cab to find him watching her with a gentle expression that made tears prick her eyes. She blinked them back. "I would really like to go home now. Can we just go home?"

JOHN PULLED HIS truck up next to Miranda's on the concrete driveway and cut the engine, waiting for her to move.

She sat in the passenger seat and was very still for a long moment before she slowly reached for the seat belt buckle and released herself from the harness. "I should call my dad and let him know." She sighed. "Although as fast as news travels in this town, he probably knows already."

Before she could move, her cell phone trilled, harsh in the silence of the truck cab. She pulled it from her pocket and checked the display. "Can I call it or what?" She got out of the truck and started toward the house, lifting the phone to her ear as she walked. "Hi, Dad."

John followed more slowly, giving her a little privacy to talk to her father about her friend's death. By the time he reached the porch, she had hung up the phone and was unlocking the door.

"The sheriff took me off the case," she said as she locked the door behind them. When she lifted her gaze to meet his, she looked more hurt than angry.

"Because you're too close to the case?"

"Yeah. And he's making me take the rest of the week off, too. I think it's just to keep me from nosing around the case, although he says it's because I need to take more time to recover from my injuries."

"Maybe that's a good idea."

The look she gave him was sharp enough to cut. "Et tu, Brute?"

He crossed to where she stood, arms folded, her brow furrowed. "I know you're tough. Hell, you were in a roll-over accident three days ago, and I just watched you clean up a wrecked house and work a crime scene without even dragging your heels. But maybe it's time to give your-self a break."

"I'm not fragile."

"I know that." He put his hands on her shoulders, run-ning his thumbs lightly over the curve of her collarbones.

She opened her mouth as if to argue, then closed her eyes, taking a shaky breath. Slowly, she dropped her arms, her hands coming to rest on his sides, just below his rib cage. She took a step closer, the delicious heat of her body sliding over him until he felt as if he was on fire inside.

"I'm glad you're here." Her voice was barely a whis-per, her breath soft and hot against his chin. He bent his head until their foreheads touched, and he drank in her sweet herb scent.

"I'm glad I'm here, too." He brushed his lips against her forehead. "I'll stay as long as you want me to."

She lifted her gaze to his. "Don't make promises. It's way too early for promises."

"Okay. No promises." He was crazy to make prom-ises, anyway, given how up-in-the-air his life was at the moment. "Why don't you lie down a while? I could fig-ure out something for supper."

"I couldn't sleep." She moved away from him in restless strides, coming to a stop at the window. She gazed out at the dying daylight for a moment, her face tinged rose by the setting sun, before turning to look at him. "I wouldn't mind supper, though. What do you have in mind?"

"I thought I'd run to that little store down the road and pick up some groceries. Maybe grill a couple of steaks and bake a potato?"

"Sounds good." She pulled her keys from her pocket and handed them to him. "The house key is the silver one there on the end. Pick up some vegetables, too, and I'll whip up a salad."

"Okay, you're on." He smiled at her as he unlocked the door. "Lock up behind me. I'll be right back."

He hurried through his shopping, not liking the idea of leaving her alone for long. Delta McGraw clearly hadn't died of natural causes. And if the attack on Miranda was connected, the stakes had just gotten a lot higher.

"I haven't found much of anything on Delta McGraw," Quinn told John when he checked in with his boss. "I have found a few things on her father, Hal, however."

"Anything that could help us figure out who killed his daughter?"

"I'm not sure. The one thing I've learned is that he was charged with extortion by an oilman in Plainview shortly before his death. Apparently he tried to blackmail the man over something the oilman's son had done—selling drugs or something. The report I got had been redacted in places. Anyway, the oilman told Hal to go do something anatomically impossible and called the cops on him for his attempted extortion."

"What happened?"

"Hal died before it ever got to court."

"Is that the only thing?" John asked.

"The only thing I've found," Quinn replied. "But if he blackmailed one person…"

"He might have blackmailed several," John added. "But I'm not sure how that relates to his daughter's death."

"Maybe the apple didn't fall far from the tree. Ask around. Stay in touch." Quinn ended the call.

Pocketing his phone, John pondered his boss's suggestion as he carried his basket of groceries to the checkout stand. The teenage boy at the cash register rang up the purchase with amusing enthusiasm, keeping up a stream of friendly chatter until John paid the bill. "You have a nice evening," he said with a grin, displaying a mouth full of metal.

He let himself in at Miranda's with the house key, expecting to find her waiting for him in the living room, where he'd left her.

But the living room was empty.

He started to call her name but stopped himself, standing still and listening instead. He heard a soft hitching sound coming from somewhere in the back of the house.

The sound went silent as he moved through the house, his footsteps on the hardwood floor seeming loud to his own ears.

The bedroom door was open, the room empty. The bathroom was empty, as well. He found no one in the kitchen, either, but he could almost feel a presence nearby. Waiting.

He set the bag of groceries on the kitchen table and eased over to the door to the unfinished room. It was only halfway open, obscuring his view of all but a sliver of the room. Reaching behind his back, he grabbed the butt of the Ruger hidden in a holster clipped to his jeans and drew it.

Slowly, he pushed open the door. It creaked, the loud sound jangling his taut nerves.

"Don't move." Miranda's voice sounded thick and hoarse, but there was no mistaking the tone of command.

He went very still. "Are you alone?"

"Are you?"

"Yes."

"Come in."

He found her sitting under one of the windows, her knees tucked up near her chest and her head leaning back against the wall. She still held her M&P 40, but the barrel was pointed toward the ground.

She'd been crying.

As he walked slowly into the room, she set it on the floor beside her. "Sorry about that."

"No worries." He nodded his head back toward the kitchen. "I brought the groceries. You still hungry?"

"I will be. Just give me a few minutes." She spoke as if she wanted him to go. But when she lifted her damp eyes to his again, he could see she really didn't want to be left alone.

He reholstered his own pistol and crossed to where she sat, easing himself into a sitting position next to her.

"What did you buy?" she asked, sniffling a little.

"Two nice sirloin steaks, two enormous baking potatoes—plus sour cream and butter, because this is no time for watching our weight. And I wasn't sure what kind of salad stuff you liked, so I might have bought out half the produce section at the grocery store. Didn't know what kind of salad dressing you'd want, so I bought small bottles of several to choose from."

She managed a watery laugh. "I'm sure I'll find exactly what I want."

"Listen, before we start supper—I need to ask you something about Hal McGraw. Did you know he was arrested for extortion shortly before his death?"

She looked up at him. "Of course. But how do you know?"

"My boss told me."

One of her eyebrows lifted. "And why would he know anything about Hal McGraw?"

"I asked him to do some research on Delta."

"Without asking me?"

He shrugged. "Do you want to know what else he said or not?"

She was quiet for a moment, then gave a brief nod.

"Well, he asked a really good question. I was wondering if you might know the answer. Do you think Hal McGraw might have been blackmailing anyone else?"

"We always figured he must have been. But once he died, it wasn't likely anybody was going to come forward to tell us about it. We figured most of the offenses were probably personal problems, not legal ones, and none of our business."

He didn't like asking the next question, considering the tear tracks still staining Miranda's cheeks. But it had to be asked. "What about Delta? Do you think she knew about her father's extortion plots?"

Her brow furrowed as she gave the question some thought. "I don't know," she admitted finally. "I guess she might have."

"Then that brings up another question, doesn't it? Did Delta pick up where her father left off?"

She turned her gaze to him again, her expression troubled. "And is that why she ended up dead?"

Chapter Eleven

"If she was blackmailing anyone, I never heard about it." Miranda poked at the remains of her baked potato, scooping out one last buttery morsel. She popped it in her mouth.

"Well, you wouldn't, would you? The whole idea of extortion is to pay for the blackmailer's silence. You done?" John reached across the kitchen table for her plate.

She pushed it toward him and sat back, feeling comfortably full. "You're not a bad cook, John Blake."

"A man's gotta know how to grill." He flashed her a smile that made her heart give a little flip. She was beginning to wonder how she'd ever thought of him as average or ordinary.

"The only wine I had in the house went down the drain," she said as she pushed to her feet and joined him at the dishwasher. "But I saw you picked up a bag of coffee. I could brew a pot if you like."

He shook his head. "I'm fine. Why don't I go start another fire while you get the dishes going, and we can just try to relax for a while? You've had a stressful day."

Stressful and upsetting, she thought, adding the word he was kind enough not to say. She'd felt a little embarrassed when he'd found her crying in the back room, but he hadn't made things worse by trying to comfort her with awkward words of sympathy. He couldn't know how she was feeling, and he knew it.

To be honest, she wasn't sure herself how she was feeling. Grief of a sort, she supposed, but Delta had never really let her get close enough for her to think of the other woman as a true friend. Still, the sight of her lying dead in the bottom of a shallow arroyo had been deeply disturbing on a number of levels, some of them personal.

She finished loading the dishwasher and set it to run, then joined John in the living room. The fire had reached a crackling blaze, helping to fend off the gathering chill of the evening, and John had moved the sofa so that it faced the fireplace.

"Hope you don't mind." As she approached the sofa, he smiled up at her, sliding one arm over the back of the sofa. "Didn't want to waste a nice fire by sitting halfway across the room."

She hesitated.

"I don't bite," he murmured in a tone that made the words sound like a lie. There was a challenge in his expression, as tempting and dangerous as the firelight reflected in his eyes.

Come on, Mandy. You're not a sixteen-year-old virgin faced with your first bad boy. He's a tax accountant. You've dated bull riders before.

She sat beside him, daringly close, her hip snugged against his. For a few moments, they sat in silence broken only by the crackle of the fire and the distant hum of the dishwasher at work.

"Tell me about Delta," he murmured a few moments later. She felt his fingers play in her hair. Lightly. Undemanding.

"She was a couple of years younger than I am. Three years behind in school because she failed a year early on, thanks to her dad dragging her all over Texas for a while. She couldn't keep up with her schoolwork as she went from town to town, so she had to start over fresh the next year, somewhere down near Abilene, I think." Delta had told the story so matter-of-factly, without a hint of how she'd felt about her rambling lifestyle with her father. "I think that wasn't long after her mother left them."

"So they weren't from here originally."

She shook her head. "You're probably wondering why they settled in a little place like this."

"The question did cross my mind."

"Mine, too. Delta never really said what made them stay, but if I had to guess? I think she told her daddy to settle down or she'd call the cops on him."

"Really. How old was she then?"

"Twelve."

"Tough little girl." John's voice held a touch of admiration.

"She was. It's so hard to think she's gone now. She endured so much. Overcame so much." Grief tangled around her heart, squeezing hard. She took a deep breath, attempting to relieve the sudden sharp stab of pain.

"I was hoping for a better ending," he murmured, his fingers warm against her cheek. He pressed his lips to her temple, a brief, uncomplicated caress.

Except her reaction to his touch was anything but uncomplicated. Her heart skipped a beat before shifting into a higher gear, and her skin prickled hot beneath his fingers.

"I wanted to believe we'd find her alive, but—"

"But you didn't really think you would?"

She let herself relax, resting her head against his jaw. "She kept a lot of things to herself, but she'd have told me if she was leaving for this long."

With a soft *prrrup* sound, Ruthie jumped up on the sofa next to her, her tail forming a question mark. She wasn't hungry, Miranda knew, because she'd fed the cats before John had returned from the grocery store.

"Hey there, Ruthie," John said in a soft voice.

The cat's ears twitched, and slowly, she turned her green eyes to look at him with a quizzical expression.

"I had a cat when I was in Johnson City," John said. "Well, sort of. He was a stray who took up with me. He'd been someone's cat before—he was tame and had already been neutered. The vet said someone might have accidentally let him out of the car on a trip or something— he was too well behaved to have lived his life outdoors for long. He wasn't microchipped, though, and my 'lost cat' ads didn't bring his real owners around, so I took him in. Let him live with me until he died."

All the while John had been speaking, Ruthie had been watching him, her ears perked as if listening. When he stopped, the tortoiseshell cat walked over Miranda's lap and reached up, claws sheathed, to touch his mouth.

"Well, then. Ruthie must like the sound of your voice."

"Or maybe she's trying to make sure I stop talking."

Miranda watched with amusement as Ruthie settled in his lap, a low purr rumbling from her throat. "That's the Ruthie seal of approval."

"She must have low standards." He scratched behind her ears, then under her chin, each stroke earning him a blissful stretch from Ruthie.

"Not at all. But if you can get Rex to sit in your lap like that, you're a miracle worker."

John stroked the fingers of his other hand lightly over the skin behind Miranda's ear, sending a ripple of pure pleasure darting down her spine. If she wasn't careful, she'd end up purring like a kitten herself.

"Miranda?"

"Hmm?" She turned her head and found his face inches from hers, his eyes gleaming with desire and intent. But he remained perfectly still, giving her the chance to make the final move.

Toward him or away from him? It was her choice.

And then, suddenly, it wasn't her choice any longer.

He leaned in and pressed his mouth to hers, his lips somehow both firm and soft. With soft, nipping movements, his kiss deepened, urging her lips apart until his tongue brushed lightly against hers. Lightly at first, then with dark seduction, making her head swirl until she found herself clinging to him just to remain upright.

His fingers threaded through her hair, holding her in place while he slowly, thoroughly kissed her until she couldn't find her breath.

Suddenly, his breath caught and he drew back, hissing with pain. A flash of fur darted from between their bodies.

John looked down at the three scratches turning red down his wrist. "I don't think Ruthie approved."

"I'm so sorry." Miranda winced as the scratch marks started to ooze blood. "She likes you, I swear."

"Yeah, I know." John stood up and started toward the hallway. Miranda followed quickly, wondering what he was going to do to poor Ruthie.

"She was just scared," she said quickly.

In the hallway, he turned to look at her, his expression

quizzical. "I know that. What do you think I'm going to do, go wring her neck?"

"I didn't know. Some people freak out when they're scratched, and—"

"I had a cat. Scratches happen." He went into the bathroom and looked around. "Where do you keep your first-aid supplies?"

"There's a kit in the cabinet under the sink."

John found the kit, a small metal box full of adhesive bandages, individual packets of antiseptic pads, antibiotic ointments and pain reliever tablets. He selected the antiseptic, ripping the packet open and dabbing the antiseptic on the three scratches. "All better now."

She was relieved that he'd handled Ruthie's reaction with such levelheadedness. She'd dated a tough cowboy once who'd nearly cried when Rex had reacted to his relentless teasing with a claws-extended swipe, despite Miranda's warnings to stop. She'd had to restrain the idiot from going after her cat, and that had been the end of that relationship.

Of course, she and John weren't really dating, were they? They were just temporarily sharing a house. With kissing benefits included, apparently.

"I'd better go apologize to Ruthie," he said after he'd finished treating the scratch. "Don't want to get on her bad side."

She watched him head down the hall in search of her miffed cat, trying to ignore the melty feeling in the center of her chest.

"CAN YOU TELL if anything looks any different?" Tim Robertson had remained in the doorway while Miranda took a slow circuit of Delta McGraw's tiny trailer. She'd been there a few times over the past few months since the tornado had wiped out Delta's previous home.

"Someone's been here," she said, taking in the disturbed places in the dust that lay in a thin layer over everything in the trailer. "They took their time, though. Nothing like the search at my place."

"Wonder why they didn't just toss this place like they tossed yours?"

"Maybe because they had more time," she suggested. "There was a narrow window of time at my place to do any sort of search. Even if I'd died in the wreck, someone would have been there within a few hours to check on the cats."

Tim nodded. "You have any idea what they were looking for at your place?"

She thought about what she and John had agreed to earlier that morning over a breakfast of instant oatmeal and the fresh strawberries he'd bought at the market the night before.

"I'm not going to tell the others at the cop shop about our suspicions that Delta's death and the attack on me might be connected," she'd told him. "Because the last thing I want is to be put on leave for my own safety. I need access to the department's resources."

"Don't you think they might figure it out on their own?" John had asked.

Miranda looked at Tim, who remained near the doorway, leaning against the wall with his arms folded over his chest. He was a good deputy, she knew. Smart and resourceful.

Would he figure it out on his own?

Maybe. But she wasn't going to help him put her own

investigation in cold storage, which would surely happen if the sheriff thought her life might be in danger.

"I don't know what they were looking for," she told Tim. That much, at least, was true. She might have a pretty good idea why they'd been searching her house, but she had no idea, yet, what they'd been looking for.

On closer inspection, she found plenty of signs that the place had been carefully searched, but if they'd taken anything, she had no way of knowing what it was. Even if she'd been Delta's closest friend, she couldn't pretend she knew that much about Delta's life outside their limited interactions. The handful of times she'd been in this trailer had been brief, usually when she stopped by to say hello after too many days, even weeks, of not hearing from Delta.

The woman had been a loner at heart. Probably the result of the kind of life she'd had with her pariah of a father.

In the end, she found the money by accident. As she walked into the kitchen one last time to make sure she hadn't missed anything, her foot caught on the edge of the linoleum in the door, sending her sprawling forward. She caught herself on the edge of the narrow counter inside the tiny kitchenette and felt it give.

Regaining her footing, she gave the counter an upward tug, and that small section of the counter lifted up on a hinge.

Underneath, a shallow square space was empty except for a thick manila envelope bound shut by a couple of rubber bands. She opened the envelope and sucked in a sharp breath.

Inside the envelope were several fat stacks of plastic-wrapped one-hundred-dollar bills.

THE FLOOR OF the unfinished room had been framed atop the existing concrete foundation, sheathed in plywood awaiting the installation of final flooring. Miranda and her father had framed the floor and the walls, she'd told John earlier that morning when they'd been discussing the next part of the building project, but they'd had professional builders handle the roofing, siding and insulation. Heating, ventilation and air-conditioning ductwork had also been added by the pros, but the rest of the work Miranda intended to do herself, with help from her father and now from John, as well.

Next job up—installing the drywall. Sheets of the plasterboard stood against one of the walls, ready to go. Miranda had already measured and cut the boards to fit the walls, helpfully marking each one with a corresponding framing board in the wall. She'd left him with her power screwdriver, a bucket of drywall screws and the smiling admonition to avoid screwing any body parts to the wall.

He started installing the drywall top to bottom, working up a nice sweat despite the mild day. Within an hour, he'd managed to screw up an entire wall and had started the next when something in the fiberglass insulation near the floor caught his eye.

Was that a split in the fiberglass batting?

He found a pair of work gloves in the toolbox in the corner. They were snug but covered his hands, protecting them from the scratchy fibers of the insulation batting as he pushed his fingers inside the split.

There was something in there. Hard and rectangular, like a box. Or a book? It moved a little when he touched it, though it seemed to fit snugly into its hiding place. He didn't want to make the slit in the fiberglass any worse, but being too careful wasn't going to make it possible to get the mystery item out of the recess.

Removing his hand, he sat back, trying to figure out if the rectangular object might have something to do with the wiring or the HVAC system. After reassuring himself it couldn't be, he pushed his hand through the opening in the insulation and tried to grab the object again.

This time, he caught it firmly between two fingers and wiggled it until it popped free. Turning it sideways, he pulled it out through the fiberglass and dusted strands of the glass fiber away from it.

It was a small, hard-backed book, wrapped in clear plastic, the end pieces of the wrap taped together at the back side of the thin book. It wasn't a novel or anything like that; the dark blue cover was made of fabric and had no title or any writing at all on the front or back.

The sound of keys rattling in the door sent a light shock through his system, and he almost lost his grip on the book. He pushed quickly to his feet, bracing himself until he heard Miranda's voice down the hall. "John?"

"In here," he called.

Miranda's footsteps rang down the hallway, moving at a fast clip. She stopped in the doorway for a second, taking in the newly installed drywall. "Wow. You've been busy."

"I have," he said, "and I may have—"

"Guess what I found at Delta's trailer this morning." If she noticed the book in his hands, she didn't give any sign.

"What did you find?"

"Ten thousand dollars in one-hundred-dollar bills." She looked both excited and troubled, and she walked back and forth in front of him, the emotions warring in her storm cloud eyes. "I have no idea where she could get her hands on that much cash, but there it was, hidden in a secret compartment in her kitchen counter, of all places."

Hidden, John thought, glancing at the book dangling from his gloved hand. "Wrapped in plastic?" he asked.

She stopped her restless pacing and turned to look at him. "Yes. How did you know?"

He lifted the book in his gloved hand and motioned toward the partially finished wall. "I was putting in the drywall and noticed there was a split in the insulation. I reached inside and found this."

Miranda took a couple of steps closer to get a better look at the book. "It looks like a journal or a diary. Maybe a ledger?"

"I didn't want to touch it with my bare hands, in case you need to process it for fingerprints."

"Good idea." She reached into her pocket and pulled out a pair of latex gloves, probably spares from her search of Delta's trailer earlier that morning. She donned them quickly and took the book from his hands. Carefully she unstuck the tape holding the plastic wrap in place. "Can you go to the kitchen and get me a gallon bag out of the box over the stove? Bring the whole box."

He retrieved the box of gallon-sized resealable bags and handed her one. "Here you go."

She passed him the book. "Gloved hands only. And try not to touch it much. I'm not sure we can get prints off that fabric surface, but you never know."

As he balanced the book flat on his gloved palm, she carefully folded the plastic wrap she'd removed from the book and slipped it inside the gallon bag he'd supplied, sealing it up and setting it on the top of the toolbox by the door. "Now let's take a look at that book."

He handed over the small blue book. She took it in her gloved hands, trying to touch only the edges and the corners as she opened it. John moved to look at the contents over her shoulder.

Small, neat writing filled the pages, but they didn't form any sort of journalistic narrative. Instead, they were line after line of notes. Names. Places. Short commentary on one or both. *Never pull a con in Vegas. Everybody already knows all the tricks.*

"This must have belonged to Delta's father," John said.

Miranda nodded, flipping through the pages slowly, giving him time to make out the neat writing. "It's almost like a how-to book on pulling cons."

As they neared the later pages of the book, some of the notes changed. Still names and places, but now notes such as "Does his wife know he's bedding boys?" and "One more DUI and he loses his license."

"And now we have blackmail," John murmured.

About ten pages from the back of the book, the writing changed abruptly from the neat, almost printlike writing to a larger, more looping cursive. "That's Delta's writing," Miranda said.

John looked down at the book. "So you're saying…"

"I'm saying Delta McGraw was following in her father's footsteps." Miranda looked down at the journal. "And this may be what got her killed."

Chapter Twelve

One of the small back rooms at Duncan Hardware served as Gil Duncan's office. Inside, he'd crammed filing cabinets, a computer and a multifunction printer. One of those functions was copying, and Miranda spent a couple of hours that afternoon making two sets of copies from Delta McGraw's journal.

"I have to take this book to the sheriff's department," she'd told John earlier, after a second read through had convinced her that the journal might contain a clue that would help the department solve Delta's murder.

"Don't you want to go back through it again a few times first?" John had asked. He'd sat quietly enough across the table from her while she gave all the journal pages a more thorough reading, but she hadn't missed the impatience creasing his forehead and feathering fine lines from the corners of his eyes.

He was right. She did want to go back through it a few more times. Once the book was in the hands of the sheriff's department, it would be off-limits to her, since Miles Randall had made it clear he wasn't going to let her be part of the investigation.

So she'd just have to run her own investigation on the

side, and to do so, she was going to need the information in that journal.

She finished copying the last page and slipped the journal back into the plastic bag. After removing her latex gloves, she took the paper from the copier and bumped the stack against the top of the copier a few times to straighten the pages into a neat sheaf. She bound them together with a couple of rubber bands.

"Here." John handed her the canvas shopping tote she'd brought with her to conceal the copied pages. She shoved the bound pages inside, and John tucked the whole thing under one arm.

They headed out the back door to the employee parking area, where she'd parked her truck.

"Do you think the sheriff will suspect you've kept a copy?" John asked as he buckled his seat belt.

"I don't know. Maybe. I don't think he's going to make a stink about it, though, unless I get in the way of his investigation."

"And will you? Get in the way, I mean."

"I'll do my best not to."

She could see suspicion in Miles Randall's eyes when she handed over the two bags of evidence, but he didn't comment as she told him where the book had been hidden and how she'd done her best to maintain any potential evidence. "I'm not sure you'll be able to get any prints off the journal. And even if you could, I'm pretty sure the prints will be either Hal McGraw's or Delta's. I think Delta must have hidden the book when she was staying at my place for a couple of weeks."

"The room was already up that soon?"

"Oh, yeah. We had the builders reframe everything and get the siding and roof up as soon as we could after the tornado. We've just been taking our time with the rest of it, working when we could. But Dad's been swamped with all the orders from other people trying to rebuild, and you know you've been keeping me busy here at the station."

Randall was silent for another moment. Miranda realized she was holding her breath and let it go in a quiet sigh.

"Okay," Randall said finally. "But you're still off this case, Duncan. Understood?"

"Understood."

Randall frowned at the plastic-encased journal. "We'll dust the outside for prints. Nobody touched this at all?"

"John Blake found it, but he was wearing gloves because it was hidden in fiberglass insulation. I wore latex gloves when I held the book. Nobody touched it without a glove."

"But you looked through it?"

"Of course."

"What's inside?"

She described what she'd read, being as truthful and complete as she could.

Randall was a good man. A smart man. He knew as soon as she began talking what they were dealing with. The disappointment in his eyes echoed the sadness in her own heart. "She'd taken up her father's work."

"Looks like it." Miranda had hoped after Hal's death, Delta would finally be free of his legacy.

Instead, it looked as if she'd chosen to embrace it.

"Guess that explains that ten grand you found at her house this morning." Randall rubbed his chin thoughtfully. "Is there anything in that book that's actionable?"

"I don't know. She made notes about things she believed to be true. But if she had any actual evidence hidden anywhere, I don't know where she hid it. All that's in there right now are leads to go on but nothing we could take to court."

"Well, we'll see what we can track down from it." As Miranda rose to go, the sheriff asked, "How're you feeling?"

"A little tired. But improving." She could probably go to work right now and be fine, but since the sheriff wasn't going to let her anywhere near the Delta McGraw case while she was wearing the uniform, it had occurred to her that having the next few days free to work the case informally might be in her favor. "I'll be fine by Monday."

"Take care to get some rest, Deputy." Randall softened the stern tone of his voice with a slight smile.

"Thanks. I'll do that." She left the sheriff's office and headed for the front exit.

Coy Taylor was just coming on duty when she passed the sergeant's desk. He flashed her a smile. "You back yet?"

"Not until Monday," she said with an exaggerated sigh. "You're on afternoon duty this week?"

"Yeah. Chambers is covering mornings for the next couple of weeks. His kid starts his first varsity spring practice at the high school this week, and I guess Chambers wanted to be there to watch." Taylor settled behind the desk. "Heard you went to Delta's place this morning. Find anything?"

"You know I can't say, Sarge. But I'm hopeful we'll get a break in the case soon, and then you'll know all the details." As a desk sergeant, Taylor wasn't given details on every case they worked, only the parts that had been released to the press. Everything else stayed strictly between the deputies investigating the case.

In fact, she shouldn't be sharing any of the stuff she'd learned with John Blake at all. But since he'd almost been a victim of the same mystery gunman who had gone after her the other day, she figured she owed him the chance to get in on the investigation.

And she could use his help, since the sheriff had more or less banned her from her own case.

"Real shame about Delta." Taylor shook his head. "She had a real rough life."

Miranda nodded. "Yes, she did."

The phone rang, and Taylor shot her a look of apology as he answered. Miranda continued out the door to where John was waiting patiently in the passenger seat of her truck.

"How did it go?" he asked as she belted herself in behind the steering wheel.

"If he knew I was not only investigating this case on my own, but bringing a civilian in on it as well, I think I'd be in serious trouble."

"So don't let him find out."

Easy to say, she thought. But maybe not so easy to do.

"I THINK WE can probably set aside anything that wasn't from the last couple of years." Miranda looked up from one set of the journal pages she'd copied at her father's store. She looked tired, John thought. Probably should be getting some rest rather than diving headfirst into the blackmail journal. But she'd rebuffed the suggestion when he brought it up.

"I don't know—Delta might have kept up some of her father's blackmail schemes."

"Yeah, but I'm not seeing anything in Hal's notes that would be worth ten thousand dollars in hush money. Are you?"

John looked at the notes he'd taken from the early set of pages. Most of the crimes Hal McGraw had chronicled in his journal might be worth a couple of thousand dollars to keep them from coming out, but ten grand?

"Of course, I suppose it's possible that money I found came from multiple sources," Miranda added.

John shook his head. "I don't think so. Not the way you described those packets of bills. It seems as if it all came from the same place."

"True." She rested her chin on her folded hands and looked at him across the kitchen table. "So what kind of crime would be worth paying a blackmailer ten grand to cover it up?"

He dropped his pen and mimicked her position. "More to the point, what kind of crime would be worth killing for?"

"Very good point." Miranda picked up her pen and started marking through a few of the listings in her notes. "By the way, did you notice that a few of Delta's last entries looked as if they were written in code?"

"I did." He looked down at his own notes and marked through a few that didn't seem likely to stir up a murderous rage. "It looks like some sort of cipher. Did Delta like things like puzzles and ciphers?"

Miranda frowned. "I don't know. She never let me that far into her life, you know?"

"Well, if her father was a con man, she probably had at least a passing knowledge of ciphers and tricks. I'm surprised Hal didn't keep his own book in code."

"I'm surprised he kept a book at all," Miranda said. "He never seemed to be the organized sort."

"Does the first entry date mean anything?" John flipped back to the first page of his copy of the journal. "Looks like the first entry was about eleven years ago. January 12. Does that mean anything?"

"That's Delta's birthday. She would have turned sixteen that year."

"Sweet sixteen."

"Actually, on her sixteenth birthday, she was declared an emancipated minor by the courts. I don't remember much about it—I was in my senior year of high school and Delta McGraw wasn't really on my mind at the time. I do know that Hal McGraw didn't try to stop her. I think he knew he wasn't exactly a great dad."

John tried to put himself in Hal McGraw's shoes. His wife long gone, his own life a series of scams and cons, the law dogging his heels and his daughter officially declaring her independence from him—would that situation make him do a little soul-searching?

Not a guy like Hal McGraw. He'd try to do something to win back his daughter.

"What if that's why he started keeping this journal?" he asked. "What if this was meant to lure Delta back all along?"

"Lure her back?"

"She declared her independence from him right about the time these entries started. Maybe he tried to buy her affection and loyalty. Made a big push to earn more money, give her a reason to stick around."

Miranda frowned thoughtfully. "Maybe. I do remember some of the girls at school talking about how she was suddenly dressing nicer and wondered how come she suddenly had money after ditching her daddy."

"He might have been trying to impress her."

"Could she have known all along what Hal was doing?"

"You tell me. You knew Delta. Do you think she knew?"

"I don't know. But clearly she knew what that book meant, and rather than destroy it, she tried to protect it." Miranda rose from the table, revealing in her restless movements the troubled state of her mind. She paced to the window and looked outside at a landscape bathed in the ruby glow of the setting sun. "She must have hidden it here when she was staying with me. She was here alone a lot."

"You said her father had made her his accomplice, right?"

She nodded, still looking out the window.

"So she'd know how to run an extortion scheme."

"Yes. She would." Miranda turned slowly to face him. "I just wanted to believe she'd put that kind of life behind her."

"She didn't have a job, did she?"

"Not recently." Miranda closed her eyes. "I should have spent a little more time trying to figure out where she was getting the money to live on if she wasn't working a job."

"But you didn't."

She shook her head. "I can be as much a loner as Delta was. I get really wrapped up in what I'm doing in my own life and I sometimes forget to touch base with people."

He could sympathize. "You can't fix what you didn't

do. Not at this point. But you can find justice for her. Right?"

"Right." She pushed her fingers through her hair like a comb, shoving the mass of auburn waves away from her face. "We had some leftovers from yesterday's barbecue. Want me to heat them up for us for dinner?"

"You sit. I'll get the leftovers."

She didn't argue, sliding back into the chair she'd vacated a few minutes earlier, then straightening the scattered pages before her into a neat stack. John retrieved the leftover steaks and baked potatoes from the refrigerator and piled them onto plates to heat in the microwave. He also grabbed the remaining salad and placed it on the table.

"Hmm," Miranda murmured as he pulled glasses from the cabinet.

"Hmm what?"

"This entry. It's in Delta's handwriting, and I don't think this notation is code, but I'm not quite sure what it means." She turned the page around so he could read it, pointing to the note in question.

Hef. Co. clerk—Rem. Alamo Fund. 50K missing?

"Heflin County is the next county over," Miranda explained. "And there's a Texas-based charity for wounded Texas soldiers called the Remember the Alamo Fund. But I haven't heard anything about missing money."

"Maybe it hasn't been discovered yet. Or someone managed to pay it all back after getting a note from Delta."

"So her blackmail was altruistic?" He tried not to scoff, but there had been several packets of hundred-dollar bills hidden in Delta's kitchen counter that would suggest otherwise.

"No, of course not." Miranda sighed. "I just mean, maybe that was the response to Delta's blackmail rather than paying the money to her."

"Paying it back would have been about covering his tracks."

"Or hers. I don't know who the Heflin county clerk is."

"Or hers," John conceded. "But if he or she was willing to go to the lengths of coming up with fifty thousand to pay back the charity—"

"He or she might have gone even further."

"Having that hanging over your head would be a nightmare. Even if the money was refunded, you'd have to worry that what you did would come out. Forget about your position with the charity. Even being accused of that sort of transgression could put your job in jeopardy."

"Especially in Texas. County clerks here oversee elections. Imagine the kind of election shenanigans a blackmailer could cause holding something over the head of the county clerk. And you know, if something like that came out and your spouse didn't know about it, it could wreak havoc on your personal life, too."

John nodded. "A person might be willing to kill to make it all go away."

"So we need to find out who the Heflin county clerk is and if he or she has any connection to the Remember the Alamo Fund." She pushed away from the table and headed down the hall to her bedroom.

John followed, stopping in the doorway while she grabbed her laptop computer from a drawer beside her bed. She plugged it in and sat on the edge of her bed, glancing at him over her shoulder. "You can come in."

He sat on the bed beside her, trying to ignore the little shiver of animal awareness that rippled through him. So many other things he'd like to do in this room besides surf the internet...

"Here we go. Jasper Layton is the Heflin county clerk." She pulled up a search engine page and entered the name. Several links came up, most of them connected to his position as county clerk.

She made a sound, and he found himself edging closer to read the screen over her shoulder.

She clicked a link and a page came up, an article from the Heflin County newspaper. "'Liver transplant miracle not without its downside—recipient and family find themselves deep in debt.'"

"His wife needed a liver transplant," John murmured, scanning the article. "Guess that might explain why he was willing to risk everything to skim money out of the charity fund."

"But how did he pay it back?"

"Good question."

Miranda picked up her cell phone and brought up the previous tab from the Heflin County website. She punched in a number. "Jasper Layton, please." Listening for a second, she frowned. "Oh. I'm sorry to hear that. Thank you."

"Sorry to hear what?" John asked as she ended the call and set the phone on the bed beside her.

She turned her head to look at him, her expression troubled. "Jasper Layton is dead."

Chapter Thirteen

"He ran his car off Wildcat Ridge. There was no evidence that he hit the brakes." Sheriff Paul Leonardi leaned back in his chair, steepling his hands over his flat stomach as he looked across the desk at Miranda and John. "What's your interest in Jasper Layton, if I may ask, Deputy Duncan?"

Miranda had anticipated the question, and she had her answer ready. "We're investigating a murder in Barstow County, and Mr. Layton's name showed up in some of the victim's personal effects. When we learned that Mr. Layton was deceased—"

"You thought you'd come talk to me."

"You said there was no evidence he hit the brakes," John said. "Do you think he intentionally ran his car off the road?"

Leonardi gave John a long, narrow-eyed look of speculation. "You're not a deputy."

"No, sir."

The sheriff flicked his gaze toward Miranda. "You bring a civilian along to all your meetings with fellow law enforcement agents?"

"Mr. Blake is a consultant," she said, as if dismissing the question. "Do you think Mr. Layton's accident was intentional?"

"Let's put it this way. The autopsy determined that cause of death was blunt-force trauma to the head. Layton went through the windshield and landed under the car. There were no signs of alcohol or drugs in his system. It was in the middle of the afternoon, so it's not likely he fell asleep at the wheel."

"But you seem reluctant to call it suicide."

"I didn't see the point of multiplying the tragedies Mrs. Layton and her children had to face." Leonardi shrugged. "It wouldn't have made any difference. He was past the two-year exception in his life insurance. They were going to get the money regardless."

Miranda glanced at John. He looked back at her, his dark eyebrows twitching upward in response.

"The article I read said this happened three weeks ago?"

"Yes."

So, she thought, soon after Delta disappeared. But quite possibly before she had died and definitely before her body was dumped on Lizzie Dillard's farm. And that meant even if Jasper Layton had been one of Delta's blackmail victims, he wasn't likely to have been her killer.

"Is there anything else I can help you with?"

"Just one thing, and I don't think you're going to like it."

Leonardi sat forward, leaning his forearms on his desk blotter. "You want to talk to Angela, don't you?"

"I do."

Leonardi's lips pressed to a thin line. "Is that really necessary?"

"I'm afraid it is."

"I'd like to be with you when you talk to her."

"If you're worried I'll tell her something about her husband's mode of death, rest assured, I won't."

"Then what's left to ask her?"

She glanced at John again. He sent back a meaningful look.

"I'd like to ask her about her husband's involvement in the Remember the Alamo Fund."

One twitch of the muscle in Leonardi's lean jaw was the sheriff's only visible reaction, but it was enough. "What about it?"

"Did you know at least fifty thousand dollars went missing from the fund earlier this year?"

"You're mistaken." His tone was dismissive.

"Are you involved with the fund?" she asked bluntly.

Leonardi rose to his feet, towering over them. "I'm a busy man, Deputy Duncan. I've answered all the pertinent questions about Jasper Layton's unfortunate accident. If you have any further enquiries, you can have your boss contact me."

"You hit a sore spot back there," John murmured a few moments later as they left the Heflin County Hall and stepped into the mild afternoon sunlight. "I think he knows the money is missing."

"Or was," she said as she unlocked the door of her truck. The interior had heated up beneath the warm Texas sun, coaxing a trickle of perspiration down her temple as she started the truck and headed its wide nose out of the parking lot.

"You think Layton paid the money back."

"If he stole fifty grand from the charity, it would come out unless it somehow got paid back before anyone figured it out."

"But how could he have paid it back?" John asked. "You saw that article about his wife. Her transplant left them in serious debt."

"That's why I wanted to talk to Angela Layton."

"You think she knows what her husband did?"

"I think if anyone would know, it's probably her." Miranda pulled the truck into a small shopping strip just off the highway, parking in front of a diner that occupied one of the glass-front shops at the nearest end. "So we need to talk to her."

"But first, we're going to have a late lunch?" He followed her as she got out of the truck and headed for the door of the diner.

"I don't know how much you know about life in a small town," she said as they neared the front door of the diner, "but if you want to know anything about anyone in town, a town diner is the place to start."

At a little after two in the afternoon, the diner was sparsely occupied. Miranda headed for the counter at the back. Within a few seconds, a pleasantly plump, motherly waitress appeared from the back and put menus on the counter in front of them. With a smile, she welcomed them to the diner.

"I'd like a cup of coffee—black, one sweetener—and a slice of your double chocolate cake," Miranda ordered with a smile.

"Same," John said.

"I've heard such good things about your chocolate cake," Miranda added, taking a chance.

"Really?" The waitress smiled with pleasure at the compliment. The rectangular name badge pinned to her light blue dress said "Vicki" in neat embossed letters. "Heard from who?" she asked, as Miranda had hoped.

"Angela Layton, for one."

Immediately Vicki's expression faltered. "That poor woman."

"These past few months have been so hard on her."

"Just when she was finally starting to see a little light at the end of the tunnel." Vicki shook her head. "Did you make it to the funeral?"

"We were still at the hospital," John said, slanting a quick glance at Miranda. "My mother was still recovering from her transplant."

"That's where we met Angela and Jasper," Miranda said. "John's mother was having a kidney transplant when Angela was in the hospital. We met Jasper in the cafeteria and, well—"

"We clicked, you know?" John flashed Vicki a smile that seemed to charm the waitress into a broad, answering smile.

"I know what you mean," Vicki said as she poured coffee for both of them. "Did you come to town just to see Angela?"

"Actually, no," Miranda answered, "we're just passing through on our way to Amarillo, but we thought we'd at least stop in here at the Lone Star Diner to try a slice of that cake."

"We had hoped maybe Angela might be feeling well enough to be here, too," John admitted. "But that was probably hoping too much."

"She hasn't felt a lot like getting out and about," Vicki said as she served them slices of the chocolate cake. "But maybe you could give her a call. I'm sure she could use some cheering up."

"That's the thing," Miranda said with a slight shake of her head. "Jasper gave John their phone number, but somewhere between the hospital and the motel where we were staying, he lost it. We were lucky to remember Heflin County."

"She's probably not in the mood for visitors anyway," John said after swallowing a bite of cake.

"Not so sure about that. She'd probably appreciate a friendly face right about now." Vicki reached under the counter and pulled out a thin phone directory. "I think they're listed."

While Vicki went to wait on a couple of customers who had just entered and taken one of the tables near the front window, Miranda quickly looked up the listing for Jasper and Angela Layton. She jotted the number and address to her phone.

"Are we really going to invade that poor woman's privacy?" John asked quietly.

"I don't want to, but if anybody's going to be able to tell us why Delta had that notation about Jasper Layton in her blackmail diary—"

"What if Jasper didn't tell his wife anything?"

"We won't know unless we ask."

Still, she had to give herself a mental pep talk during the mile-and-a-half drive from the diner to the small ranch-style house on Prescott Road, including most of the walk up the flagstone path to the front door, before she found the courage to knock.

The woman who answered was plump and cheerful, and definitely not the woman whose photo had been part of the online article Miranda had found during her internet search for Jasper Layton. She introduced herself as Angela's aunt Laura.

"Angela's resting in the sunroom," Laura told them when they asked. "Are you friends?"

"We actually knew Jasper," John lied. "Through his work with the Remember the Alamo Fund."

Laura's expression fell. "Poor Jasper. Poor Angela, for that matter. Finally starting to feel better, a whole new future ahead of her, and then this."

"We wanted to see if she needed anything. If there was anything we could do for her," Miranda said, and meant it. She might have questions for the woman, but maybe if she could find the answers about what really happened to Jasper, it would give Angela Layton some comfort.

At least, she hoped it would. She hoped she wasn't about to make everything worse.

"I'll ask if she's up to having visitors." Laura disappeared down a hall, returning a few moments later. "She'll see you. Down the hall, first room on the left."

Miranda and John followed the directions and found a slim, blonde woman sitting on a colorful sofa in front of a wall full of curtainless windows. Bright sunlight and warmth flowed into the room through the wall of glass, bathing the blonde in golden light.

Angela Layton looked considerably better than she'd appeared shortly after her liver transplant surgery, but beneath the glow of improving health was the pallor of grief. She rose to greet them as they entered the sunroom, extending a slim hand. "Aunt Laura said you knew Jasper?"

Miranda felt like a creep. "Actually, we didn't. Not personally."

Angela sank to the sofa again, looking at them through narrowed eyes. "Are you reporters?"

"No." Miranda gestured at the round ottoman sitting in front of the sofa. "May I?"

"Who are you?"

"My name is Miranda Duncan. I'm a deputy sheriff with the Barstow County Sheriff's Department."

Angela's expression went from wary to confused. "Barstow County?"

"Did you know anyone named Delta McGraw?"

Something shifted subtly in Angela Layton's eyes. "Should I?"

"I believe she might have been blackmailing your husband."

For a moment, Angela looked as if she was about to order them to leave. But after a second of tension, she slumped back against the sofa cushions and closed her eyes. "He paid it all back."

"To the Remember the Alamo Fund?"

Angela nodded, her eyes still closed. "We were so desperate for money. All of our savings were gone. Jasper had borrowed all he could against his 401K and it just wasn't enough. One of the doctors at the hospital in Dallas was making a big stink about getting his fees, and I was still feeling so sick, I couldn't even go to work part-time to try to pick up the slack."

"And there were the funds at the charity, so easy to get his hands on," John murmured.

"It wasn't easy for him," Angela snapped, anger flashing in her blue eyes. "It broke him. Do you really think that accident that killed him was an accident?"

Miranda glanced at John, whose expression was carefully neutral. But she was beginning to be able to read the subtle clues to the emotions he kept in check. There was a grim cast to his hazel eyes that echoed the dismay burning in her own chest.

"He held onto the funds for a long time. I think maybe he was hoping something would happen to save us." Angela passed a thin hand over her face. "Then one day, he told me someone knew what he'd done."

"Delta."

Angela nodded. "Delta."

"How did Jasper know Delta? Or did he?"

"He told me he knew her through his job as county clerk. Apparently her father had owned some property here in Heflin County and she'd come here after his death to deal with some probate issues. He wasn't sure how she figured out what he'd done, but the next thing he knew, she called him and told him she knew he'd skimmed the funds from the charity and if he wanted her silence, he had to pay her ten thousand dollars."

Miranda's heart sank. Intellectually, she knew that Delta had to be involved in extortion, but hearing it laid out so baldly was a blow.

"What did Jasper do?" John asked.

"He couldn't pay her. He hadn't even really decided whether he could keep the money to pay our bills. So he told Delta why he'd taken the money and told her he would put it back."

"What did she say?"

"She said if he did, she wouldn't tell anyone what she knew."

"For a price?"

Angela looked up at them. "Jasper said no. That once she heard why he'd taken the money in the first place, she backed off. She just said she'd know if he put it back or not, and if he didn't, she'd double her price."

"So he put it back?" John asked.

"Yes. And then three weeks later he drove off Wildcat Ridge." Tears glittered in Angela's eyes, but they didn't fall.

"I'm so sorry." Miranda started to reach across the

space between them to touch Angela's hand, but the expression on the woman's face stopped her. She dropped her hand back to her lap. "You clearly don't think it was an accident."

"It wasn't. He left the life insurance policy sitting on the desk in his study. I found it there before I even heard about the crash." She brushed away the tears welling on her lower eyelids. "He'd left a sticky note on top."

"What did it say?" Miranda asked.

"It said the two years were up."

"The suicide clause," John murmured.

Angela nodded. "He took the policy out four years ago, when I was first diagnosed with liver failure. I'd contracted hepatitis B when I was working as a nurse at a clinic down on the border a few years ago. I got over it quickly enough and didn't really think anything more about it, until my liver started failing." She shook her head. "Jasper went out and bought a life insurance policy that day. Until then, I guess we thought we were invincible."

"His insurance will cover your bills, won't it?"

This time, Angela didn't stop the tears. "There'll even be some left over so I can keep the house until I'm recovered enough to go back to work."

Miranda looked at John. He gave a slight nod, and she stood. "Mrs. Layton, I really am very sorry for your loss. And I'm sorry I had to bother you this way."

Angela didn't rise to see them out, but she did speak as they were turning to go. "Did you find out what you wanted to know?"

Miranda turned back to look at her. "Yes. Your husband was a good man. Don't ever let anyone make you think otherwise."

For the first time since they'd entered the room, Angela managed a faint smile. "I know."

Back in the hot truck cab, Miranda leaned against the headrest and closed her eyes. "I wish we hadn't done that."

"It answered a few questions."

"At what price?" She opened her eyes and looked at John. "There's no way Jasper Layton killed Delta."

"But we couldn't really know until we talked to her whether Angela Layton might have done it."

"We're back to square one."

John held up the bundle of copied pages he'd brought with them. "We still have these."

"Well, then, you look through those pages and see what you can find while I hunt down a gas station."

John flipped through the pages while she navigated the side streets until she found a gas station near the highway that would take them back to Barstow County. When Miranda got back into the truck after pumping the gas, he looked up at her with a slight smile.

"Does this mean anything to you?" he asked, looking down at the page he was holding. "'Jarrod Whitmore. Trainor and 7,'" he said. "Why does the name Jarrod Whitmore sound familiar?"

"Ever heard of the Bar W Ranch?"

"Of course. It's just a couple of miles down the highway from where I'm staying. I pass the place all the time."

"Bar W is owned by Cal Whitmore. Jarrod is his youngest son. He's always been a little on the wild side."

"What about the rest of it? 'Trainor and 7'?"

"I'm not sure. Trainor is a road that crosses Route 7 about five miles south of the ranch, but I don't know…" She froze in the middle of putting her key in the ignition as the answer hit her like a hammer blow. "Oh, my God. Trainor Road and Route 7."

"What is it?" John asked.

She turned to look at John, hear stomach roiling. "Do you remember that lady you met at my dad's place the other day? Rose McAllen?"

He frowned. "You mean the one with the little girl?"

"Right, her granddaughter, Cassie. Rose's daughter, Lindy—Cassie's mother—was killed in a hit-and-run on Route 7. To be more specific, she was killed on Route 7 right at the Trainor Road crossing. About a year after Hal McGraw's death. She was walking on the highway and a vehicle struck her and kept going. We've never found the person responsible."

John looked down at the page he was holding. "This is Delta's handwriting, isn't it?" He showed her the copy.

Miranda nodded.

"So Delta—"

"She knew," Miranda interjected. "She knew that Jarrod Whitmore was the one who hit Lindy McAllen and left her to die. In fact, she was blackmailing him about it."

"We *were* looking for a crime someone might be willing to kill for," John murmured.

Miranda met his troubled gaze, her stomach in knots. "I think we just may have found it."

Chapter Fourteen

By the time they arrived back in Cold Creek, the sun was already dipping well toward the western horizon. Miranda pulled into the parking lot of the hardware store and shut off the engine to make a phone call to the Bar W Ranch, while John ran into the store to pick up some paint he was going to need when he got back to the work on his own place.

By the time he returned to the truck with his purchase, Miranda was off the phone, sitting with both hands tightly gripping the steering wheel and a frustrated look in her gray eyes.

She turned her head to look at him as he climbed into the passenger seat. "Got Mr. Whitmore's housekeeper. She said the Whitmores are in Montana looking at a couple of bulls for sale and won't be back until Monday. And Jarrod's in Ireland."

"Ireland?" John asked, surprised. "What's he doing in Ireland?"

"The housekeeper didn't offer any other information."

"Well, at least we have an extradition treaty with Ireland."

"First we have to figure out if he was the person driving the vehicle that killed Lindy McAllen."

"You'd have access to the case files, wouldn't you?"

Miranda started the truck and pulled out of the parking lot. "Yeah. I should be able to access them from my laptop at home, though. I noticed Sheriff Randall's truck was still at the station when we drove by. I don't want him asking questions about why I keep showing up at the station when I'm supposed to be on medical leave."

"So let's pick up dinner somewhere, go back to your place and try to relax a little," John suggested. He was beginning to think she was overtaxing herself so soon after the crash. She'd been rubbing her head for most of the drive back to Cold Creek, as if she was trying to ward off a headache, and her pale face and the dark circles under her eyes were starting to concern him.

"We have so many more pages to work through," she protested.

"And they can wait until tomorrow," he told her firmly. "Right now, you need some food, a nice hot bath and a good night's sleep. In that order."

She slanted a look at him but didn't say anything else until they reached the small roadside barbecue stand near her house. They picked up barbecue brisket, baked beans and tangy vinegar slaw to share and were back at Miranda's house by five thirty.

Rex and Ruthie both greeted them at the front door when they entered, as good a sign as they were likely to get that nobody had tried to break into the house while they were gone.

John fed the cats in the kitchen while Miranda pulled an old folding card table and two chairs onto the front porch. By the time John went outside, she'd already laid out their meal on the table and had kicked back, her feet propped on the porch railing, sipping iced tea through a straw while she watched the ruby sunset sinking into the western horizon.

"Every time I wonder why I haven't moved out of this little bitty town, I look at one of those sunsets, breathe in the clean air and listen to the killdeer calling and I remember why I'm still here."

"It's very different than where I'm from." He took a sip of his own tea and followed her gaze toward the sunset. "But just as beautiful in its own way."

"Miss the mountains?" She dropped her feet to the porch floor and turned to spoon a couple of slabs of brisket onto her plate.

"Some. Not as much as I would've thought." There was a wild beauty in the flat scrubby plains of the panhandle that spoke to something inside him he hadn't even realized existed, a hunger for wide open spaces and endless horizons that couldn't be found in the hills of home.

"I used to think of this place as untouchable." She added beans and slaw to her plate and poked a fork into a piece of brisket. "Crime didn't really exist here, you know? Not like in the bigger cities. I could count on my hand the number of serious crimes in the past ten years. Until now."

"Can't keep the world out forever."

"No." She dropped her fork. "Now we have a murder, and an unsolved hit-and-run and God knows what else we're going to find once we figure out what kind of code Delta was using—"

"You can't keep the world out forever," he repeated, reaching across the table and closing his hand over hers. "But maybe we should try to keep it out for tonight?"

She looked at him for a long, tense moment, then

turned her hand so that her palm touched his. "Do you think we can really do that?"

"We could try."

She gave him a narrow-eyed look for a second, then smiled. "Okay. No shoptalk for the rest of the evening."

They settled in to a comfortable silence as they ate, but soon, with their stomachs full, the leftovers put up in the refrigerator and the card table restored to the hall closet, Miranda sat on the sofa across from John and shot him a questioning look. "What now?"

"What do you usually do when you have men over?"

Her gaze skittered away. "I don't usually have men over."

"Ever?"

"I don't have a lot of time to date these days," she said, sounding mildly defensive. "And when I do, we generally drive in to Plainview or Lubbock for dinner and maybe a movie, and then it's late, so I have to come home so I can get a decent night's sleep before work in the morning." She pressed her face into her hands. "God, that sounds pathetic."

"Yeah, well, the last woman I went out with didn't even know my real name, so I don't exactly have room to judge."

She managed a smile. "I don't think this is what you had in mind when we agreed to no shoptalk."

"Relax. I don't have anything in particular in mind." He joined her on the sofa, sitting close enough that he could touch her if he liked, but not so close he would send her nervously skittering into the next zip code.

"Maybe we could ask each other questions," she suggested. "You know, getting-to-know-you kind of questions."

"Sure. You want to start?"

"Okay." Her smile was a little nervous, but she turned her body toward him, giving him a nice view of her long neck and the ripe curves of her breasts beneath her thin blue T-shirt.

Progress, he thought, trying not to stare too obviously.

He must have failed, he realized a moment later when a look of amusement lightened her gray eyes and her nerves seemed to settle in a heartbeat. "I've already done a background check on you, so no easy questions from me," she warned with a widening smile. "Let's start with a hard one. Ever milked a cow?"

He laughed. "Yes, actually. On my granddaddy's farm. He had a place west of the mountains, where he raised chickens and pigs and he had a milk cow and a couple of swayback mares he'd let us ride until we got too heavy for them."

"You and your brother and sister?"

"Yeah. Josh, Julie and me."

"All your names started with *J*?"

"Not one of my parents' better decisions. My poor mom went through the whole list every time she was trying to call any one of us."

Miranda laughed, the sound warm and inviting, drawing him closer despite his intention to keep his distance. "My dad just had me, but when he gets mad, he uses my full name."

He leaned even closer. "Which is?"

"Miranda Crockett Duncan."

"Crockett? As in Davy?"

"Remember the Alamo," she said with a sheepish laugh. "My dad tells me it was a compromise. He wanted to name me after his mother, Geraldine, and my mother wanted to name me after her best friend in grammar school, Mercedes Gonzales."

"Miranda Mercedes Duncan?" He couldn't hold back a wince. "Yeah, I think Crockett was definitely the way to go."

"You'd think. But there was this one kid in summer camp who found out my middle name and kept singing the Davy Crockett TV show theme whenever he saw me."

"Summer camp where?"

"Down near San Antonio. Of course."

"And you went to college at Texas Tech."

"Wreck 'em, Tech!" she said with a big grin.

"So, have you ever actually left Texas?"

"Of course. I drove across the state line into Oklahoma once. Quickly." She shot him a big grin. "Seriously, of course I've been other places. I went to Spain for a semester my junior year of college. I've seen Notre Dame in Paris and once talked my way onto a sculling crew practicing on the Thames."

"What did a girl from Cold Creek, Texas, know about sculling?"

"Not a damn thing." She laughed. "But the guys thought I was cute, so they nearly capsized the boat trying to teach me how it worked."

He could picture the scene all too easily. There was something about Miranda Crockett Duncan that made a man want to do things he never realized he could. Or should.

He touched her cheek because it was there, softly curved and tempting, within his reach. Her smile faded and her gray eyes grew large and luminous as she gazed back at him in breathless anticipation.

He kissed her. Her response was swift and fierce, her

hands threading through his hair and drawing him closer. Her lips parted, inviting him in, and before he knew quite how they got there, she was lying on her back beneath him, her hands sliding under his shirt until they touched his skin, her fingertips leaving a shivery trail of need the farther they traveled.

Suddenly, her fingers pressed against a tender place above his shoulder, and he couldn't quite swallow the hiss of pain it evoked.

She went still, drawing her head back to look at him. "Did I hurt you?"

"No," he lied, dipping his head toward her again.

But she wriggled out from beneath him, pushing him back into a sitting position. "That was a bullet-wound scar."

"I told you about that."

"You said they were hunting you, but I didn't realize they actually shot you. I thought maybe you just got assaulted or something." She reached for the collar of his shirt, tugging it aside until she found the corresponding entry wound scar. "How many other scars like this do you have?"

He nudged the waistband of his jeans down to show her where he'd taken a bullet just above his hip. "That wasn't much more than a flesh wound."

"Is that it?"

He let the jeans fall back into place and lifted the bottom of his shirt to bare his right side. The wound there was the worst of his scars because it had taken surgery to remove the bullet lodged a few inches away from his hepatic artery. It had nicked his liver, but the damage to that organ had been minimal and it had healed on its own, once the surgeon had removed the bullet from its dangerous hiding place.

"How much damage did it do?" she asked quietly, her eyes wide with dismay.

"Not as much as it could have."

"What did you do that made the Blue Ridge Infantry put you on their most-wanted list?"

He frowned. The night wasn't going the way he'd hoped at all. "I thought we weren't going to talk shop."

"I don't consider this talking shop," she said with a frown. "What did you do to cross them, exactly?"

"Remember I told you about that tough lady named Nicki who helped bring down the Virginia branch of the militia?"

Miranda nodded.

"Nicki was deep undercover. She had no contact with our boss, Alexander Quinn, except through me. I guess you could say I was sort of her handler."

"And the BRI found out what you were doing?"

"Not exactly. What put me on their radar was my part in helping Nicki sneak their top man's wife and kid out of their cabin in the woods."

Miranda's eyes narrowed. "Were they being held hostage?"

"Not exactly." He settled back against the sofa cushions with a sigh. "Nicki had been trying to get close enough to find out the identity of the militia leader. People talked about him in hushed, almost reverent tones, but they never called him by name. The only thing she'd learned was that he had a medical condition that needed nursing care, and she made it her goal to be chosen as his medical caretaker."

"What kind of condition?"

"Diabetes. The story was, he was having trouble stabilizing his blood sugar and he didn't trust doctors or hospitals."

"And Nicki was a nurse?"

"She had paramedic training."

"So she managed to get them to trust her?"

"We thought they did. One day, they told her she was in and arranged for her to go meet the leader." There were some fuzzy places in his memory of what had happened next, but one thing he'd never forgotten was the gutting fear that had come over him when he'd realized the Blue Ridge Infantry was on to Nicki's scheme. "It turned out, Nicki had been working for the leader of the Virginia BRI the whole time she was in River's End. He was her boss at the diner where she'd worked as a fry cook."

"My God. And she never had a clue? What about the diabetes—if he was having so much trouble getting his blood sugar regulated, didn't he show signs of it?"

"That's the thing. It was never Trevor Colley who was sick. It was his little boy."

Miranda lifted her hand to her mouth. "Juvenile diabetes?"

He nodded. "The kid was really sick, and Colley let his fear of doctors and hospitals put that kid in danger. They took Nicki hostage and made her try to help the little boy while they waited for Nicki's backup to arrive so they could take them out."

"Which is where you and your bullet wounds come in."

"More or less. Nicki had gotten involved with someone else, someone in nearly as much trouble as she was, and he helped me get to her once the operation went crossways. Nicki convinced Colley's wife that they needed to get the little boy to a real doctor. That if they didn't do something soon, he'd die. Nicki's friend, Dallas, helped her get the woman and the boy to safety."

"While you were doing what, offering a diversion for Colley and his men?"

He didn't answer. He didn't have to.

"My God, you let them shoot at you so the others could get to safety?"

"I didn't know what else to do. I'd had one job—keeping Nicki as safe as possible while she did her very dangerous job. I had to see it through."

She just stared at him for a moment, her heart in her eyes. Then she reached out and caught his face between her long-fingered hands. "You crazy, amazing man." Bending, she kissed him firmly, not resisting when he pulled her into his arms.

The kiss deepened, but only so far. He didn't know if he was the one keeping things in check or if it was Miranda, but in the end, he didn't suppose it mattered. They ended up holding each other quietly, the fire of desired tamped down beneath an odd sort of survivor's communion.

"I was serious when I said you should take a hot bath and get a good night's sleep," he said a while later, long after the lingering light of day had disappeared into cool, blue night.

"But then I'd have to move," she grumbled against his throat. "And I'm so comfortable."

"I might be persuaded to give you a back rub once you got out of the bath."

She leaned her head back and looked up at him. "You're playing with my emotions now."

As he opened his mouth to respond, her cell phone

rang, the sound muted where her hip pressed against his side. She wriggled out of his grasp and pulled out the phone. "It's a local number," she murmured, pushing the button to answer. "Miranda Duncan."

He saw her brow furrow as she listened to whoever was on the other end of the line. "I see," she said finally. "Okay, I understand." She hung up the phone, her expression still troubled.

"Who was that?" John asked when she didn't say anything else.

"It was Rose McAllen." She leaned forward, resting her elbows on her knees. "She told me to stop looking into her daughter's death."

"Why?" he asked.

She turned her head to look at him. "She didn't say, but I could tell she was worried. Maybe even scared."

"Do you think someone's threatened her?"

"I don't know." She rubbed her chin with her fingertips before she turned to look at him. "It's odd, don't you think, that I make a call to the Bar W Ranch, wanting to talk to Jarrod Whitmore about Lindy McAllen's death, and a couple of hours later, Rose calls and asks me to stop looking into her daughter's case?"

"You think Whitmore threatened her?"

She frowned, as if giving the question real thought. "I don't know. Honestly, it doesn't sound like Cal Whitmore's style."

"He's a wealthy, ruthless cattleman, and you don't think threats seem like his style?"

"He's a wealthy, successful cattleman," she amended. "And most people around here like him. They don't fear him."

"Maybe because they've never had to cross him."

"He tends to grease the skids with money, not threats." She looked at him, still frowning. "Do you remember when we saw Rose and Cassie the other day at the hardware store? I told her then that we'd never stop looking for the person who killed Lindy. And she gave me the strangest look, as if she wanted to say something. But then she just turned away."

"And you think it's because she doesn't want you to keep looking?"

"I think she already knows that Jarrod Whitmore was the one who did it. And I think Cal Whitmore has paid her for her silence."

"But how could she have known it was Jarrod? Did she witness it?"

"No," Miranda answered, an odd look in her eyes.

"Then how?"

Miranda pushed to her feet, pacing toward the fireplace. The afternoon had been warm, so they hadn't bothered with a fire, but now that night had fallen, there was a definite chill in the air, and John could see her looking with almost wistful longing at the cold hearth before she turned to face him, wrapping her arms around herself.

"Remember earlier today, when Angela Layton told us that after Jasper met with Delta, he decided to pay the money back to the charity?"

"Yes."

"Doesn't that seem like a strange thing for someone to do in response to a blackmailer's demands?"

"It could have been the only way to make her go away."

"Or maybe it's what she wanted from him all along." She rubbed her hands up and down her arms as if fighting off a chill. "Maybe it's what she demanded from Jarrod Whitmore, too."

He stood up to face her, finally understanding what she was getting at. "You think Delta—"

"Wasn't blackmailing people for money," she elaborated. "I think she was trying to make them do the right thing."

Chapter Fifteen

Miranda's cell phone rang shortly after six the next morning. She grabbed it from the bedside table, rubbed her eyes and checked the display. It was the station. "Duncan," she answered, her voice hoarse with sleep.

It was Sheriff Randall. "Waller and Mendoza are both in the hospital in Lubbock. They took their wives into town for dinner and got broadsided by a dump truck on the way home."

She sat up quickly, her stomach knotting with anxiety. "How bad?"

"Broken bones, shaken up, but everybody's going to recover."

"Thank God."

"But we're shorthanded now."

"No worries. I'll be right in." She hung up the phone, grabbed her robe and headed for the bathroom to shower.

By the time she finished dressing, she could smell bacon frying in the kitchen. She secured her hair in a ponytail and followed the aroma down the hall, where John stood at the stove, flipping strips of bacon. "You're up early."

He looked at her. "And you're dressed for work."

"Two of our deputies were in a car accident last night.

They're going to be all right, but they're still in the hospital, which means we're shorthanded at the station. So I'm going in this morning." She eyed the bacon. "Once I eat, that is."

While she poured orange juice for both of them, he whipped up a quick batch of scrambled eggs, added them to the bacon and buttered toast on a couple of plates and joined her at the table. "You sure you're ready to go back to work?"

"I was ready two days ago," she said, dismissing his worries with a wave of her hand. "But that means you're on your own with Delta's journal. I can't be caught with my copy of the pages at work."

"I was already planning to try to figure out what kind of cipher she used on the last few pages of the book," he told her. "So I'll work on that and maybe by the time you get home, I'll have figured some of it out."

"That would be great." She smiled at him over her glass of orange juice, keeping her tone light. "You know, John Blake, if you're not careful, I could really get used to having you around."

"Would that be a bad thing?" He sounded serious.

She set the glass on the table, considering the question. "If you were going to stick around long-term, maybe not. But if you're just some stranger passing through—"

He didn't say anything, looking down at his plate of food. "I don't know what happens next," he admitted.

She swallowed an unexpected rush of disappointment. "Then maybe we should just keep things casual. No strings, no expectations. No taking things too far."

He followed her to the door when she started to leave, catching her hand as she was about to step through the doorway. "Does kissing count as taking things too far?"

She turned to look at him, torn between amusement at the hopeful look on his face and uncertainty about the wisdom of continuing to tempt fate when neither of them could make any promises. But amusement, and the delectable memory of his kisses, won out. "Kisses are okay."

"Good." He leaned forward and pressed a sweet, hot kiss against her lips. "I'll try to have a breakthrough on the code by the time you get home."

"You do that." She gave him another swift kiss and headed out to her truck.

All the talk at the station was about Wallace and Mendoza, with photos of the horrific crash scene already floating around from deputy to deputy. "Amazing they survived at all," Tim Robertson told Miranda as he passed her the photos the Lubbock Police Department had emailed over.

The twisted, crumpled metal that had been Mendoza's SUV looked as if it couldn't possibly have protected the occupants from mortal injuries, but when Randall stopped by the bullpen around midmorning, he told them that both Wallace and Mendoza were expected to be released from the hospital the next day. "They'll both be out a while until their broken bones heal, but everybody's going to recover sooner or later. Thank God."

He stopped by Miranda's desk on his way out. "Sorry I had to call you in. I know you could have used a little more recovery time yourself."

"I'm fine," she assured him. But after he left, she took another look at the crash photo and felt a little shudder run through her.

Her cruiser hadn't looked nearly as bad as Mendoza's SUV, but something about the photo triggered a brief memory of the day of the crash, an image of a dark blue sedan coming up quickly behind her cruiser as she was heading back to the station.

She'd tried to see through the windows, but they were darkly tinted, only the reflection of the snowfall and her own cruiser, with its flashing blue and cherry lights, visible in the opaque glass.

She handed the photo back to Tim Robertson and rubbed her gritty eyes. In some ways, the wreck seemed as fresh in her mind as the kiss John had planted on her lips that morning as she headed out to work.

But in other ways, it seemed more like some misty, mysterious dream.

By ten that morning, most of the other deputies were out on calls that Bill Chambers seemed to make sure went through to any phone but hers. Only Tim Robertson remained, poring over some photos spread out on his desk. He looked up briefly from the photos and smiled at her. She managed to smile back, but she wasn't sure if she had been able to cover her growing sense of annoyance.

She was on glorified desk duty, it appeared. The orders had probably come straight from Miles Randall himself. She might as well have stayed home and helped John with the ciphers.

"What're you looking at?" she asked Robertson.

"Photos from Delta McGraw's trailer."

She got up and crossed to his desk, looking over his shoulder. "And what are you looking for?"

Robertson gave her a doubtful look. "I thought the sheriff took you off this case."

"What's it going to hurt for me to take a look? I knew Delta. I might see something in those photos that you wouldn't even notice." She leaned closer to look at the photo he held. It was a close-up of Delta's bed, which was slightly rumpled but clearly not slept in. One edge of the bedside table was also in the photo, the round base of a lamp and the corner of a book just visible near the image edge. She couldn't make out much about the book cover, except the little triangle she could see appeared to have what looked like a series of numbers and letters on it.

"Do you have a full shot of the bedside table?" she asked.

Robertson flipped through the photos until he came across a close-up of the bedside table. The book cover was indeed covered by numbers and letters. The title *Ciphers and Code Made Easy* filled the top half of the book in bright blue letters.

Robertson looked up at her, his eyes slightly narrowed. She could tell he understood the significance of the book, but he wasn't going to share what he knew with her, thanks to Randall's insistence that she not be involved in the investigation.

"Hmm," she said. "Not what I thought." She handed the photo back to Robertson and returned to her desk. She pulled up a search engine and typed in the name of the book. It came up in several links, including an online bookstore that included a preview of the book's table of contents. As she hoped, the chapter listings were essentially the names of the codes included in the book. One of them, surely, would be the code or cipher Delta had used to encrypt the last few pages of the journal.

But she didn't have a copy of the pages with her, not wanting to risk getting caught with them at the station.

She grabbed her cell phone and called John.

He answered on the second ring. "Miss me already?"

"Maybe a little," she said with a smile. "I may have a shortcut for you and your deciphering." She told him about the book and gave him the website address for the online bookstore. "You can probably look up the types of ciphers and codes listed in the table of contents and compare them to what Delta was using in the journal."

"It's really killing you that you can't do this for yourself, isn't it?" he asked.

"Yes."

"I'll figure it out for you. Promise." He lowered his voice, even though there was nobody else to hear him. "I miss you already, too."

"You're just trying to torment me," she murmured.

"How's the first day back at the station?"

"Boring." Almost as soon as the words escaped her mouth, the phone on her desk rang. "But maybe it's about to pick up. Talk to you later." Pocketing her cell phone, she picked up the desk phone receiver, wondering who'd call her direct number. "Deputy Duncan."

"Deputy, it's Phil Neiman from the old Westlake Refinery. You helped me out a few months ago when I had some break-ins, remember?"

"I do. How are you?" The refinery had long since ceased operation, but it was something of a historic site from the early Texas oil boom days and Phil Neiman had bought the place to keep it from being bulldozed, determined to keep it viable as a tourist attraction.

"I've been better. There's been another break-in. I was hoping you could come on out here and write me up a report for my insurance."

"Of course," she said. "I'll be there in a few minutes."

She grabbed her jacket and headed for the fleet parking lot to grab a cruiser, telling Bill Chambers at the front desk where she was going. It wasn't exactly an exciting call, she thought as she drove up the highway toward the Westlake Refinery, but it was good to be in the saddle again.

JOHN HIT PAY dirt on Chapter Seven of *Cyphers and Code Made Easy*, titled "Vigenère." He was familiar with Vigenère, a fairly simple cipher built off a keyword. Delta McGraw's scribblings looked as if they might be encrypted using a Vigenère table.

The hard part would be figuring out the keyword. He knew next to nothing about Delta McGraw's life, except that her father had been a con man. He supposed that was a place to start.

He had actually been trained how to decrypt Vigenère ciphers algebraically, but he had a hunch that there was probably somewhere on the internet where he could simply enter the cipher and try decrypting it automatically by guessing at the keyword.

He found just such a page on the first page of his search list. Starting with the last entry in the journal, he typed in the cipher:

Oicl Tlrx ulrqhr, Btriayiqe. Eoihmnmi 3. Cbb Tmgcoe ln Btriayiqe jazh dmg. Tayo Guzc's suiqvus fdip rfha zae i toc.

Now to figure out the keyword.

He started with the most obvious: *HalMcGraw.* The result was more gibberish. He then tried variations on the name—first name, last name, Harold spelled out, on the assumption that Hal was short for Harold, and the last name, McGraw by itself, as well. All to no avail.

He was pondering other options when his cell phone rang. It was Miranda.

"I'm out on a call, but I thought I'd see if you've had any luck."

"Maybe." He told her his theory about the cipher being a Vigenère cipher. "But I don't know much about Delta, so it's hard to guess at her keyword."

"I'm not sure I knew her well enough for that," Miranda admitted ruefully. "Like I told you, Delta didn't have friends. I was probably as close as she got." Her last few words crackled through the phone line, as if she was driving through an area where the cell service was spotty.

"You're breaking up," John told her.

"I…can't… I'll call…back." The call ended abruptly.

John laid his phone on the table and went back to his laptop. She hadn't used her father's name. He didn't know her birth date or where she'd been born. He didn't even know her mother's name, although he supposed he could do a search of her name and see if there was any sort of internet trail he could follow.

He sat back in the kitchen chair, his gaze wandering to the doorway to the unfinished room, where he'd found the journal in the first place.

Why had she left the book here? She obviously hadn't wanted it found, but why leave it here in Miranda's house? Had she felt threatened in some way? Was Miranda the only person she felt she could trust?

Miranda.

He scratched his chin and looked at the blank box for the keyword. With a little shrug, he typed in the word *Miranda*.

A readable set of words appeared in the decryption

box. With a flood of satisfaction, he read Delta McGraw's last journal entry.

Call Girl murder, Plainview. November 3. Coy Taylor in Plainview same day. Call Girl's friends said john was a cop.

Coy Taylor. A niggle of recognition tickled his brain. Why did the name Coy Taylor sound so familiar?

THE WESTLAKE REFINERY was a shell of its former self, little more than a long, rectangular corrugated steel building surrounded by the rusting remains of tanks. Miranda pulled up in front of the main building, surprised not to see Phil Neiman's old yellow Cadillac convertible parked near the door. She pulled out her cell phone to give him another call, but once again, she had no signal.

Frowning, she gazed down the highway at the tall cell tower only a mile away. Why didn't she have a signal?

She radioed to the station as she approached the silent building. "I'm at Westlake Refinery," she told Bill Chambers when he responded. "Can't see Neiman anywhere, but I'm heading inside."

She tried the door, half expecting to find it locked. But the handle turned easily in her hand.

"Mr. Neiman?"

There was no answer.

Frowning, she eased inside the open door and looked around. The place was quiet and still, though she spotted smudges in the dust on the floor that might have been footprints. No sign of tread marks, though. She started to crouch to take a closer look when she heard footsteps behind her.

"Hey there, Deputy." Phil Neiman's voice echoed faintly in the cavernous building.

She rose and turned around with a smile. "Hey, Phil, I was wondering where you…" Her voice faltered as she saw the man standing behind her. "What the hell?"

Coy Taylor stood behind her, holding a large Smith & Wesson pointed at her heart. "I thought you'd never get here."

MIRANDA WASN'T ANSWERING her phone. In fact, it seemed to be going straight to voice mail. John left his third message in the last fifteen minutes, not sure whether he was more frustrated or worried.

Someone needed to see what he'd found. It was possible, he supposed, that the sheriff's department had already decoded the entries themselves, but what if they hadn't? If Miranda was available, he'd ask her who Coy Taylor was, but since she wasn't answering, what was he supposed to do now?

He needed to find out who Coy Taylor was, for starters. And if he couldn't ask Miranda, maybe her father would know.

Gil Duncan answered on the third ring. "Duncan Hardware."

"Mr. Duncan, it's John Blake."

"Hey, John. What can I do for you?"

"Can you tell me who Coy Taylor is?"

There was a brief pause on Duncan's end of the call. "You haven't asked Miranda?"

"She's back on duty today and out on a call. I haven't been able to reach her, and I just needed to know why the name sounds so familiar."

"Oh. Well, easy enough. He's one of the desk sergeants at the sheriff's department."

John's blood iced over. "I see. I guess that's why it's familiar. Thanks."

There was an odd tone to Duncan's voice when he replied, "Anytime."

John hung up and stared at the deciphered note from Delta McGraw's journal.

Call Girl murder, Plainview. November 3. Coy Taylor in Plainview same day. Call Girl's friends said john was a cop.

Did Coy Taylor know that Miranda had found Delta's journal? And if so, what was he planning to do about it?

He retrieved his wallet and pulled Miranda's business card out of one of the pockets. Besides her personal phone number, the card also listed the sheriff's department main number.

Would Coy Taylor answer?

"Barstow County Sheriff's Department."

"Is this Coy Taylor?"

"No, sir," the voice on the other end replied. "He comes in after three. You want to leave a message for him?"

"No. Is Sheriff Randall available?"

John's question seemed to catch the other man by surprise. "Who's calling?"

"John Blake. I'm the man who helped Deputy Duncan the other day after her crash."

"Right. Okay. I'll see if the sheriff has time to talk to you."

After a brief pause, a different voice answered. "Mr. Blake, what can I do for you?"

"Sheriff, have you had a chance to examine that journal Delta McGraw left at Miranda's house?"

"I'm looking at it now."

"Then you've seen the ciphers."

There was a long pause on the other end of the line. "Ciphers?"

"The last two pages of the journal were written in cipher form." He'd spent the last few minutes testing the rest of the encrypted entries using the Vigenère decryption website and the keyword *Miranda*. The rest of the entries had been about petty crimes like shoplifting, theft and another embezzlement case similar to the one involving the late Jasper Layton.

"These don't look like ciphers," Randall disagreed.

John flipped back a couple of pages. "What's the last entry in the journal?"

"I can't share that with a civilian."

"Sheriff, I'm looking at a copy of the journal."

"You're what?"

"What's the last entry in the journal?"

After a tense pause, Randall said, "It's about a ranch hand at the Bar W who's been stealing money from the ranch's petty cash."

John found the entry. It was on the last page before the encrypted entries started about halfway down the next page.

"Look at the journal—can you see any signs that pages have been removed?"

After a brief pause, Randall's voice rumbled over the phone. "You're telling me someone tampered with this journal?"

"Who entered the journal into evidence?"

"What kind of question—"

"Who?"

There was a rustling noise as the sheriff apparently checked the label on the evidence bag the journal was probably kept in when it wasn't being used. "Coy Taylor."

Son of a bitch, John thought. "Sheriff, I think we have a big problem."

Chapter Sixteen

"What the hell's going on, Taylor?" Miranda dragged her gaze from the barrel of Taylor's Smith & Wesson to his face. "Where's Phil Neiman?"

"At home, I suppose." Taylor gave a slight shrug. "How'd you like my Phil Neiman impression?"

"Not much."

"It got you here." Despite his smug tone, Taylor's gun hand shook a little, making Miranda's heart skip a beat, but he got the twitching under control. "Did you make copies of the journal?"

"What?"

"The journal." His voice rose with tension. "Did you make any copies before you turned it in?"

Miranda's initial confusion and alarm had settled into a sort of alert tension. If she lied and told him no, what would keep him from shooting her on the spot?

Nothing.

"Yes," she answered.

"Where are they?"

"If I tell you, you'll shoot me."

"I'm going to shoot you anyway." Taylor's tone remained calm, but she saw a hint of unease behind his dark eyes. "But if you'll tell me where to find the copies, at least your daddy might be spared."

"Coy, this isn't you."

His expression flattened. "Miranda, you don't know me. Nobody in this town really knows me. Nobody's ever really bothered to."

Anger flared hot in her belly. "So that's why you're pointing a gun at me? Because you're so misunderstood?"

"Where are the copies of the journal? How many did you make?"

"Why does that matter?"

"How many did you make?" Taylor's voice rose, his face reddening.

"One. I made one." She let her gaze fall back on his gun hand, trying to gauge her chances of disarming him. It would have helped a lot if she'd already drawn her gun before entering the building, but she hadn't suspected she'd be facing an armed man with murder on his mind. "You know the sheriff has the journal already. Whatever you're hoping to hide—it's too late."

"He has part of the journal. He doesn't have all of it." Taylor's lips curved in a nasty smile. "One of the perks of being the person who enters evidence into the properties room."

"What did you do? Tear out the incriminating page?"

"Pages," he said with a little shrug of his shoulders. "She put it in some sort of code. I removed the two coded pages."

Why was he telling her this? Why hadn't he just shot her already? Because she had copies of the pages where his name was mentioned?

"How do you even know you're mentioned in that journal, then?"

"Because Delta tried to blackmail me, the stupid little bitch!" The last words came out in a spittle-flecked rage. "Did she think I'd do what she wanted because she had the goods on me? I'm not some sniveling little coward she could manipulate."

"What did she want?"

"Money. She wanted money for that stupid whore's kids." He shook his head. "She didn't know who she was messing with."

"You killed her."

Taylor looked at her as if she was an idiot. "Of course I did."

"You're the one who drove me off the road."

He didn't answer.

"Why? What did I do?" She looked at him through narrowed eyes. "Or was it that you needed to get into my house and poke around a while?"

"I couldn't risk your coming back home before I had a chance to find it." For a moment, Taylor almost looked troubled. "It's not what I wanted. I just didn't have any choice."

"You knew about the journal already."

He looked at her for a long moment. "Remove the mike."

"What?"

"Your shoulder mike. Detach it from the receiver." As she reached for it, he added, "Slow. No sudden movements."

She unplugged the mike from the unit and held it out.

"Toss it on the floor in front of me."

She did as he asked. He stomped on it with the heel of his boot. The plastic mike crunched under the blow, splitting apart. He gave it another hard stomp, mangling the wires inside.

"Phone?"

"It's not getting any reception."

"I know. I'm blocking it." He held out his free hand. "Hand it over."

She pulled her phone from the pocket of her uniform pants and handed it to him.

He shoved it in his back pocket. "Now your weapon. Remove your utility belt. Don't touch the pistol."

She unbuckled her belt and held it in front of her. He took it with his free hand and nodded toward her feet. "You packing an extra?"

"No."

"Lie to me again and I'll call your daddy down here to join us."

Biting back a furious retort, she pulled up the leg of her trousers and removed the ankle holster holding her spare pistol. She handed over the second holster, as well.

"Other leg?"

She lifted the pants leg to show him there wasn't another weapon.

"All right. We're getting in my car and we're going wherever you've got that copy of the journal hidden."

"I'd be stupid to do that. You'd kill me the second I handed it over."

"Don't you get it, Mandy? You're dead either way."

"Then why should I help you?"

"Because I know where your daddy lives. And that might be the very next place I go to look for those pages if you don't lead me to them right now."

She looked at Taylor, took in the ruddy cheeks, sandy

hair and brown eyes she'd seen nearly every day for most of her life and realized she didn't even know who he was.

"What did you do? What did she have on you?"

He laughed. "Get moving. Out the back."

She turned around slowly, her mind racing to piece together the fragments of the puzzle Coy Taylor's treachery had just presented. What had he said before? *She wanted money for that stupid whore's kids.*

What kids? What woman?

"Who else did you kill?" she asked as she moved slowly toward the refinery building's back exit.

He didn't answer.

"You said Delta wanted money for someone's kids. Did you kill a woman?"

"She tried to roll me."

"A prostitute?"

"Keep moving."

The murder of a prostitute would be a big deal in Cold Creek. Not that they were exactly flush with prostitution in a town that size, where everybody knew everybody else's business.

But maybe Plainview. Or even Lubbock. He could have killed someone there.

"Was it an accident?" She tried to infuse her voice with sympathy. "Things just got out of hand?"

"Don't try to play me, Mandy."

She was getting close to the door. Her options for escape were pretty slim at this point and getting slimmer all the time.

"Open the door," Taylor ordered. "Slow."

She opened the door slowly and started outside. Then, with a sharp spurt of action, she slammed the door shut behind her and started running for the front of the building.

She heard the door whip open behind her, the crack of Taylor's pistol and the ringing clang as the round hit the building only a couple of feet from her. She increased her speed, running all out, her long legs eating up big chunks of real estate.

She just had to get to the cruiser. The keys were still in her pocket and the car radio should still work.

It was her only chance at escape.

She skidded in the gravel as she took the corner and reached the front of the building, where her cruiser was parked. She had already made it to the front door when she realized something wasn't right.

Both tires on the driver's side were flat.

"Nowhere to run, Miranda!" Taylor called as he came around the building, laughter in his voice.

There was a shotgun in the trunk of the cruiser, but she'd never reach it before he ran her down and killed her.

To hell with that, she thought, and jerked open the car door. Scrambling inside, she ducked instinctively when she heard the next shot, though by that time, the bullet had already hit the back door with a hard thump.

Please start, she begged the cruiser as she stuck the key in the ignition and turned.

It rumbled to life, and a bubble of bleak laughter escaped her lips as she jerked it into gear and started driving.

The flat tires were less of a problem than they might have been, since the cruiser had been equipped with run-flat tires. But when she reached for the dash-mounted radio, she saw that Taylor hadn't settled for simply slashing her tires. The mike was missing on the dash unit, as well.

She looked around frantically in the seat and on the

floorboards in the futile hope that he might have left the mike in the car. But it wasn't anywhere in sight, rending her radio useless.

And her phone was with Taylor.

Drive, she thought. *Just drive. You may be miles from the next outpost of civilization, but you still have a chance. And make it harder for him to kill you without getting caught.*

Make it harder for him.

Lifting her chin and gritting her teeth, she hit the siren switch.

"Where did you get these?" Miles Randall frowned at the pages John laid on the desk in front of him.

There was no point in trying to cover for Miranda. "She made copies before she turned it in. She didn't want to be left off the Delta McGraw case."

Randall's frown deepened, but John thought he spotted a hint of admiration in the sheriff's blue eyes, as well. "You deciphered this gibberish?" he asked, eyeing the ciphers Delta had used to encode the latter entries of the journal.

"I've had some experience dealing with ciphers." John showed him the translation of Delta's notes about Coy Taylor. "Does this make sense to you?"

Putting on a pair of bifocals, Randall took a closer look at John's decryption. "Plainview, November 3?"

"Delta seemed to think it was significant that Taylor was in Plainview the same day as the hooker murder."

"Seems pretty slim evidence."

"Have you heard anything from Miranda yet?"

"No," he admitted. "We tried radioing her a few minutes ago, but she's not answering. We also tried calling

Phil Neiman, the man she was supposed to meet at the refinery, but he hasn't answered his phone yet."

"Maybe that call she got wasn't legit."

Randall frowned. "I can try Neiman again."

John paced impatiently while the sheriff picked up his phone and made a call. After a moment, Randall spoke. "Phil? This is Miles Randall. We got a call from you earlier today about a break-in at the refinery?" As the sheriff listened to Neiman's response, his frown deepened to a scowl. "So, you didn't call? And there hasn't been a break-in?"

No, John thought, his chest tightening with fear. God, no.

"Thanks." Randall hung up the phone and looked intently at John before he pushed the intercom button. "Bill, radio all available units. We need everyone we've got at the Westlake Refinery immediately." He turned and grabbed the jacket hanging on his chair.

"I'm going, too," John said as the sheriff tried to brush past him.

"Let us do our job."

"I'm going," John insisted, falling into step with Randall. "I can come along with you or I can go myself, but I'm going."

Randall looked as if he would argue, but finally he gave a nod of defeat. "You ride with me."

IT HADN'T TAKEN long for Taylor's blue Ford Taurus to catch up with the crippled cruiser, since the run-flat tires couldn't easily handle speeds above fifty miles per hour. Once she spotted the Taurus coming up fast behind her, however, she took the risk, pushing the speedometer needle over sixty-five.

At the higher speed, the cruiser shimmied and shook, forcing her to muscle the steering wheel to keep the cruiser on the road. But the alternative was to let him catch up with her. And if that happened, she wasn't sure she'd live through whatever he had planned for her.

But if she could hold on a little longer, there was a chance to get out of this mess alive. For the past few minutes, her dashboard radio had squawked with calls from the sheriff's department, trying to find her. She'd also heard a call to all available units to converge on the Westlake Refinery.

There were only so many ways to get to the refinery from Cold Creek, and she was driving down one of the main roads that led there. Sooner or later, one of those units would find her.

She just hoped it wouldn't be too late.

She passed a turnoff, tempted to take it, but she knew there wasn't an occupied dwelling down that road for another two miles. The road was bumpier and would be that much harder to navigate with the ruined tires, too. And it wasn't one of the main ways to reach the refinery.

She forced herself to keep going, focused on keeping the cruiser from spinning off the highway.

How could the killer be Taylor? She'd worked with him at the sheriff's department for the past six years. She'd known him a lot longer than that; he was a frequent patron of her father's hardware store. How could he be a cold-blooded killer and nobody realize it?

She didn't know much about his background, she realized. He wasn't a Cold Creek native; he'd moved there more than twenty years ago, when he was in his early twenties. He'd married a local girl, but the marriage hadn't lasted more than a year. His ex-wife was living somewhere in Dallas, Miranda thought. Or at least, that was the last thing she'd heard.

Was that when he'd started frequenting hookers?

Behind her, the sedan was moving closer, but she'd gotten a decent head start back at the refinery. Taylor had been forced to run back to retrieve his vehicle, a familiar-looking blue sedan with tinted windows that brought nerve-rattling memories of the day of her crash rushing back to her, including a few images she hadn't remembered before.

The Taurus had pulled even with her, a hulking, mysterious presence in the driving snow. She'd tried to pull him over, she remembered, but he'd responded by falling back to perform a PIT maneuver that had driven her off the road.

He could have killed her. It had probably been his intention. He just hadn't planned for John Blake to come to her rescue, had he?

Oh, John. She longed to talk to him now, the urge so powerful it felt like an ache in the center of her chest. Just to hear his voice, to somehow find words to tell him—

What? What did she want to tell him? That in the past few days, he'd made her feel more vibrant, more whole, than she'd ever felt before? That her life would feel empty without him?

That was crazy thinking. She barely knew him.

But crazy or not, it was true.

The cruiser gave a hard lurch and she forced herself to pay attention to the road ahead. She was coming up on another crossroad, but again, there was little hope for help down the road in either direction, so she stayed on the highway, pressing her foot on the accelerator when she saw that her speed had begun to drop.

She had to stay alive.

She had to see John again.

In the rearview mirror, the Taurus had almost caught up with her. And the odds were good that he'd make the same move here he'd made the day of the snowstorm, weren't they?

People were, after all, creatures of habit.

Come on, Taylor. Make your move.

I'll be ready.

"Is THAT A cruiser ahead?" John peered down the dusty road, certain he was seeing a flicker of red and blue lights somewhere in the hazy distance.

"I think it is." Sheriff Randall gestured toward the cruiser's glove box. "There's a set of binoculars in there. See what you can make out."

He found the binoculars and lifted them to his eyes, adjusting the dials until he got a clear look at the vehicle moving toward them. It was probably four miles down the road, which meant they'd intercept it in a couple of minutes at their current speed.

Was it Miranda? Or one of the other units the sheriff's department had called to action?

"Could that be one of the other responding units?" he asked the sheriff.

"If so, he's going the wrong direction. The Westlake Refinery is about five miles farther down this road."

"If it's Miranda, why isn't she answering your radio calls?" John tried to get a better look at the cruiser's driver, but the sun glinted off the windshield, obscuring any view of the driver. He shifted the binoculars down to see the license plate, reading off the numbers and letters. "Is that the cruiser Miranda was driving?"

"I don't have it memorized," Randall growled, but he radioed the number to his dispatcher, who came back a few seconds later with confirmation.

"It's the cruiser Duncan signed out."

"Something's wrong with the tires," John said, trying to get a better look through the binoculars. "They look flat."

Randall muttered a profanity.

John dropped the binoculars to his lap and looked up. A dark-colored sedan pulled up next to the cruiser, edging closer in an apparent attempt to drive her off the road.

Suddenly the cruiser slowed, letting the other car move ahead. Then the cruiser made a sharp inward turn, hitting the other car on the rear panel.

The darker car went into a 360-degree spin, ending up off the road.

Unfortunately, so did the cruiser, sliding sideways into a shallow arroyo on the other side of the road.

The sheriff's cruiser was closing in on the scene fast, close enough that John spotted the driver's door of the blue sedan opening. A dark-clad figure emerged from the car, one arm outstretched. Sunlight glinted on something he held in his hand.

"No!" John shouted, but it was already too late.

The man fired on the wrecked cruiser.

Chapter Seventeen

The cruiser hadn't rolled. But the crack of gunfire and the crunch of the cruiser's back driver's side window shattering were stark reminders that Miranda was still in grave danger.

At least this time, help was on its way. She'd seen another cruiser heading her way at a fast clip, less than a mile down the road now, before she pulled the PIT maneuver to drive Coy Taylor's car off the road. But she hadn't managed to wreck him.

And she was still unarmed.

She slid into the passenger seat and opened the door, swearing when the bottom of the door caught on the edge of the arroyo the cruiser had slid into. The opening was far too small for her to escape through.

Damn it!

Another shot fired, this one zinging through the driver's side window. If she hadn't moved, she'd have taken the bullet in the head. A hard shudder raced through her as she squeezed herself into a tight crouch in the passenger floorboard. It wouldn't be enough, she knew. Not if he kept firing.

Where the hell was that other cruiser?

There was the sudden boom of a shotgun, and she

heard a cry of pain from somewhere outside the cruiser. Seconds later, she heard the cruiser's door creak open.

"Miranda?"

She lifted her head and met the frightened hazel eyes of John Blake. He crouched in the doorway, his gaze shifting to look her over, as if searching for signs of injury.

"I'm fine," she told him quickly, pushing herself up into the passenger seat. She stayed there a few seconds, catching her breath as her pulse galloped like a thoroughbred in her chest. "Taylor?"

"He took some buckshot. The sheriff's got him cuffed and disarmed." John held his hand out to her. "You sure you're not hurt?"

"I'm sure." She took his hand. A spark of heat and energy seemed to flow from his fingers into hers, bolstering her strength. She slid up the slight incline of the cruiser's bench seat and let John help her out onto the shoulder of the road.

A few yards down the highway, the sheriff was shoving Taylor into the back of his cruiser, ignoring the injured man's groans. Randall turned and gave Miranda a nod. "You okay?" he called.

"Fine," she answered, no longer certain she was telling the truth. Now that the danger had passed, her limbs had started trembling wildly and she felt as if the world beneath her feet had begun to shift like quicksand.

She caught John's arm, and he turned to look at her in alarm. "Miranda?"

"I'm okay," she said through chattering teeth.

"No, you're not." He put his arm around her and led her over to the sheriff's cruiser. She bumped gazes with Miles Randall, who stood in the cruiser's open door, talking on the dashboard radio. "Suspect in custody. All units to—" Here he stopped and looked around him before continuing. "West Highway, north of mile marker 210."

John had his arms wrapped tightly around her waist, holding her as the tremors dashing through her slowly started to dissipate. "You're okay," he murmured in her ear.

Finally, she started to feel it.

"PLAINVIEW IS GOING to look into a series of unsolved prostitute murders, but we're not even sure we can tie Taylor to the one Delta mentioned in her journal." Miles Randall leaned back in his desk chair and looked briefly at John before his gaze settled on Miranda, who sat straight backed in the armchair next to John's. Over an hour had passed since they'd arrived at the sheriff's department in Tim Robertson's car and went their separate ways for a formal debriefing.

During their time apart, Miranda's condition had improved considerably, John noted. She had stopped shaking altogether and her color had returned. She'd also been reunited with her utility belt, extra weapon and cell phone, retrieved by one of the deputies processing the crime scene at the old refinery. She'd already strapped on the belt and her service weapon again, as if donning armor. "It's possible Delta had more evidence hidden somewhere. Or maybe when we track down the dead prostitute's friends, they can help us figure out what Delta knew and how she knew it," Miranda suggested. "Is Plainview going to allow us to aid in the investigation?"

"I've talked to the Plainview chief of police. He's agreed to combine our resources in the investigation,"

Randall said. "But you're not going to be on the case, Duncan."

"What?"

"Taylor tried to make you his victim. Twice. Like it or not, that makes you entirely too close to the case to be objective."

The muscle in Miranda's jaw worked violently, but she managed to keep her mouth shut, John saw. He couldn't blame her for her frustration, however. He hated like hell being left out of the final roundup of the Blue Ridge Infantry's straggling holdouts.

He needed to call Quinn, he reminded himself as he listened to Randall tell Miranda what her new assignment would be.

"Even decrypted, some of Delta's notes are a little hard to figure out," the sheriff told her. "She seems to have chronicled a few serious crimes and we need to determine if any of her allegations are actionable. I'm putting you and Tim Robertson on working those leads."

Miranda's tension seemed to ease a bit, though John's own level of annoyance rose considerably at the thought of Miranda working closely with tall, good-looking and clearly smitten Deputy Robertson.

What right do you have to care? You're out of town as soon as Quinn gives you the all clear, aren't you?

"Take the rest of the day off," Randall told Miranda, slanting a look at John. "Get some rest and be ready to start fresh in the morning."

John half expected Miranda to protest, but she merely stood and gave the sheriff a businesslike nod of agreement. She headed out of the sheriff's office with a glance at John.

He rose and started to follow, but the sheriff called his name. "A moment, please?"

John glanced back at Miranda, who was standing in the doorway, looking at him. "I'll catch up," he told her. "Meet you at your place?"

"See you there." She inclined her head briefly and closed the door behind her.

John sat again in the chair across from the sheriff. "Is something wrong?"

"I'm not sure," Randall admitted. "First, I guess I need to tell you that I've done a little bit of investigation myself. Of you."

John managed not to bristle. He couldn't fault the sheriff for wanting to know whether the stranger in town playing bodyguard to one of his deputies was on the up-and-up. "And what did you learn?"

"I know you were working for a man in Tennessee named Alexander Quinn." At the slight narrowing of John's eyes, Randall smiled. "I may look like a small-town hick sheriff, Mr. Blake, but I assure you I'm not."

"Don't suppose you tried calling Quinn?" John asked, faintly amused at the thought.

Randall laughed softly. "I did. Not exactly a success."

"I don't imagine so."

"But there were other ways to find out some of the things I wanted to know. Tennessee law enforcement, for example. And I had an interesting discussion with the Dudley County sheriff."

John sat up a little straighter. Dudley County included River's End, Virginia, the tiny mountain town where he'd nearly met his maker at the end of Del McClintock's Remington 700.

"It seems you were known by a different name when you were in that area. John Bartholomew, I believe?"

"I was undercover."

"Indeed." Randall leaned forward. "I'll just get to the point. I know there's a dangerous man looking for you. A man named Delbert McClintock. And that McClintock is believed to be somewhere near Altus, Oklahoma, at the moment."

"So I hear."

Randall's expression darkened. "Then you need to know what we found on Coy Taylor's cell phone."

Miranda unlocked the front door of her house and entered, realizing for the first time in days she didn't feel as if she had to go in low, weapon drawn, looking for trouble in every corner.

It was nice to feel as if she finally had her house back. Her haven.

And John would be here soon.

The thought should have warmed her, but something she'd seen in John's eyes earlier had left her feeling unsettled. A reminder that as close as they'd become over the past few days, he was still little more than a stranger in Cold Creek. Like so many, he was just passing through.

Unless she could give him a reason to stay.

She slumped on her sofa and leaned forward, pressing her hands to her face. How, exactly, did she plan to give him a reason to stay? Seduction? Sex might hold him in place a day or two longer, but it wasn't enough to keep a man around indefinitely.

She'd tried a couple of times before to hold on to a man who already had one foot out of town, and both relationships had fallen apart sooner rather than later.

Maybe she had to face the idea of leaving Cold Creek and following John wherever he wanted to go.

Could she do that?

Her head said no. But her heart whispered yes.

If John wanted her to go with him, she could do it. Couldn't she?

"If he even wants you," she muttered.

Frustrated and anxious, she pushed to her feet and stripped off her utility belt, removing all the tools and storing them in the locked drawer in the corner, where she kept them when she was off duty. She left the service pistol in the drawer of the side table next to the sofa and headed into her bedroom to change clothes.

She looked at her undressed body in the mirror on her closet door. Not too bad, she had to admit. She might be a little on the big-boned side, and she'd never have a tiny waist or delicate arms and legs, but she was lean and toned, with curves in the right places. And, okay, there were a few fresh new bruises here and there on top of the fading bruises from her earlier crash, but those would fade.

Besides, John had scars from his own brush with death. She'd felt them beneath her fingertips while they were kissing—

She finished dressing, slipping on her most flattering sweater and her favorite pair of jeans, grinning a little sheepishly at her unaccustomed spurt of vanity. She checked her reflection and noticed with dismay that she'd lost her ponytail holder at some point during her escape from Taylor. As a result, her hair was tangled and wild.

Definitely not seduction material.

She gave her hair a brisk, ruthless brushing, saw it wasn't going to be tamed without washing it and starting over, so she settled for pulling it back into a neat pony-tail. She even grabbed a tube of lipstick from the back of her sorely neglected makeup drawer and dabbed a bit of the warm peach tint on her lips. Fortunately, she'd inherited her father's dark eyelashes and could skip mascara.

Taking a deep breath, she looked at her reflection. "You can convince a man to stick around a little Texas town, Miranda Duncan," she murmured to the woman in the mirror. "Oh, yes, you can."

Then, laughing at the absurdity of her self-directed pep talk, she walked out of her bedroom and straight into a bearded stranger.

With a gasp, she tried to run down the hall to where she'd left her pistol, but the intruder's hands curled around her arms with cruel strength, jerking her back against his hard body.

A voice rumbled in her ear, deep and thick with a mountain drawl. "Uh-uh, darlin'. You ain't goin' any-where. You're going to help me find somebody I've spent months lookin' for."

As cold fear washed over her, she realized her captor's identity.

"You're Del McClintock," she said, barely keeping her voice steady.

"That I am," he said with a low laugh. "And you're the woman who's going to bring John Blake to me without a fight."

"HE'S NOT HERE." John and the sheriff had walked a thorough circuit of his rental house twice now, finding no sign that Del McClintock had ever been there. He was on the phone with Alexander Quinn now, relaying the news that Randall had shared with him back at the sheriff's department.

"Maybe he just hasn't arrived yet," Quinn suggested.

"No way. Taylor's phone call to Altus was hours ago," John disagreed. "It's a two-hour drive. He'd be here by now."

"What if Taylor didn't send McClintock to you?" Quinn asked quietly.

The question struck John like a thunderbolt. "Miranda—"

Across the living room, Randall looked up from his phone, his expression instantly worried.

"Is she with you?" Quinn asked.

"No." John passed a shaking hand over his mouth and chin. "I haven't even told her yet—"

"On it," Randall murmured, dialing his phone.

"She went home," John told Quinn. "I was supposed to meet her there, but what the sheriff told me about Taylor's call—"

"Understandable," Quinn said quickly. "But you need to make sure she's okay. You know the BRI will use people as pawns to get what they want."

"At least she's armed," John said.

Except she was at home, finally free of the fear that had come with Coy Taylor's first attack on her. With no reason to think she wasn't alone.

Or that she needed to be armed.

"I've got to go, Quinn. I'll be in touch." He hung up and looked at Randall, who met his gaze darkly and shook his head.

Damn it.

"I can have backup at Miranda's place in minutes."

"No," John said, unlocking the chest where he kept his Ruger. He checked the magazine, chambered a round and grabbed a second magazine in case he needed it. He clipped the holster to his waistband and secured the pistol in place. "We don't want an armed standoff. Get them there, but make them stay back. No lights, no sirens. And we'll take my truck."

Randall nodded and made the call on the way out of John's house.

As John locked up behind him, his cell phone rang. A shudder of relief ran through him as he saw Miranda's name on the display. "Miranda," he answered. "I'm so glad—"

"I know," she interrupted quickly, her voice cheerful. "I know we agreed to meet at your place, but I've gotten sidetracked here at the house."

John froze on the top step of the porch. They certainly had not agreed to meet at his place.

But before he could respond, she continued in the same overly bright tone. "Could you come here instead?"

"Of course." He tamped down the flood of dread washing over him and tried to keep his voice normal, in case someone else was listening on her end of the line. "I can be there in five minutes or so."

"I'll be waiting." She hung up without saying goodbye.

John forced his shaky legs down the steps and across the yard to where Randall was waiting by the truck. The sheriff took one look at John's face and asked, "What's happened?"

"Miranda just called," John said bleakly. "And I'm pretty sure she's not home alone."

"Good job, sugar." Del McClintock's deceptively friendly drawl sent ripples of revulsion down Miranda's spine, but she made sure it didn't show. "He's on his way?"

"Should be here soon." She was sitting beside him on

the sofa, trying to look anywhere but at the side table just a foot away from her, where her M&P 40 was currently hidden from view.

McClintock had traded out his rifle, which now lay propped against the wall by the fireplace within easy reach, for a large deer-hunting knife that looked lethally sharp. Could she get to the pistol before he could sink the knife into her back and give it a fatal twist?

She wasn't ready to risk finding out. Not yet, anyway.

She'd given John a clue that everything wasn't normal, but had he understood her? His voice had sounded a little tight at the end, but not so strange that she could be certain he'd gotten the message.

"Why is this so important to you?" Miranda asked as the silence in the room stretched painfully tight. "From what John told me, you did a real number on him, not the other way around."

"He told you about Nicki Jamison, didn't he?"

"No," she lied.

"Sure he did. How else would your buddy Coy have known to give me a ring when he figured out who your boyfriend really was?"

"He's not my boyfriend. And Coy's not my buddy. And I don't know how he figured out who John really was."

"Not really of that much interest to me, to tell you the truth," Del said with a shrug. "All I care about is finding him. So I owe ol' Coy a big thank-you."

"I can take you to him and you can thank him in person."

"No, that's all right." He flashed a mean smile at her. "He sure ain't real fond of you, though, sugar. What did you do to get on his bad side?"

"Well, today I arrested him for murder," she answered flatly.

The sound of a vehicle slowing on the highway outside broke through the tension, and Del rose to his feet, grabbing Miranda's arm. He tugged her with him, and she went without a struggle, dropping her hand to the side-table drawer pull as she trailed behind him. The drawer opened just wide enough to reach her hand inside if she got the chance.

But Del didn't allow her the chance, giving her a sharp tug as her feet tangled in the throw rug. "Watch it," he warned, shoving the tip of his knife blade under her nose.

She got her feet under control and stayed close as he flicked the front window curtains open just far enough to see the dark blue Ford pickup truck pulling into the driveway to park next to Miranda's truck.

Beside her, Del McClintock laughed softly, excitement bright in his eyes.

"Showtime, sugar," he said.

Chapter Eighteen

"He's in there," John said quietly. "He's at the front window and I'd bet he has Miranda with him."

Randall looked up at him from the floorboard of the truck cab, grimacing. "I'm too old to stay in this position long."

"I know. Just let me get inside and I can distract him." John opened the truck door, leaving his keys in the ignition. The truck's rhythmic warning bell grated on his nerves and he closed the door quickly behind him to stop the noise.

There was a chance Del McClintock would take a shot at him as soon as he opened the door. That's why he'd agreed to don the lightweight Kevlar vest the sheriff had offered him before they left John's house. It might not save him, but it could keep him on his feet long enough to save Miranda.

At least, he hoped so.

He took the porch steps two at a time and knocked on the door, trying to anticipate what would happen.

McClintock would send Miranda to the door. Could he pull her out and shield her with his body until Randall could get out of the truck?

No. Too big a risk. Miranda could be caught in the cross fire too easily.

The door opened. As he expected, Miranda stood in the doorway. "Hey, there," she said with a weak smile. "I thought you'd never get here."

"You know me. Can't keep me away."

Her smile faded, and she took a step backward, her eyes shifting hard to her left, where the open door must be shielding McClintock from sight. "Come in."

She stepped back as he entered, and he grabbed her, giving her a hard shove away from the door with his left hand as he grabbed his Ruger from the holster at his waist, slamming the door with his elbow to reveal McClintock hiding behind the door.

The other man was caught off guard, but only for a second. As John brought up his pistol, Del swept his hand up toward John's hand. John caught a glint of metal just before the blade sliced into his arm above his wrist, sending pain shrieking up to his shoulder. His grip on the Ruger went slack and the pistol fell to the floor with a clatter.

A second wave of agony raced through his rattled nervous system when McClintock pulled out the knife and dove for the Ruger. John forced his sluggish reflexes into action and he drove his knee into McClintock's chin, sending his head snapping back before he could reach the errant pistol.

He kicked the pistol out of reach and dodged McClintock's furious swipe of the knife toward his leg.

"Back away, John!" Miranda's voice broke through the cacophony of pain and adrenaline raging in his brain, and he stumbled backward, looking for her.

She stood a few feet away, holding her M&P 40 aimed

at McClintock's heart. "Drop the knife," she said in a low, deadly voice.

McClintock looked up at her, his shaggy hair in his eyes. A slow smile spread across his face, half hidden by his beard. "I do like a lady who knows how to handle a gun," he said, letting the knife fall to the floor in front of him with a clatter.

"Kick it over here," she ordered.

"Do it," John growled as McClintock hesitated. He didn't know if he could be much good to her if McClintock made a move. His right arm was nearly useless. Blood had already soaked most of the bottom half of his sweater sleeve and was dripping into a puddle at his feet.

McClintock had risen to a crouch and gave the knife a sideways kick. Then, suddenly, he grabbed John by the bad arm and dug his fingers into the wound, driving John to his knees.

John took a swing at him with his good hand, but McClintock had already moved, diving for the Ruger.

He came up with it before John could tackle him, swinging the barrel toward Miranda.

Instinct made John want to grapple with him, but he ignored it and fell back, out of the cross fire.

A gun barked. He wasn't sure, at first, which of them had fired, until McClintock hit the floor face-first. The Ruger fell to the floor again and skittered away.

John turned to look at Miranda, terror squeezing the breath from his lungs. Only when he saw her standing tall, her pistol still aimed at McClintock's prone body, could he breathe again.

He heard footsteps on the porch outside. At the same moment, Miranda swung her pistol toward the door.

"Don't!" John held up his hands. "It's the sheriff."

He pushed to his feet and opened the door with the only hand that still worked. "Situation under control," he said quickly as the sheriff looked ready to enter with his gun drawn.

Randall looked around quickly, assessing the situation with one sweep of his sharp eyes. He holstered his pistol and nodded at John's bloody arm. "Gunshot?"

"Stab wound." His legs were starting to feel rubbery, he realized.

Randall radioed in the situation and called for paramedics as Miranda hurried to John's side and led him over to the closest armchair.

"I'm bleeding on your rug," he said. His tongue felt thick and his head was starting to swim.

"I can get a new rug," she said and started to cry.

"It looks worse than it really is," the doctor told Miranda a couple of hours later in the waiting room of the Plainview Memorial ER. "It missed any major veins or arteries, and the nerve damage appears minimal. He might have minor numbness in his fingers for a month or two, but everything should return to normal after that."

She took a deep breath. "Good. Thank you."

"It didn't require surgery. We just stitched him up and bandaged the wound. I told him he should keep it in a sling for at least a week. Two would be better. He doesn't need to use it much for eight to ten days, and frankly, he's not going to want to."

"Is he in a lot of pain?" she asked, afraid to hear the answer.

"More than he needs to be. He's refusing anything but ibuprofen."

Of course he was. "Can I see him?"

"We tried to talk him into staying overnight, just because he lost a decent amount of blood and his blood pressure is a little low, but he declined, so we're letting him go. He's being checked out right now, and an orderly will bring him out in a wheelchair in just a moment."

"Thank you." She smiled at the doctor as he walked away.

Her father had been waiting with her. He held out his hand to her as she returned to the seat beside him. "Good news?"

She nodded. "He's going to be okay. They're about to release him."

"He's going home with you?"

"My place is a crime scene. I'll take him to his place and stay with him there instead." She smiled at the look in her father's eyes. "If I can convince him to let me."

Gil smiled. "Piece of cake."

"I need to check in with the sheriff." Eyeing the no–cell phones sign on the wall, she headed for the nearby exit and made her call from outside.

Randall answered on the first ring. "What's the news?"

She told him what the ER doctor had said. "I'm going to try to talk him in to letting me stay with him, at least until we can give our formal statements."

"I've been getting calls from his boss since I got back into the office, wanting an update. Apparently Blake's not answering his phone."

That was because it was out in her truck, locked in the glove compartment. "Tell him what I told you. I'm sure John will call him back as soon as he gets settled at home."

"You've had a hell of a day today, Duncan. I think you ought to take another couple of days off, let all the dust settle. We're going to be dealing with the fallout from Coy's mess anyway. Better for you to stay clear of that until it's sorted out."

"I'm not going to argue this time," she said. Movement out of the corner of her eye caught her attention, and she turned to see a female orderly pushing John into the waiting room in a wheelchair. "John's coming out now. I'll be in touch."

John pushed himself up as soon as the wheelchair rolled to a stop, swaying a little but regaining his balance before Miranda reached his side. His right arm was in a sling, and he looked a little pale and glassy-eyed with pain, but he managed a slight smile as she wrapped her arm around his waist and draped his left arm over her shoulder. "Hey, there."

She smiled back at him. "'Hey, there' to you, too."

"Mr. Duncan." He nodded at Miranda's father.

"Gil," her father said firmly. "Seeing as how you've saved my girl's life three times now."

"She saved me," John said firmly, giving Miranda a look that turned her insides to fire.

"She's got a way of doin' that," her father agreed, giving her a different sort of look but one that left her feeling nearly as warm. "She wants to stay with you at your place, and I reckon you ought to let her, because if you don't, she'll just park outside your house and sleep in her truck."

"Daddy."

He grinned at her. "Reckon he ought to know who he's dealing with."

He stayed with John while she went to the parking lot for her truck. After helping John into the passenger seat and closing the door, he gave a wave and a smile, patting the side of the truck to tell her it was safe to go.

"He's a good man," John murmured.

"I know."

"I'm not going to argue if you want to stay at my place for a few days." His voice softened. "Or weeks."

She glanced at him, but his eyes were closed and his head lolled against the headrest as if he had already fallen asleep.

"I thought they didn't give you the good drugs," she murmured.

He didn't answer.

He woke quickly enough when she got him back to his place, however, and managed to unbuckle his seat belt on his own by the time she opened the passenger door. He stumbled a little getting out but made it into the house without having to lean on her.

"Oh, I forgot." She got him safely seated on his sofa and went back outside, returning a few minutes later with his phone. "Sheriff Randall said your boss has been trying to call you."

John groaned and took the phone, checking the missed calls. "Guess I should call him."

While he was talking to Alexander Quinn, Miranda went into the kitchen in search of some fluids. Even without hitting any major veins or arteries, he'd bled enough to deplete some of the fluids in his body. Rehydration would make him feel better quickly.

She returned to the living room with a large glass of apple juice from his refrigerator. She gave it to him after he laid his phone on the coffee table in front of him. "Did you get everything settled with Quinn?"

"Not everything," he said, taking a couple of big gulps of the apple juice. "Thanks. I needed that."

"What do you mean, not everything?" She sat next to him.

"Well, he was very happy about McClintock, but the sheriff had already caught him up on all of that." John winced as he shifted his injured arm so that he could turn to face her. "But he was a little surprised when I told him I might not be heading back east, even though it should be safe for me to do so now."

"Oh? You're not going back there?" She tried to not read anything into his words, but her heart had started pounding like a jackhammer.

"I'm not."

"Why's that?"

He tipped up her chin, forcing her to look at him. What she saw in his warm hazel eyes did nothing to slow her racing heart. "I guess maybe I'm in a Texas state of mind these days."

"The ol' Lone Star worked its magic?" she asked with a smile.

"*You* worked your magic." He bent until his forehead touched hers. "If you want to tell me I'm crazy, I wouldn't blame you. I know you're a practical kind of woman, and I swear, I usually am a practical kind of guy, too." His eyes closed and his voice softened to a murmur. "But I don't think I can leave you."

Tears stung her eyes, but she blinked them away. "Good. Because I'm not against using force to keep you here."

His eyes snapped open and he laughed. "So you don't think I'm crazy?"

"Oh, no, I never said that." She grinned at him, feeling about a thousand pounds lighter. Her heart was still beating wildly, but it was joy, not fear, that drove its cadence. "I think we're both crazy. Because if you hadn't wanted to stay here, I was going to do my damnedest to talk you in to taking me with you."

He kissed her, lightly at first, then with a fierce hunger that made her head swim. When he pulled away, she had to hold on to his good arm to keep from sliding to the floor.

"You wouldn't have had to work very hard," he said with a laugh.

"I should warn you, despite my considerable skills as a law enforcement officer, I'm not exactly known for my feminine wiles."

"I think your feminine wiles are outstanding," he murmured as he slid his hand over the curve of her hip and bent to kiss the side of her neck. She tugged him closer but made the mistake of clutching his injured arm. He made a hissing sound against her throat and she drew back, horrified.

"I'm so sorry! See what I mean?"

He touched her face. "I'm not exactly known for my way with women, either, so clearly, we're made for each other."

She smiled. "Clearly."

"Of course, you're going to have to teach me a few things about living in Texas," he warned, threading his fingers through her hair and drawing her close again.

"Such as what?"

"Such as how to deal with all this flat land as far as the eye can see."

"It grows on you."

"And where I'm going to find a job to support us and our eight children."

She drew back in horror. "Eight?"

"Not enough?" he asked with a laugh.

"We'll negotiate that point later. And as for a job—there's always the hardware store. Dad's been wanting to hire someone to take over for him when he retires, you know."

"And if I offer myself as a sacrifice, he'll quit bugging you?"

She grinned. "Well, I wasn't going to put it that way."

"I thought you might suggest I take a job with the sheriff's department instead," he said thoughtfully. "Any reason you didn't?"

"Is that what you want to do?" She had come entirely too close to losing him that afternoon to feel sanguine about the idea of his wearing a badge and a gun daily, but with time, she supposed, she could deal with it. "Because if that's what you want—"

"I'm not sure it is," he said seriously. "I'm not sure what I want yet, to tell the truth. I've spent a lot of my life trying to figure out my place in this world, and while I'm not saying working as a deputy definitely isn't that place, I'm not ready to say it is, either."

"I get that."

"I know you do." He caressed her face. "You get me in a way nobody ever has. Which is why the one thing I'm starting to believe is that whatever else I'm supposed to be doing with my life, my place in this world is with you."

Tears pricked her eyes again, and this time she couldn't stop them from falling. "I feel the same way."

He traced the track of her tears with his thumb, kissing her eyelids. "Yup. Two of a kind, you and me. Crazy as coots."

Crazy in love, she corrected silently as she lifted her face for his kiss.

Her favorite kind of crazy.

* * * * *

WHAT HAPPENS ON THE RANCH

USA TODAY Bestselling Author

DELORES FOSSEN

Chapter One

Anna McCord figured she had committed a couple of sins, maybe even broken a few laws, just by looking at the guy in the bed. He was naked, so it was hard not to have dirty thoughts about him.

Drool, too.

Mercy, he was hot.

Thick blond hair all tousled and bedroomy. Lean and muscled. At least what she could see of him was muscled anyway. He was sprawled out on his stomach, his face cocooned in the fluffy feather pillows of the guest bed. He reminded her of a Viking just back from a good pillaging, minus the bed and feather pillows, of course.

But who was he?

Even though she should have bolted out of there the moment she opened the guest room door and saw a partially exposed butt cheek, Anna stayed put. Someone had obviously glued her feet to the floor. Glued her eyeballs to the hot guy, too.

She glanced around the room and spotted a clue as to who he was. There was a military uniform draped over the back of a chair and a duffel bag on the floor near the bed.

Anna didn't actually need more clues to know he was

an Air Force officer and likely a friend that her brother Riley had brought home. But she also saw the dog tags. The ball chain holding them was still around the hot guy's neck, but the tags themselves were lying askew on the bed like smashed nickels.

Maybe he sensed she was there, because he opened an eye, and the seconds trickled by before it must have registered in his mind that he had a woman ogling him.

He made a grunting sound mixed with some profanity and rolled over, no doubt because that was the fastest way he could reach the sheet to cover himself. However, the rolling over gave her a view of his front side.

Definitely more dirty thoughts.

"Sorry, I didn't know anyone was in here," Anna said, as if that explained the gawking. The drool. The long, heated look that she was giving him.

But both the heated stuff and the drool came to a quick halt when Anna got a better look at his face. "Heath?"

He blinked. "Anna?"

Good gravy. It was Heath Moore, all right. Well, a grown-up Heath anyway. The last time she'd seen him had been nine and a half years ago when he was barely eighteen, but he had filled out a lot since then.

Oh, the memories she had of him came flooding back.

He'd been naked then, too—for part of those memories anyway, since she'd lost her virginity to him. Though she certainly hadn't seen as much of him during that encounter in the hayloft as she'd just witnessed. He had filled out *everywhere*.

He sat up, dragging the sheet over his filled-out parts, and still blinking, he yawned and scrubbed his hand over his face. More memories came. Of his memorable mouth. The equally memorable way he'd kissed her.

She fanned herself like a menopausal woman with hot flashes.

"Why are you here?" she asked at the same moment that Heath asked, "Why are you here?"

Anna figured he was going to have a lot better explanation than she did. "I thought I might have left a book in here," she told him.

A total lie. She had been in search of a book that the housekeeper, Della, had said she'd left in her room on the nightstand. But when Anna had seen the guest room door slightly ajar, she'd opened it and had a look.

She made a show of glancing around for a book that had zero chance of being there since it was all the way at the end of the hall.

"This is your room now?" Heath asked.

"No. But I come in here sometimes. For the view." Anna motioned to the massive bay window. She wouldn't mention that every bedroom on the second floor had similar windows, similar views. As did her own room on the first floor.

Heath glanced in the direction of the bay window as if he might get up to sample that view, but his next glance was at his body. Considering he was naked under the sheet, he probably didn't want to get up until she'd left, and that was her cue to leave. First though, she wanted an answer to her question.

"Why are you here?" she repeated.

"Riley. He saw me at the base in San Antonio and said I needed some…R & R before I left on assignment. He was headed back here to the ranch to finish out his leave, and he asked me to come."

All of that made sense because Riley, too, was an Air Force officer and had indeed been at the base the day before. Yes, it made sense except for Heath's hesitation before R & R.

"You weren't here last night when I went to bed." She would have noticed Heath, that's for sure.

"We stopped for a bite to eat, then to visit some mutual friends, and we didn't get in until late. We didn't want to wake anyone up so Riley just sent me here to the guest room." Heath paused. "Riley's my boss."

Uh-oh. That wouldn't play well with Riley if he found out about her lustful thoughts over his subordinate. It wouldn't play well with Heath, either, since he probably didn't want to do or think anything—or have *her* do or think anything—that would cause his boss to hit him upside the head with a shovel.

A threat that Riley had first rattled off nine and a half years ago when he thought a romance was brewing between Heath and her.

If Riley had known what had gone on in the hayloft, he might not have actually carried through on the shovel threat, but Anna would have never heard the end of it.

And there was that whole underage-sex thing.

When Heath had first started working at the ranch, he'd been eighteen. But she'd been only seventeen. Riley and her other brothers had made a big deal about the attraction they'd sensed going on between Heath and her.

The term *jail bait* had been thrown around.

Since Heath had been making a big deal of his own about going into the military, it was an issue. Heath wanted to go into special ops, which would have required a lengthy background check for a top-secret clearance, and Riley had brought up her age for the sole purpose of scaring Heath into keeping his jeans zipped.

It had worked. Until the day Anna turned eighteen,

that is. After that, she'd made the trip to the hayloft with Heath, and she had the memories of the orgasm to prove it.

Heath smiled at her, but it felt as if he'd had to rummage it up just to be polite. Again, the nudity was probably driving that. But the nudity didn't stop him from looking at her with those sizzling blue eyes. Also bedroomy like his hair. He slid his gaze from her head to her toes, lingering in the middle. Lingering especially on her breasts. Perhaps because she was wearing a T-shirt and no bra.

"Riley didn't mention you'd be here at the ranch," Heath said.

"Oh? Well, usually I leave the day after Thanksgiving, but I decided to stay a little longer." Since it was already two days after Thanksgiving, she probably hadn't needed to add that last part. "I'm in law school at University of Texas, but I finished my courses early this semester. I'm also planning a transfer. I need a change of scenery...or something."

And a life.

And perhaps sex, but she'd only gotten that idea when she'd seen Heath naked.

"Yeah, a change of scenery," he repeated, as if he were aware of what she meant by the *or something*.

"So, how long will you be here?" Anna tried to keep her eyes directed just at his face, but her gaze kept drifting a bit to that incredibly toned chest. Either he'd gotten very good with contouring body paints or the man had a six-pack.

"Until the cows come home," he said.

That's when she realized both her eyes and her mind had seriously drifted off, and she didn't have a clue what he'd been talking about before that.

The corner of his mouth lifted. A dreamy smile, and he hadn't had to rummage up this one. It was the real deal.

"I'll be here about two weeks," he said. Probably repeated information. "How about you?"

"Two weeks. More or less. I was going to stay until the final exams were over and the campus was less busy. Then, the plan was to talk to my advisor about the transfer."

"For that change of scenery or something?" Heath made it sound like a question.

Anna pretended not to hear it. No need to get into all that. Instead, she glanced at his left hand, the one part of his body she'd failed to look at during her gawking. No ring.

"I'm not married," Heath volunteered. "Never have been." He looked at her left hand, too, where she was still wearing the opal ring her Granny Ethel had left her.

Anna shook her head. "No I-do's for me, either." Close, though, but best not to get into that after her change-of-scenery slip. "So, catch me up on what you've been doing."

"Maybe I can do that after I've put on some clothes? Or we can talk like this?" Another smile.

He was flirting with her, a ploy she knew all too well since she'd been on the receiving end of his flirting that summer. Well, she could flirt, too.

"I guess I can restrain myself for a quick catch-up," she joked. "A *quick catch-up*," she emphasized. "What are you doing these days? I mean, other than sleeping naked, that is. How's the job going?"

The smile faded, and she was sorry she'd taken the conversation in that direction. Of course, it was something a normal nondrooling woman would have asked the man who had been her first.

Even though it was a dumb-as-dirt thing to do, she went closer. Much closer. And she sat down on the bed. Not right next to him, though, because she didn't want to move into the dumber-than-dirt category, but it was still too near him. Six miles would have been too near.

"Sorry," she added. "Didn't mean to hit a nerve. And I should have known better because Riley doesn't like to talk about his assignments, either. I think he believes it'll worry me, but whether he talks about it or not, I still worry."

"You shouldn't. Riley's been on plenty of deployments and hasn't gotten a scratch. Some guys are just bullet-proof, and Riley's one of them."

Maybe. But Anna had a bad feeling about this deployment coming up. A bad feeling she definitely didn't want to discuss with Heath. Or Riley. If she didn't mention it aloud, maybe the feeling would go away. Maybe the danger would as well, and her brother would come back with his bulletproof label intact.

"You okay?" Heath asked.

That was a reminder to push aside her fears and get on with this catch-up conversation. "Riley always says if he tells me about his job, he'll have to hit me with a shovel afterwards. Riley really likes that shovel threat."

"I remember." Heath took a deep breath, causing the muscles in his chest and that six-pack to respond. "Well, shovels aside, I can tell you that I just finished up a deployment in a classified location where there was a lot of sand, followed by eight months in Germany where there was a lot of paperwork. That's where Riley became my boss. Small world, huh?"

Yes. Too small, maybe. "Riley and you are in the same career field?"

"For now." The short answer came out so fast. As did his hand. He brushed his fingers over the ends of her hair. Even though he didn't actually touch skin or anything, it was enough of a distraction. "Your hair is longer," he said.

"Yours is shorter." And yes, she achieved dumber-than-dirt status by touching his hair, as well. Since it was on the short side, she also touched some skin.

She felt everything go still, and even though Anna was pulling back her hand, it seemed to be in slow motion. The only thing that was in the revving-up mode was this flamethrower attraction that had always been between Heath and her.

"Yeah," he drawled. No other words were necessary. They were on the same proverbial page along with being on the same actual bed. The flamethrower had had a go at him, too.

"I, uh…" Anna stuttered around with a few more words and syllables before she managed to say something coherent. "This could be trouble."

"Already is." He drawled that, too. Hitched up another smile.

The past nine and a half years just vanished. Suddenly, Anna was eighteen again and was thinking about kissing him. Of course, she hadn't needed vanishing years for that to happen, but it was as if they were back in that hayloft. On all that warm, soft hay. Heath had taken things so slow. Long kisses. His hand skimming over various parts of her body.

Then, into her jeans.

That had been the best part, and it'd all started with a heated look like the one he was giving her now.

Even though they didn't move, the foreplay was in full swing. His gaze lingered on her mouth. She picked up the rhythm of his breathing—which was too fast. Ditto for her heartbeat. Everything was moving in sync.

"Anna, we're playing with fire," he whispered. It was a drawl, too.

She was near enough to him now that his breath hit against her mouth like a kiss. "Yes," she admitted, but she was in the "fire pretty" mindset right now, and she inched closer, her drifting gaze sliding from his mouth to his abs.

"Is it real?" she asked, but was in the wrong mindset to wait for an answer. She touched that six-pack.

Oh, yes. Definitely real.

It probably would have been a good time to snatch back her hand and be outraged that she'd done something so bold, but she kept it there a moment and saw and heard Heath's reaction. He cursed under his breath, and beneath the sheet his filled-out part reacted, as well.

He cursed some more, but it was all aimed at himself. "I really do need you to leave now so I can get dressed. Once I can walk, that is. Maybe you can shut the door behind you, too."

That caused the last nine and a half years to unvanish. Heath was putting a stop to this. As he should.

Anna was about to help with that stopping by getting to her feet and doing something that Heath clearly would have trouble doing right now—walking. But before she could budge an inch, she saw the movement in the doorway.

And saw the source of that movement.

Riley.

His eyes were so narrowed that it looked as if his eye-lashes were stuck together.

"What the hell's going on here?" Riley growled. He opened his eyes enough to look at her. Then at Heath. Then at the other *thing* that was going on. "And what are you doing with my sister?"

No way was Heath going to be able to explain with the bulge of his filled-out part beneath the sheet. And neither could Anna.

Chapter Two

Well, hell in a big-assed handbasket. This visit was off to a good start.

Heath had known it wasn't a smart idea to come to the McCord Ranch, and he was getting a full reminder of why it'd been bad, what with Riley glaring at him.

"Get dressed," Riley ordered, and yeah, it was an order all right. "And we'll talk." Then he turned that ordering glare on his sister.

But Anna obviously wasn't as affected by it as Heath was, even though Riley was in uniform and looked thirty steps past the intimidation stage. Still, Anna matched Riley's glare with a scowl and waltzed out.

Thankfully, Riley did some waltzing as well and left, shutting the door behind him. Though it was more of a slam than a shut. Still, he was gone, and that gave Heath some time to take a very uncomfortable walk to the adjoining bathroom for a shower. Cold. Just the way he hated his showers. And if he stayed on the ranch, there'd be more of them in his near future.

It was time for a change of plans.

Not that he actually had plans other than passing time and moping. Yeah, moping was a definite possibility. At least it had been until Anna had shown up in the doorway. Difficult to mope in his current state.

Regardless, Anna was off-limits, of course.

He repeated that while the cold shower cooled down his body. Repeated it some more while he dressed. Kept repeating it when he went down the stairs to apologize to Riley and tell him that he'd remembered some place he needed to be. Riley would see right through the lie, but after what he had witnessed in the guest room, he'd be glad to get Heath off the ranch.

Heath made his way downstairs, meandering through the sprawling house. Since he was hoping for some coffee to go along with the butt-chewing he would get from Riley, he headed toward the kitchen.

He heard women's voices but not Anna's. He was pretty sure they belonged to Della and Stella, sisters and the McCords' longtime housekeeper and cook. Yep. And Heath got a glimpse of them and the coffeepot, too, before Riley stepped into the archway, blocking his path.

"I know," Heath volunteered. "You want to hit me on the head with a shovel."

"Hit who with a shovel?" Della asked, and when she spotted Heath, she flung the dish towel she was holding. Actually, she popped Riley on the butt with it and went to Heath to gather him into her arms for a hug. "It's good to see you, boy."

Heath hadn't even been sure the woman would remember him after all this time, but clearly she did. Or else she thought he was someone else.

"Nobody's gonna get hit with a shovel in this house," Della warned Riley, and then she added to Heath, "Have you seen Anna yet?"

"Earlier," Heath settled for saying.

"Well, I hope you'll be seeing a lot more of her while you're here. Never could understand why you two didn't just sneak up to the hayloft or somewhere."

Heath choked on his own breath. Not a very manly reaction, but neither was the way Riley screwed up his face. Della didn't seem to notice or she might have used the dish towel on him again.

"Have a seat at the table, and I'll fix you some breakfast," Della offered.

"Heath and I have to talk first," Riley insisted.

"Pshaw. A man's gotta have at least some coffee before he carries on a conversation. Where are your manners, Riley?"

"I think I left them upstairs."

Della laughed as if it were a joke and, God bless her, she poured Heath a cup of coffee. He had a couple of long sips, figuring he was going to need them.

"Thanks. I'll be right back," Heath said to Della, and he followed Riley out of the kitchen and into the sunroom.

No shovels in sight, but Riley had gone back to glaring again, and he got right in Heath's face. "Keep your hands off Anna, or I'll make your life a living hell."

Heath had no doubts about that. He didn't mind the living hell for himself so much, but he didn't want any more of Riley's anger aimed at Anna. "I'll get my things together and head out."

Riley's glare turned to a snarl. "And then Anna, Della and Stella will think I've run you off."

Heath had some more coffee, cocked his head to the side in an "if the shoe fits" kind of way. Because in a manner of speaking, Riley was indeed running him off. Except that Heath had already decided it was a good idea, too. Still, he didn't acknowledge that. He was getting some perverse pleasure out of watching Riley squirm a little.

"I'm guessing Anna, Della and Stella will make your life a living hell if they think you've run me off?" Heath asked. And he said it with a straight face.

Riley opened his mouth. Closed it. Then he did a wash, rinse, repeat of that a couple more times before he finally cursed. "Stay. For now. And we'll discuss it later. I've got to do some more paperwork at the base. Just keep your hands off Anna while I'm gone. Afterwards, too."

His hands were the least of Riley's worries, but Heath kept that to himself. Besides, Riley didn't give him a chance to say anything else. He lit out of there while growling out another "Stay" order.

Heath would stay. For the morning anyway. But it was best if he put some distance between Anna and all those parts of him that could get him in trouble.

He went back into the kitchen, got a hug and warm greeting from Stella this time, and the woman practically put him in one of the chairs at the table.

"How do you like your eggs?" Della asked.

"Any way you fix them." Heath added a wink because he figured it would make her smile. It did.

"Tell us what you've been doing with yourself for the past nine years or so," Della said as she got to work at the stove. "I seem to recall when you left here that summer you were headed to boot camp."

Heath nodded, took a bite of the toast that Stella set in front of him. "I enlisted in the Air Force, became a para-rescuer and took college classes online. When I finished my degree, I got my commission and became a combat rescue officer."

"Like Riley," Stella said.

"Yeah, but he outranks me."

"How is that? Didn't you go in the Air Force before Riley did?"

Heath nodded again. "Only a couple months earlier, though. We've been in the service about the same amount of time, but for most of that I was enlisted. I've only been an officer for three and a half years now. And Riley's my boss. Well, until the rest of my paperwork has cleared. That should be about the time Riley leaves for his assignment in two weeks."

Della stopped scrambling the eggs to look at him. "You won't be going with him?"

There it was. That twist to the gut. Heath tried to ease it with some more toast and coffee, but that was asking a lot of mere food products. And Della and Stella noticed all right. He'd gotten their full attention.

"No, I won't be going with Riley this time," Heath said.

He still had their attention, and judging from their stares, the women wanted more. Heath gave them the sanitized version. "The Air Force feels it's time for me to have a stateside assignment. It's standard procedure. A way of making sure I don't burn out."

His mouth was still moving and words were coming out, but Heath could no longer hear what he was saying. That's because Anna walked in. Or maybe it was just a Mack Truck that looked like Anna because he suddenly felt as if someone had knocked him senseless.

She'd changed out of her sweats and T-shirt. Had put on a bra, too. And was now wearing jeans and a red sweater. Heath tried not to notice the way the clothes hugged her body. Tried not to notice her curves. Her face.

Hell, he gave up and noticed.

Not that he could have done otherwise. Especially when Anna poured herself a cup of coffee, sat down next to him and glanced at his crotch.

"Back to normal?" she whispered. Then she gave him a smile that could have dissolved multiple layers of rust on old patio furniture. Dissolved a few of his brain cells, too. "So, did Riley try to give you your marching orders?"

Since Della and Stella got very, very quiet, Heath figured they were hanging on every word, so he chose his own words carefully and spoke loud enough for the women to hear. "Something came up—"

Anna glanced at his crotch again and laughed. Obviously, a reaction she hadn't planned because she clamped her teeth onto her bottom lip after adding "I'm sorry." Too late, though. Because Della and Stella weren't just hanging on every word but every ill-timed giggle, too.

"Well, I'm sure whatever came up—" Della paused "—you can work it out so you can stay here for at least a couple of days. That way, Anna and you have time to visit."

"Especially since Anna needs some cheering up," Stella added.

Anna certainly didn't laugh that time. She got a deer-about-to-be-smashed-by-a-car look. "I'm fine, really," Anna mumbled.

Which only confirmed to Heath that she did indeed need some cheering up. Maybe this had to do with the "change of scenery or something" she'd mentioned upstairs.

Well, hell.

There went his fast exit, and no, that wasn't the wrong

part of his body talking, either. If Anna was down, he wanted to help lift her up.

Stella dished up two plates of eggs for Anna and him, and she smiled at them when she set them on the table. "You two were as thick as thieves back in the day." She snapped her fingers as if recalling something. "Anna, Heath even gave you that heart necklace you used to wear all the time. It had your and his pictures in it."

Hard to forget that. Heath referred to it as the great engraved debacle. He'd spent all his money buying Anna that silver heart locket as a going-away gift. Something to remember him by after he left Spring Hill and the McCord Ranch. It was supposed to be engraved with the words *Be Mine*.

The engraver had screwed up and had put *Be My* instead.

Since Heath hadn't had the time to get it fixed, he'd given it to Anna anyway, but he hadn't figured she would actually wear it. Not with that confusing, incomplete *sentiment*.

"Where is that necklace?" Della asked.

"I'm not sure," Anna answered, and she got serious about eating her breakfast. Fast. Like someone who'd just entered a breakfast-eating contest with a reprieve from a death sentence waiting for the winner.

Della made a sound that could have meant anything, but it had a sneaky edge to it. "I think Heath needs some cheering up, too," Della went on. "And not because Riley was going on about that shovel. That boy needs to get a new threat, by the way," she added to her sister before looking at Anna again. "I get the feeling Heath could use somebody to talk to."

Heath suddenly got very serious about eating his

breakfast, as well. Either Della had ESP, or Heath sucked at covering up what was going on in his head.

Anna finished gulping down her breakfast just a bite ahead of him, gulped down some coffee, too, and she probably would have headed out if Stella hadn't taken her empty breakfast plate and given her a plate of cookies instead.

"I need you to take these cookies over to Claire Davidson at her grandmother's house."

"Claire's back in town?" Anna asked, sounding concerned.

Heath knew Claire. She'd been around a lot that summer he'd worked at the McCord Ranch, and if he wasn't mistaken Claire had a thing for Riley. And vice versa.

"Her grandmother's sickly again. Thought they could use some cheering up, too." Della shifted her attention to Heath. "And you can go with Anna. Then maybe she could show you around town."

"Spring Hill hasn't changed in nine and a half years," Anna quickly pointed out.

"Pshaw. That's not true. The bakery closed for one thing. And Logan bought that building and turned it into a fancy-schmancy office. It has a fancy-schmancy sign that says McCord Cattle Brokers. You can't miss it."

Logan—one of Anna's other brothers who ran the family business and probably also owned a shovel. Ditto for Logan's twin, Lucky. At least the two of them didn't stay at the ranch very often, so Heath might not even run into them. Well, he wouldn't as long as he avoided the fancy-schmancy office and any of the local rodeos since Lucky was a bull rider.

"I thought I'd go out and see if the ranch hands needed any help," Heath suggested.

That earned him a blank stare from the women. "You don't have to work for your keep while you're here," Stella said. "You're a guest."

"I know, but I like working with my hands. I miss it." He did. Not as much as he'd miss other things—like having the job he really wanted—but grading on a curve here, ranch work was missable.

"All right, then," Della finally conceded. "At least walk Anna to the truck. There might be some ice on the steps. We had a cold spell move in."

"Now, go," Stella said, shooing them out. "Della and I need to clean up, and we can't do that with y'all in here."

This wasn't about cleaning. This was about match-making. Still, Heath grabbed his coat so he could make sure Anna didn't slip on any ice. He only hoped Anna didn't ask why he needed cheering up, and he would return the favor and not ask her the same thing.

"So, why do you need cheering up?" Anna asked the moment they were outside.

He groaned, not just at the question but also because it was at least fifty degrees with zero chance of ice.

"Is it personal or business?" she added.

"Is yours personal or business?" he countered.

She stayed quiet a moment and instead of heading toward one of the trucks parked on the side of the house, she sat down in the porch swing. "Both. You?"

"Both," he repeated. But then he stopped and thought about her answer. "Yours is personal, as in guy troubles?"

For some reason that made him feel as if he'd been hit by the Anna-truck again. Which was stupid. Because of course she had men in her life. Heath just wasn't sure he wanted to hear about them.

She nodded to verify that it was indeed guy trouble.

No, he didn't want to hear this, so he blurted out the first thing that popped into his head. He probably should have waited for the second or third thing, though.

"I had a girl break up with me once because I kept calling her your name," he said.

"*My* name?" She didn't seem to know how to react to that.

"Uh, no. I kept saying *your name* because I couldn't remember her name." And he added a wink that usually charmed women.

But, of course, it'd been Anna's name. The way stuff about her often popped into his head, her name had a way of just popping out of his mouth.

"Any other confessions you want to get off your chest and/or six-pack?" she asked. And she winked at him.

Man, that's what he'd always liked about Anna. She gave as good as she got. "Let me see. I don't wear boxers or briefs. I like mayo and pepper on my French fries. And my mother's in jail again."

All right, so that last one just sort of fell from his brain into his mouth.

Anna didn't question the *again* part. Maybe because she remembered the reason he'd ended up at the McCord Ranch all those years ago was that his mother had been in jail then, as well.

In jail only after she'd stolen and spent every penny of the money that Heath had scrimped and saved for college. She'd also burned down their rental house with all his clothes and stuff still in it.

Heath had snapped up Riley's offer of a job and a place to stay—since at the time Heath had had neither. His father hadn't been in his life since he was in kindergarten, and what with him being broke and homeless, he'd had few places to turn.

If it hadn't been for his jailbird mom, he would have never met Anna. So, in a way he owed her.

In a very roundabout way.

"Want to talk about why your mom's in jail?" Anna asked.

Well, since he'd opened this box, Heath emptied the contents for her. "Shoplifting Victoria's Secret panties. She'd stuffed about fifty pairs in her purse—guess they don't take up much room—and when the security guard tried to stop her, she kicked him where it hurts. Then she did the same to the manager of the store next door. Then to the off-duty cop who tried to stop her. My mom can be a real butt-kicker when it comes to high-end underwear."

Anna smiled, a quiet kind of smile. "I do that, too, sometimes."

"What?" And Heath hoped this wasn't about butt-kicking or stealing panties.

"Diffuse the pain with humor. I'm not very good at it, either. Pain sucks."

Yeah, it did, and he thought he knew exactly what she was talking about. "You lost your parents when you were a teenager."

"Yes, they were killed in a car accident before you and I met. I was fourteen, and I thought my world was over. That was still the worst of the *world's over* moments, but I've had others since."

"Is that why you need cheering up?" he asked.

She didn't answer. Anna stood. "I should deliver these cookies before the ice gets to them."

Heath put his hands in his pockets so he wouldn't touch her as she walked away. Not that he would have had a chance to do any touching. Because someone pulled up in a truck. Not a work truck, either. This was a silver one that Della would have labeled as fancy schmancy. It went well with the cowboy who stepped from it.

Logan McCord.

The top dog at the McCord Ranch and the CEO of McCord Cattle Brokers. He made a beeline for the porch, passing Anna along the way. She said something to him, something Heath couldn't hear, but it put a deep scowl on Logan's face.

"Smart-ass," he grumbled. "She threatened to hit me with Riley's shovel if I didn't make you feel welcome. So—welcome."

Warm and fuzzy it wasn't, but at least it wasn't a threat. Not yet anyway.

"Riley called," Logan continued. "He said I was to come over here and convince you to stay."

"Because of Anna, Della and Stella."

Logan certainly didn't deny that, and his gaze drifted to Anna as she drove away before his attention turned back to Heath. "You're only going to be here two weeks at most, and then you'll leave, right?"

Since that pretty much summed it up, Heath nodded.

"Well, the last time you did that, it took Anna a long time to get over you. *Months*," Logan emphasized. "We all had to watch her cry her eyes out."

Hell. Crying? Months? This was the first Heath was hearing about this, but then he hadn't been around to see those tears. He'd been off at basic training at Lackland Air Force Base. He'd written her, of course. In the beginning at least. She'd written back to him, too, but she damn sure hadn't mentioned tears.

Logan took a step closer, got in his face. So close that

Heath was able to determine that he used mint mouthwash and flossed regularly. "You won't hurt my kid sister like that again."

"The shovel threat?" Heath asked, aiming to make this sound as light as a confrontation with Logan could be. Heath wasn't sure friendly bones in a person's body actually existed, but if they did, Logan didn't have any.

"Worse. I'll tell Della and Stella what you've done and let them have a go at you. If you piss them off, the shovel will be the least of your worries."

Heath didn't doubt that. In fact, the whole McCord clan would come after him if he left Anna crying again. And that meant Anna was way off-limits.

He'd survived months in hostile territory. But Heath thought that might be a picnic compared to the next two weeks with Anna and the McCord brothers.

Chapter Three

Heath had been avoiding her for the past three days. Anna was certain of it. And she was fed up with it, partly because if Heath avoided her, it was like letting her knot-headed brothers win.

The other *partly* was that she couldn't get him off her mind, and she didn't know what riled her more—her brothers' winning or her own body whining and begging for something it shouldn't get.

Shouldn't.

Because another fling with Heath would only complicate her life and possibly get her heart stomped on again. That was the logical, big-girl panties argument, but the illogical, no-underwear girl wanted Heath in the hayloft again.

And the hayloft was exactly where she spotted him.

He was standing in the loft, tossing down bales of hay onto a flatbed truck that was parked just beneath. He was all cowboy today: jeans, a blue work shirt, Stetson, boots. Oh, and he was sweaty despite the chillier temps.

She wasn't sure why the sweat appealed to her, but then she didn't see a single thing about him that didn't fall into the appeal category.

Anna stood there ogling him, as she'd done in the bedroom, and she kept on doing it until his attention landed on her. Since she should at least make an attempt at not throwing herself at him, she went to the nearby corral and looked at the horses that'd been delivered earlier. It wasn't exactly the right day for horse ogling, though, because the wind had a bite to it.

An eternity later, which was possibly only a couple of minutes, the ranch hands drove off with the hay, and Heath made his way down the loft ladder. Then he made his way toward her.

"You've been avoiding me," she said. All right, she should have rehearsed this or something. For a soon-to-be lawyer, she was seriously lacking in verbal finesse when it came to Heath.

"Yeah," he admitted in that hot drawl of his. And he admitted the reason, too. "Your brothers are right. I'm not here for long, and they said you cried a lot the last time I left."

Her mouth dropped open, and the outrage didn't allow her to snap out a comeback. But her brothers were dead meat. Dead. Meat.

"They told you that?" She didn't wait for an answer. "I didn't cry. That much," Anna added.

Heath lifted his eyebrow, went to her side and put his forearms on the corral fence. "The fact that you cried at all tells me that I should keep avoiding you."

"Should?" she challenged.

He cursed, looked away from her. "You know I'm attracted to you. You saw proof of that in the bedroom."

She had, indeed. "And you know I'm attracted to you."

There, she'd thrown down the sexual gauntlet. But it caused him to curse again.

"I don't want to hurt you," he said.

"And I don't want to get hurt—"

A commotion in the corral nipped off the rest of what she was about to say. And it wasn't a very timely commotion.

Sex.

Specifically horse sex.

It went on a lot at the ranch. So often in fact that Anna rarely noticed, but because Heath was right next to her, she noticed it now. And he noticed that she noticed.

With all that noticing going on, it was amazing that she remembered how to turn around, but she finally managed it. She took hold of Heath's arm and got him moving away from the corral and toward the pasture.

Where she immediately saw cow-and-bull sex.

Dang it. Was everything going at it today?

Heath chuckled. "The Angus bull was getting restless, trying to break fence, so the hands brought in some company for him."

The ranch's version of Match.com. And the icy wind definitely didn't put a damper on things. Not for the bull anyway, but it did for Anna. She shivered and wished she'd opted for a warmer coat instead of the one that she thought looked better on her. It was hard to look your best with chattering teeth and a red nose.

"In here," Heath said. He put his hand on her back and maneuvered her into the barn.

"The scene of the crime," Anna mumbled. She'd fantasized about getting Heath back in here, but not like this. Not when she needed a tissue.

He glanced up at the hayloft, his attention lingering there a moment before coming back to her. The lingering lasted more than a moment though, and he took out a handkerchief and handed it to her.

"I should probably take you back to the house so you can warm up," he offered.

She considered it just so she could blow her nose. It was tempting, but Riley was inside. Della and Stella, too. So Anna touched the handkerchief to her nose and hoped that did the trick. In case it didn't, she went for what Riley would have called a tactical diversion.

"I'm surprised you're not off somewhere enjoying some *company* like that bull before you leave for your deployment," she said.

Anna figured that would get Heath to smile. It didn't. And she saw it again—the look on his face to remind her that he needed to be cheered up about something. Apparently, it had something to do with his assignment.

"Unless a miracle happens, I won't be deploying," he finally answered. The strewn hay on the floor was suddenly riveting because he stared at it. "The Air Force wants me to take an instructor job in Florida."

With the hay-staring and the gloomy look, Anna had braced herself for something a lot worse. "You make it sound as if you're being banished to Pluto."

"In a way, it is like that for me. I trained to be a combat rescue officer, like Riley. I didn't go through all of that to work behind a desk."

Anna wasn't sure how far she should push this so she just waited him out. Waited out the profanity he muttered under his breath. Waited out more hay-staring.

"I feel washed up," he added.

Ah, she got it then. "But the instructor job is temporary, right? You'll go back to being a combat rescue officer?"

"In three years."

She got that, too. It was an eternity for someone like Heath or Riley.

Anna touched his arm, rubbed gently. "The three years will fly by. Look how fast the past nine and a half years went."

The hay finally lost its allure for him, and he looked at her. "Yeah." Not so much of a sexy drawl this time. The hurt was still there. Time to pull out the big guns and do a little soul-baring.

"Remember when I told you I needed a change of scenery? Well, what I really need is to get away from my ex-boyfriend," Anna confessed. "We had a bad breakup."

Evidently, Heath didn't like this soul-baring so much because he frowned. "Are you telling me this is rebound flirting you've been doing with me?"

"No. The breakup happened two years ago, but he's getting married to one of my classmates. And they're having a baby. Twins, actually. The classmate is a former Miss Texas beauty pageant winner."

He nodded, made an "I got it" sound. "You're still in love with him."

"No!" And she couldn't say that fast or loud enough. "He's a lying, cheating weasel. My need for a change of scenery isn't because I still care for him but because I'm sick and tired of everybody walking on eggshells around me."

Her voice had gotten louder with each word, and she couldn't stop the confessions now that the floodgates were open.

"Poor pitiful Anna McCord got dumped for the beauty queen," she blathered on. "It reminds me of the stuff my brothers pull on me, and I'm tired of it. Tired of being treated like someone who needs to be handled with kid gloves."

She probably would have just kept on blathering, too, if Heath hadn't slid his hand around the back of her neck, hauled her to him and kissed her.

All in all, it was the perfect way to shut her up, and Anna didn't object one bit. In fact, she would have cheered, but her mouth was otherwise occupied, and besides, cheering would have put an end to this kiss.

She didn't want it to end.

Apparently, neither did Heath, because he put that clever mouth to good use and made the kiss French. And deep. And long.

All the makings of a good kiss even if Anna's lungs started to ache for air.

Heath broke the kiss just long enough for them to take in some much needed oxygen, and he went in for another assault. Anna was no longer shivering, could no longer feel her nose, but the rest of her was hyperaware of what was happening. The heat zoomed from her mouth to her toes, but it especially fired up in her orgasm-zone.

Soon, very soon, the kiss just wasn't enough, and they started to grapple for position. Trying to get closer and closer to each other. Heath was a lot better at grappling than she was because he dropped his hands to her butt and gave her a push against the front of his jeans.

Anna saw stars. Maybe the moon, too. And she darn near had an orgasm right then, right there while they were fully clothed.

Her heart was pounding now. Her breath, thin. She was melting. And there was a roaring sound in her head. That roaring sound was probably the reason she hadn't heard the other sounds until it was too late. Not horse or bull sex this time.

Footsteps.

"Interrupting anything?" someone asked.

Not Riley or Logan. Her brother Lucky.

And he was standing in the barn doorway with a shovel gripped in his hand.

ONCE AGAIN HEATH was facing a McCord brother when he was aroused. Hardly the right bargaining tool for dealing with Anna's older siblings who were hell-bent on protecting their sister.

Anna stepped in front of him as if she were his protector, but Heath remedied that. He stepped in front of her. But that only prompted her to attempt another stepping in front of him, and Heath put a stop to it. He dropped a kiss on her mouth, a chaste one this time hoping it would get her to cooperate.

"I need to talk to your brother alone," Heath told her.

"No way. He's here to browbeat you, and he's got a shovel."

Lucky shrugged. Propped the shovel against the wall. "Riley said I should bring it and do my part to remind Heath that he should keep his jeans zipped around you." He shrugged again when he glanced at the front of Heath's jeans. "The zipper's still up, so my work here is done."

Lucky turned to walk away.

"That's really all you've got to say?" Anna asked.

Her brother stopped, smiled in that lazy way that Lucky had about him. Heath knew Lucky loved his sister, but he'd never been as Attila the Hun as Riley and Logan. Heath suspected that's because Lucky got out all his restless energy by riding rodeo bulls. And having lots of sex.

"Should I ask you two to stay away from each other?" Lucky didn't wait for an answer though. "Wouldn't work. You two have the hots for each other, and there's only one way to cool that down." His gaze drifted to the hayloft before he turned again to leave.

Was Lucky really giving them his approval?

No.

This had to be some kind of trick.

Heath went after Lucky. Anna, too, and they caught up with him by the porch steps. However, before Heath could say anything else, the door opened, and Della stuck her head out.

"Anna, you got a call on the house phone. It's Claire."

Anna volleyed glances between Heath and her brother and then huffed. "Don't you dare say anything important before I get back."

She hurried inside. So did Lucky and Heath, but they stopped in the sunroom.

"Zippers and haylofts aside," Lucky said. "I don't want Anna hurt again. She sort of fell apart the last time you left."

"Yes. I heard about the crying from Logan." Heath paused. "Define *fell apart*."

"It wasn't just the crying." Lucky paused, too. "It was the pregnancy scare."

Heath felt as if all the air had just been sucked out of his lungs. Out of the entire planet. And if there was air on Pluto, it was also gone.

"Anna doesn't know that I know," Lucky went on. "No one does, and I'd like to keep it from my brothers. If Riley and Logan find out, they'd want to kick your ass. And mine since I didn't tell them. Then I'd have to kick theirs. If you don't mind, I'd rather not have to go through an ass-kicking free-for-all."

"Pregnancy?" Heath managed to ask. Considering there was still no air, he was doing good to get out that one word.

Lucky nodded. "A couple of weeks after you left, I went into Anna's bathroom to get some eye drops, and I saw the box for the pregnancy test in her trash can. She'd torn up the box, but I was able to piece it together to figure out what it was."

Heath managed another word. "Damn."

"Yeah. Two words for you—safe sex."

"I used a condom."

Lucky shrugged again. "Then, it must have worked because when I found the pee stick—it was in the way bottom of the trash can, by the way—it had a negative sign on it."

Heath heard the words. Felt the relief at that negative sign. Then managed another word.

"Hell."

Anna had gone through a scare like that, and she hadn't even told him.

"The only reason I dragged this up now was so that you'd understand why I'm protective of her," Lucky went on. "Now, go find her. Confront her about all of this. Then use a condom when you have makeup sex."

There'd be no makeup sex. Because Heath wasn't touching her again. Hell. She could have had his kid.

Heath went looking for Anna, and when he didn't find her in the kitchen or any of the living areas, he went to her bedroom. Of course she was there. The one room in the house where he shouldn't be alone with her. The door was open, and she was still on the phone, but she motioned for him to come in. He did, but only because he wanted answers and didn't want to wait for them.

But he had to wait anyway.

He listened to Anna talk niceties with Claire. Several "you're welcomes" later, she finally ended the call and looked at him. The smile that was forming froze on her mouth though when she saw his expression.

Heath shut the door just as he blurted out, "You had a pee stick in the bottom of your trash can."

Anna gave him a blank look.

"The pregnancy test from nine and a half years ago," he clarified. "Lucky found it and just told me about it. I'm wondering why I had to hear it from him."

She laughed. Hardly the reaction he'd expected. "It wasn't my pee on that stick. It belonged to Kristy Welker. I bought it for her so her folks wouldn't find out, and she did the test here."

Heath had vague memories of this Kristy. Anna and she had been friends, and Kristy had come over a couple of times that summer.

Anna's laughter quickly stopped. "What the heck was Lucky doing in my bathroom?"

She was using her sister voice now, and it wouldn't have surprised Heath if she'd gone running out of there to confront her brother about it. She might have done that if Heath hadn't done something so unmanly as having to catch on to the wall to steady himself.

"Whoa. Are you all right?" She slipped her arm around his waist, led him to the bed.

Heath didn't even try to say he didn't need to sit down. He did. "I thought... Well, I thought..."

"Trust me, if you had knocked me up, I would have told you about it."

Of course she would have. But it might take a year or two for his heart rate to settle down.

She gave his arm another rub like the one she had in the barn. "Relax. You were my first, but I wasn't totally clueless." She stopped, paused. "I wasn't your first though, and that's why you knew to bring a condom to the hayloft."

Even though Heath was still coming down from the shock-relief whammy, he heard her loud and clear. She'd given him something that a girl could only give once. Her virginity. That upped the encounter a significant notch, and maybe she was looking for some kind of assurance that she'd given it to the right guy.

"You were the first one that mattered," he said. "I risked being hit by a shovel to be with you. That should have told you something."

No smile. No more arm rub, either. "And yet you left."

He nodded, tried to ignore the sting of that reminder. "I was leaving for basic training, and you were barely eighteen."

Anna waved that off. "I know where this is going. We were too young for it to have been real love."

"No, we weren't too young."

Okay, he hadn't meant to say that, and it was another opened box with contents that Anna was clearly waiting to be spilled.

"What I felt for you was real," Heath said. And strong.

He hadn't cried as Anna had done, but leaving her had left a hole in his heart. Best not to mention that, especially since he would be leaving again soon.

"I knew I couldn't give you a good life," he added. "Not when I was still trying to figure out my own life."

She stayed quiet a couple of seconds. "Fair enough. And if you'd stayed, you would have resented me because you gave up your dream of being in the military. Your wanderlust and need for an adrenaline fix would have come into play. We would have fought, broken up, and all these years later we would have cursed the mere mention of each other's names."

Heath frowned. He didn't like that version of what could have been, but she was probably right. Probably. Now he was cursing her name for a different reason. Because it reminded him of how much he wanted her.

"I still have the need for that adrenaline fix," he admitted. "The need to be...something. Somewhere. It's easier if I stay on the move."

"I get it." She motioned around the room. "That's why it's hard for me to be at the ranch sometimes."

He was pretty sure they were talking about her parents now, about the hole in her heart that their deaths had no doubt left. "Are the memories of your folks harder to deal with while you're here?"

"Every now and then. But sometimes it's hard no matter where I am. Sometimes, I wake up, and I can't remember what they looked like. That sends me into a panic. So I run to grab one of the photo albums just to remember their faces."

"It's your way of keeping them in your life," Heath said around the lump in his throat.

"Yes. The past has a way of staying with you like that." Anna took a deep breath, then sighed. "And you can't run away from your past. I know, I've tried. It's like that little mole I have on my right butt cheek. It just goes with me everywhere." She looked at him. "I know what you're thinking."

Because he thought they could use some levity, Heath asked, "You have a little mole on your butt cheek?"

"All right, I didn't know what you were thinking after all. I thought you might be wondering if I was trying to outrun my past by transferring colleges."

That hadn't even crossed his mind, mainly because he wondered why he hadn't noticed that mole on her butt cheek. He was also wanting to see that mole. Clearly, he had a one-track mind here.

He shook his head. "I didn't think the transfer was about running, more like ulcer prevention. No need for you to have to face a daily dose of Mr. Wrong and his new family."

"Exactly." She smiled in a triumphant *I didn't think you'd get that* kind of way.

Heath got it all right. He got a lot of things when it came to Anna. A lot of things because of her, too. Like that tug below his belly that nudged him to kiss her again. That was his red-flag warning to get moving, and he would have done just that if he hadn't spotted the silver heart locket on her nightstand.

When she saw that he'd spotted it, she tried to put it in the drawer, but Heath took hold of her hand to stop her.

Yes, it was the locket he'd given her all right.

"After Della asked about it, I found it in my old jewelry box," she said. Then, she frowned. "All right, I wear it sometimes. Okay?"

She didn't sound especially happy about that, but it pleased Heath that she still had it. Pleased him even more than she occasionally wore it. What didn't please him was the reminder of the two words engraved on it.

"Be my." Anna ran her fingertips over it. "I wasn't sure what you were saying—be my heart, be my locket. Be my lay in the hay." She chuckled, poked him with her elbow.

"It was a fill-in-the-blank kind of thing," he joked, poking her back with his elbow.

"It sounds to me as if you didn't know what you wanted to say." No elbow poke that time.

"I was eighteen. I didn't know."

"And now?" she asked.

For two little words, it was a mighty big question. One that he didn't have to answer because there was a knock at the door, and the knocker didn't wait for an invitation to come in. The door opened.

Riley.

Well, at least Anna and he weren't in a butt-grabbing lip-lock as they'd been in the barn when Lucky had found them.

"I need to talk to you," Riley said, looking at Heath. Then his gaze swung to his sister. "And no, this isn't about you. It's business."

Damn it. That didn't sound good.

Anna must have thought so, too, because she gave Heath a sympathetic look as Riley and he headed out. They didn't go far, just into the foyer.

"I just found out that you're still trying to get out of your instructor assignment, that you put in a request to go on another deployment," Riley threw out there.

Heath cursed. He wasn't exactly keeping it from Riley. Okay, he was, but he didn't want to justify what he was trying to do.

"You've already had two back-to-back deployments as

an officer," Riley reminded him. "Before that, you had back-to-back-to-backs as a pararescuer."

"You're going on another one," Heath reminded him just as fast.

"I've had breaks in between. In the past ten years, the only time you've been stateside is for leave and training." He put his hand on Heath's shoulder. "You don't have anything to prove."

"No disrespect, *sir*, but I have everything to prove. To myself anyway."

Riley huffed. "You can prove it by being the best Air Force instructor you can be."

"That sounds like a recruitment pitch."

"It is." Riley took his hand from Heath's shoulder, and his index finger landed against Heath's chest. "And here's some more advice—sometimes life gives you crap, and you just have to make crappy lemonade out of it."

Heath frowned, thinking he might never again want another glass of lemonade. Or another lecture from Riley. Of course, there wouldn't be any more Riley lectures if Heath got stuck with that instructor job he didn't want. Then Riley would no longer be his boss.

Frowning, too, possibly over that bad lemonade analogy, Riley walked away. Heath would have, as well. He would have headed back to the pasture to do something, anything, to burn off some of this restless energy inside him.

Yeah, he needed an adrenaline fix *bad*.

He figured in that moment that his thought must have tempted fate, because his phone dinged with a text message. There was that old saying about when the gods wanted to punish you, they gave you what you wanted. Well, it wasn't from the gods.

It was from Anna.

And the text flashed like neon on his phone screen. A sort of warning from the gods out to punish him.

Meet me in the hayloft in one hour.

Chapter Four

Anna figured she wasn't just going to be able to sneak out of the house without anyone seeing her.

And she was right.

As she was cutting through the sunroom, Della spotted her. Anna smiled, tried to look as if she weren't up to something, but that was sort of hard to do considering she had a six-pack of beer in a plastic grocery bag. A six-pack Anna had just scrounged from the fridge.

Della glanced at the bag and its distinctive shape. Then gave Anna no more than a mere glance.

"What are you up to?" Della asked.

Anna shrugged. "I'm considering playing with some fire. Running with scissors. Taking candy from some guy I don't know."

Falling hard for an old flame she shouldn't fall hard for was something Anna could add to that list of no-no's.

"So, you're going to the barn again with Heath," Della said. It wasn't a question.

"No. Yes," she admitted when Della gave her that liar-liar-pants-on-fire look. Anna huffed. "Don't give me a hard time about this. I'm tired of everyone babying me."

"They do that because you're the baby."

"Was the baby," Anna corrected. "I'm a grown woman now, but none of them can seem to accept it."

"They love you," Della pointed out.

"And I love them, but I want the key to my own chastity belt."

Della smiled that sly little smile of hers which meant she could be up to something. But she only kissed Anna on the cheek. "Honey, you've had that key for a long time now. Might be time to see if it works the way you want it to work."

Anna opened her mouth to respond, but she had nothing to say. Not a word. Instead, she returned the cheek kiss, tucked the beer under her arm so the bottles wouldn't jiggle and clang, and headed out the back.

No brothers in sight. No ranch hands, either.

But she also didn't see Heath.

Since it was—Anna checked the time on her phone— three minutes to rendezvous, she'd hoped she would see him waiting for her. He better not have blown her off. Except Heath wouldn't do that. Well, he might have done it with a text, call or chat, but he wouldn't do an unannounced blowing-off.

And he hadn't.

The moment she stepped in the barn, she saw him. Not in the hayloft, but standing by the steps that led up to the loft.

"You came," she said.

"Of course I came. I'm a guy and I'm not stupid. All right, maybe I am stupid, but the guy part's still true, and I've got the junk to prove it."

She smiled, chuckled. All nerves, and she hated the nerves because they didn't go well with this blistering attraction. "Yes, I got a glimpse of your junk. You're definitely a guy."

He smiled, too. "Beer?" he asked, tipping his head to the bag.

"I thought you might be thirsty. It was either this, milk or a questionable green smoothie."

"You made the right choice. I've already had my quota of milk and questionable green smoothies for a while."

He reached out, took her by the fingertips. That was it. The only part of her he touched. It was like being hit by a really big dose of pure, undiluted lust.

"You may have made the right choice with the beer," he added a heartbeat later. "But asking me to meet you here might fall into the stupid category."

"Might?" she repeated. Well, it was better than an out-and-out "this ain't gonna happen."

"Is this going to happen?" Anna came out and asked.

With only that teeny grip on her fingertips, he inched her closer. So close that when she breathed, she drew in his scent. Mixed with the hay and the crisp November air, it gave her another dose of lust.

"It shouldn't happen," Heath said. "I've tried to talk myself out of it."

"And?" She was still breathing, through her mouth now. Still taking in that scent. Still feeling him play with her fingers. "I hope you're really lousy at talking yourself out of things."

He closed his eyes a moment. Groaned. And, as if he were fighting—and losing—a fierce battle, he brought her another inch closer. She figured if the lust doses kept coming that she was going to launch herself into his arms.

"I'm leaving soon," he reminded her. "And I'm trying to do the right thing here."

She wanted to point out that unless he was leaving within the hour, then this could indeed happen, but that would just make her sound needy. Which she was. So very, very needy.

He let go of her fingertips, and she figured this was it. Heath would send her on her way. But he took the beer from her, and as if he had all the time in the world, he set the bag next to a hay bale.

"So, what now?" she asked.

Heath didn't answer her. Not with words. He reached out, and just when she thought she was going to get more fingertip foreplay, he took hold of her, snapped her to him and kissed the living daylights out of her.

Anna forgot all about the stupid argument that he was leaving soon. She forgot how to breathe. But other feelings took over, too. Probably because Heath didn't just kiss.

He touched.

He slipped his hand between them and ran his fingers over her right breast. Nice, but he double-whammied it with a neck kiss, and Anna felt herself moving. At first she thought it was just her body melting, but nope, she and Heath were walking.

"What are we doing?" she asked.

"Complicating the hell out of things."

"Good. I like complications." At the moment she would have agreed to a lobotomy.

Heath kept kissing her, kept moving. Not up the steps of the hayloft but rather toward the tack room. Maybe because it had a door. Maybe because it didn't require the coordination of step climbing with an erection. Maybe because it was just closer.

It was the erection thing, she decided, and since she

could feel it against her stomach, Anna added some touching of her own. She worked her hand over his zipper and would have gotten that zipper down if Heath hadn't stopped her.

She heard herself make a whiny sound of protest, but then he put her against the back of the door that he'd just shut, and he lifted her. Until his hard junk was against her soft junk. Everything lined up just right to create a mind-blowing sensation.

"Let's play a game," he said. And yeah, he drawled.

Anna nodded. She would have agreed to a second lobotomy.

"On a scale of one to ten, rate the kisses, and then I'll know which parts to concentrate on."

She wasn't sure she could count to ten, much less rate kisses, but Heath jumped right into the game. He kissed her mouth.

"A ten," she said after he left her gasping for air and reaching for his zipper again.

He put his hand over hers to stop her, but Anna just used the pressure of his hand to add pressure to his erection.

"We'll play that particular game later," he promised.

Heath moved on to the next kiss. He placed one in the little area just below her ear, and he must have remembered that was a hot spot for her because it didn't seem like a lucky guess.

"Fifty," she blurted out. If Heath hadn't held her in place with his body, she would have dropped like a rock. There were no muscles in her legs, and her feet had perhaps disappeared.

"I'll definitely put that on my playlist," he said and

added a flick of his tongue in that very hot spot that needed no such licking to further arouse it.

She went after his zipper for a third time, and the only reason she failed, again, was because he pushed up her sweater, pushed down her bra and did that tongue-flicking thing over her nipples.

"A seventy," she managed to say.

"Scale of one to ten," he corrected.

"Ten plus sixty."

He chuckled, which made for some very interesting sensations since he still had his mouth on her nipple.

"And this one?" he asked. He went lower, kissed her stomach.

"Ten," she admitted, and she was about to pull him back to her to breast and neck.

Then he went down a few more inches.

Heath clearly had some experience in zipper lowering. *Fast* zipper lowering. He slid down, unzipping her and dragging her jeans just low enough so that he could plant the next kiss on her panties.

Anna threw back her head, hitting it against the door and perhaps giving herself a concussion. She didn't care if she did. That's because the only thing that mattered now was the pleasure. Such a puny word for the incredible things Heath was doing with his mouth.

"Your rating?" he asked, and mercy, he added some breath with that question.

"Six million," she managed to say.

He laughed.

"One more kiss," he said. "Then it'll be your turn."

Oh, she wanted a turn all right. Wanted it badly. Until he shimmied down her panties, put her knee on his shoulder and kissed her again. A special kiss.

Tongue flicks included.

After a couple of those flicks, Anna went into forget mode again. The thought of taking her turn went right out of her head. Everything vanished. Except for the feeling that she was about to shatter. And fall. And shatter some more.

Heath made sure he gave her the *more* she needed for shattering. One last well-placed kiss. An equally well-placed tongue flick. And all she could do was fist her hand in his hair and let him shatter her.

She had to take a moment to gather her breath. Another moment to keep gathering it. But even with the ripples of the climax tingling through her, she wanted to get started on her turn. And she was going to torture the hell out of Heath and his junk.

"Damn," Heath growled.

It took her a moment to realize that he was reacting to something he heard.

A knock at the tack room door.

"Heath?" Riley called out.

Hell.

"Uh, Heath, I need to talk to you," Riley added. "It's important."

Unless the world was about to end and Heath could stop it, then it wasn't that important, but Anna conceded that was the lust talking.

"How important?" Heath asked.

"Very."

Heath and she both cursed.

"Anna's in here with me," Heath volunteered.

It took Riley several snail-crawling seconds to respond to that. "Yes, I figured that out. Didn't think you'd go into the tack room alone and close the door. But this isn't about Anna. It's about your assignment."

Heath groaned, stood back up, helping her fix her jeans and panties. "You can wait in here if you want," he offered.

"Not a chance," Anna argued. "Riley knows what we've been doing. Or rather what we started doing, and the assignment thing could be a ruse to draw us out so he can ambush you with a shovel."

He brushed a kiss on her mouth. "You've got a very active imagination." Though she knew there might be a grain of truth in her theory.

Heath went out ahead of her, and Riley was indeed right there. He was sitting on a hay bale, drinking one of the beers. She braced herself for him to say something snarky like had she been trying to get Heath drunk or why did she have this thing for barn sex?

He didn't.

Riley did give her a look that only a big brother could have managed, but it had some, well, sympathy mixed in with the brotherly snark. A strange combination.

"I just came from the base," Riley said to Heath. "They want to see you about your deployment request."

"Deployment request?" Anna repeated. "I thought Heath was going to Florida."

Riley remained quiet, clearly waiting for Heath to explain.

"I asked to be diverted from the instructor job to another deployment," Heath said.

Riley's arrival had been a killjoy in the sexual-pleasure department, but hearing about Heath's request was a different kind of killjoy. Although obviously not for Heath since this was something he wanted.

Very much.

After all, he'd told her that the instructor job made him feel washed up, and maybe now he wouldn't have to feel that way because he could go back to one of those classified sandy locations. Where people shot at him and where he could be hurt or killed.

Mercy.

That felt as if she'd been slammed with a truckload of bricks. And there was no reason for it, because this was Heath's job. No logical reason anyway. But Anna wasn't feeling very logical at the moment.

"They want to see you out at the base right away," Riley added.

Heath nodded, looked at her as if he needed to say something, but Anna let him off the hook. She smiled, brushed a kiss on his cheek.

"Go," she insisted, trying to keep that smile in place. "We can talk when you get back."

Heath hesitated, gave another nod and then walked toward the house. Anna managed to keep her smile in place until he was out of sight. Riley opened a bottle of beer and handed it to her.

"Will he get to come back here to the ranch if the deployment is approved?" Anna asked, though she was afraid to hear the answer. "Or will they send him out right away?"

"Hard to say."

Or maybe not. The next thing Anna saw was Heath leaving the house, carrying his gear. He put it in his rental car and drove off. Obviously, he was prepared to go.

Anna took a long swig of that beer and wished it was something a whole lot stronger.

"Best to forget him," Riley said as they watched Heath drive away. "Heath isn't the settling-down type."

If only that weren't true.

"It's just a fling," Riley added. "That's what it was nine and a half years ago, and that's what it is now."

If only that were *true.*

Chapter Five

The McCord brothers were waiting for Heath when he got back from the base, and they didn't even try to make it look like a friendly, casual meeting. They were in the living room just off the foyer, and the moment Heath stepped inside, they stood.

No shovels. Not physical ones anyway.

"Where's Anna?" Heath asked. "You didn't lock her in her room, did you?"

The joke didn't go over so well, but Heath didn't care. He was tired, frustrated and wanted to talk to Anna, not the kid-sister police.

"Anna's Christmas shopping in San Antonio," Logan answered. "She'll be back any minute now."

Good. Well, sort of good. Heath definitely wanted to see her even if she probably hadn't liked his news. Hell, he hadn't liked it much, either.

"My request for deployment was denied," Heath explained. "The Air Force wants me to report to the base in Florida day after tomorrow so I'll have to cut my visit here short."

He expected them to jump for joy. Or at least smile. They didn't.

Riley immediately shook his head. "I didn't have anything to do with that."

Heath nearly snapped out "Right," but he knew in his gut that Riley was telling the truth. He wouldn't do anything like that even if it meant saving his sister from having sex with a guy Riley didn't think was right for her.

And Riley was spot-on.

Heath wasn't right for her. End of subject.

"I'll leave tomorrow," Heath added. "I just want a chance to say goodbye to Anna first."

None of the brothers objected, and Heath wouldn't have cared if they did. Yeah, it was the pissed-off mood again, but he had to get something off his chest.

"I know you think I'm a jerk, that I'm here only to try to seduce Anna, but I do care about her. Always have. If I hadn't cared, I would have never had sex in the hayloft with her nine and a half years ago."

There. He'd said it. But they weren't saying anything back to him. Maybe because Riley and Logan hadn't known about the sex. Lucky had, of course, because of the pee stick discovery, but even Lucky might have been stunned to silence to hear the de-virgining had taken place in the barn.

"Anna cares about you, too," Lucky finally said.

"She'll cry a lot again when you leave," Logan added.

"She'll be hurt," Riley piped in.

Maybe. Probably, Heath silently amended. Yeah, he was a jerk all right, but he was a jerk on orders, and that meant leaving whether he wanted to or not.

And he did want to leave, Heath assured himself.

He did.

Silently repeating that, Heath went to the guest room so he could finish packing.

HER BROTHERS WERE waiting for Anna when she got home. Hard to miss them since they were on the sofa in the living room.

She so didn't have the energy to deal with them now.

"You're all grounded," Anna said, going on the offensive. "Now, go to your rooms."

Of course, they didn't budge. Well, except to stand, and judging from the somber looks on their faces they had something serious to tell her. But she had something to say, too.

"I already know about Heath's deployment being denied. He texted me right after he got the news. He was at the base and couldn't talk, but he wanted to let me know that he's leaving tomorrow."

They stared at her as if expecting her to sprout an extra nose or something. Then Riley's hawkeyed gaze moved to the Victoria's Secret bag she was holding.

"Yes, I bought it for Heath," Anna admitted. "For me to wear for Heath," she amended when their stares turned blank. "It's red and slutty, and if you don't quit staring at me like that, I'll give you lots of details about what I want Heath to do to me while I'm wearing it."

Logan's eyes narrowed. Riley's jaw tightened. Lucky shrugged and went to her. He pulled her into his arms despite the fact she was as stiff as a statue from the mini hissy fit she'd just thrown.

"I've got two words for you," Lucky whispered to her. "Condom."

She pulled back, looked at him. "That's one word."

"If you wear what's in that bag, you'll need two condoms. Three if you skip what's in the bag all together and just show up in your birthday suit. Either way, condoms."

In that moment he was her favorite brother. Lucky had

always been her champion and not judgmental. Most of the time anyway. Plus, he was the only brother who talked safe sex with her. Or any kind of sex for that matter. He wasn't just her brother, he was her friend.

Anna kissed his cheek. "Thanks."

He shrugged in that lazy but cool way that only Lucky or a Greek god could manage. It was as if he drawled his shrugs. And his life.

Lucky returned the cheek kiss and apparently considered his brotherly/friendly duties done because he strolled toward the door and headed out. Logan went to her next.

"I love you," Logan said. "And no matter what happens, I'll be here for you. You can cry on my shoulder all you need. Or if you prefer, I can kick Heath's ass for you. Your choice."

She had to fight a smile, but she didn't have to fight it too hard because the nonsmiling emotions were just below the surface. "I don't want his ass kicked, but I might need the shoulder."

Logan tapped first one shoulder, then the other. "Any time. They're reserved just for you, and I swear *I told you so* will never cross my lips or my mind. You're a grown woman, and if you want to wear what's in that bag, then you have my blessing."

In that moment she loved Logan best. Logan had been her father more than her brother, mainly because he'd been the one to step up after their folks died. He'd been the one to bust her chops when she needed it and had been a whiz helping with her math homework.

Logan would walk through fire for her and not once complain. Well, maybe he would complain, but he'd still do it.

He kissed her forehead and headed off, not out the

door but to his old room. Since he lived in town and no longer spent many nights at the ranch, Logan must have wanted his shoulders to be nearby in the event of an impending crying spell.

Uh-oh.

It was Riley's turn.

"If Heath makes you cry again, I'm hitting him with the shovel," Riley growled. "And wear a robe with whatever's in that bag."

Anna sighed. The support of two out of three wasn't bad.

Riley sighed as well, and he pulled her into his arms. "FYI, Heath did some crying, too, after he left here that summer."

Anna wiggled out of his grip so she could see if he was serious or not. He was.

"I don't mean he actually shed tears," Riley went on, "but he cried in his own man kind of way."

"How do you know that?" she asked.

"Because I'm the one who drove him to his basic training." A muscle flickered in his jaw. A sign that he was remembering that day as unfondly as she was. Some of the anger returned. "Heath asked me to make sure you were okay. Can you believe it?"

"The bastard," Anna joked.

"He said it as if I needed to be reminded of it. I didn't. Not then, not now. If you need someone to make sure you're okay, I'll do it. As long as I don't have to hear any sex details. Or see what's in that bag. And I'll do that—minus the exceptions—because you're my sister."

Anna blinked back tears. In that moment, she loved Riley best. Yes, he was hardheaded, and they had a history of sibling squabbles. Plus, there was the time when he'd ruined all her dolls with camo paint and duct-tape combat boots, but still she loved every stubborn, camo-painting ounce of him.

Riley wasn't her father or her friend. He was her brother.

And sometimes, like now, that was exactly what a sister needed.

Chapter Six

Heath paced. Cursed. He figured this much debate hadn't gone into some battle plans, but a battle plan would have been easier than trying to figure out what to do about Anna.

Or better yet what to do *with* Anna.

If he went to her room, sex would happen. Then tomorrow he would leave—just as he'd done nine and a half years ago. That hadn't turned out so well, what with all the crying and her brothers wanting to shovel him.

If he didn't go to her room, sex wouldn't happen. But then he would have to leave things unsettled between them—again—as he'd apparently done before.

He was screwed either way, so Heath decided he might as well go for it. He threw open the door and nearly smacked right into some idiot wearing a hoodie and an army-green vinyl poncho.

Except this was no idiot. It was Anna, and in addition to the garb, she was also carrying a blue sock.

She practically pushed him back into his room and shut the door. "Shhh," she said. "Della and Stella's book club is meeting tonight."

He was still wrapping his mind around the fact that Anna was there, that she had come to him, and maybe that's why Heath couldn't quite wrap his mind around the book club or the poncho.

"There are six of them in the living room, and I had to sneak past them," Anna added when he gave her a blank look.

When Heath kept that blank look, Anna pulled off the poncho, and he saw the hoodie. No pants. No shoes.

Just a pair of really tiny devil-red panties.

He was sure his blank look disappeared because his mouth dropped open. This was the best kind of surprise.

"I didn't have a robe here at the ranch, and the plastic poncho felt sticky against my skin so I put on the hoodie," she explained. Then she unzipped it.

No top. No bra. Just the Be My heart locket dangling between her breasts. Heath thought maybe his tongue was doing some dangling, too.

"And the sock?" he asked.

She smiled and emptied the contents onto the bed. Condoms. At least a dozen of them.

"I took them from Lucky's bathroom," Anna explained. She was still whispering, but it had a giddiness to it. "The poncho and hoodie didn't have pockets so I put them in the sock. I only brought the normal-looking ones. Some had pictures on them and some were glow in the dark." Anna looked at him. "Why would a man need that?"

Heath didn't have a clue. He didn't need any illumination to find anything on Anna's body. His most vital organ agreed. In fact, it wanted to go on that particular search mission right now.

But there was a problem.

"You got my text saying I was leaving, right?" he asked.

She nodded. "Tomorrow. That's why I didn't want to wait until after the book club left. Sometimes they hang around until midnight if Della breaks out the tequila, and we don't have much time."

Not if they were planning on using all those condoms, they didn't, but Heath had to make sure that Anna was sure. She stripped off the hoodie, and he was sure she was sure.

At least he wanted her to be.

He wanted that even more when she slipped into his arms and kissed him. Heath was stupid and weak so it took him a moment to break the kiss.

"Anna, I don't want you hurt," he said.

She frowned. "I think that ship's sailed. I'll be hurt, but I'll get over it. And tonight you'll give me some really good memories to help me get over it, right?"

Yeah.

Whether they had sex or not, Anna would be hurt. Or at least she would be sad to see him go. Ditto for him being sad to leave her. But at least this way they'd have new memories, and they didn't need glow-in-the-dark condoms to do it.

Now that he had a clearly defined mission, Heath pulled her back to him to kiss her. One of those kisses that reached scorch level pretty darn fast. But Anna was aiming for fast, too, and not with just the kisses. She was already going after his zipper.

"We're going to play that scale-of-one-to-ten game," she insisted.

Maybe. But the way she was tugging at his zipper, it was possible she was also trying to finish this all way too fast. Tonight, he didn't want the kissing game, and he didn't want fast.

Heath stopped what she was doing by catching on to her wrists and putting her against the wall. He liked walls because it gave him some control…

Damn.

He had no control. Anna ground herself against him, sliding her leg up the outside of his so that the millimeter of red lace was right against his crotch. Apparently, the orgasm she'd had earlier in the barn hadn't done anything to take the edge off because she was going for another one very quickly.

Again, Heath tried to slow things down. With her leg still cradling his, he turned her, intending to put her against the dresser, but he tripped over the poncho and fell onto the bed.

With Anna on top of him.

"Let's play a game," she said. Definitely not a virginal tone or look. "I'll use just my tongue to find all your special spots. You don't have to give it a number rating. Just a grunt for pleasure. A groan for find another special spot that's more special."

"Men only have one special spot," he told her. Heath took her hand and put it over his sex.

She laughed. Not a humor kind of laugh but the sound of a woman who'd come to play. Or maybe give a little payback for the things he'd done to her in the tack room. Well, Heath wanted to play, too. After all, he had a nearly naked Anna straddling him, and her breasts were making his mouth water.

He managed a quick sample of her left nipple before she moved away. Anna didn't waste any time. With her hand still on his special spot, she went in search of others. His earlobe.

He grunted, but Heath didn't know if that was because, at the same time, she started lowering his zipper.

"That wasn't a loud enough grunt," she said and went after his neck.

Heath grunted. Again, mainly because she lowered the zipper, and when she did that, her breasts got closer to his mouth again. She didn't grunt when he kissed her there, but she did make that silky sound of pleasure that Heath would never tire of hearing.

He would have kept on kissing her breasts, but apparently it was special-spot search time again because she scooted lower and ran her tongue over his own left nipple.

Oh, yeah. He grunted.

Grunted some more when she circled his navel with her tongue. All that tonguing and circling though didn't stop her from getting his zipper all the way down, and as he had done to her earlier, she shimmied his jeans lower.

"You really do go commando," she said.

"Yep—"

He might have added more. Something clever or at least coherent, but her hands were on him. The condom, too. Heath wasn't sure when she'd opened one of the packets. Nor did he care. The woman had clever hands after all—

Hell.

He grunted loud enough to trigger an earthquake when she dropped down onto him. That's when he figured out really, really fast that the panties were crotchless and that he was in her warm and tight special place all the way to the hilt.

"That's not your tongue," he said through the grunts.

"So, I cheated."

The woman was evil. And damn good. Heath usually

liked to be the alpha when it came to sex, but even more than that, he liked taking turns with Anna. Apparently, she was going to make the most of her turn, too. She had the whole *ride 'em, cowgirl* motion going on. So fast that Heath knew this would all end too soon.

Of course, sixteen hours was going to be too soon.

As if she'd read his mind, she slowed. Anna put her palm on his chest and, still moving against his erection, leaned down and kissed him.

"After this," she said, "I want you all the way naked."

Heath thought that was a stellar idea. He wanted those panties off her, too, even though they fell into the *why bother* category of women's undergarments.

The locket whacked him in the face, but even that didn't put a damper on the moment. Heath just pushed the locket aside, gathered her close and let his cowgirl screw his brains out.

Chapter Seven

Anna wished there were some kind of anticry shot she could take. Even one that worked for just an hour or so would do. She figured she'd do plenty of crying after Heath had left, but she didn't want any tears shed in front of him.

Or in front of her brothers.

She wanted Heath to remember her smiling. Or maybe naked, since that's how he'd seen her for a good portion of the night. It was certainly how she wanted to remember him.

With that reminder/pep talk still fresh in her mind, Anna left her bedroom and went in search of Heath so she could give him that smiling goodbye she'd practiced in the mirror. But he wasn't in his bedroom. Or the living room. Or the kitchen. In fact no one was, and she figured they'd all cleared out to give her a chance to have a private goodbye with Heath.

Or maybe they'd cleared out because Heath was already gone. She had several moments of panic when she sprinted to the back porch to make sure his rental car was still there.

It was.

And so was Heath.

He was at the fence pasture, looking at some cows that'd been delivered that morning. He made a picture standing there with his foot on the bottom rung of the fence, his cream-colored cowboy hat slung low on his face.

He must have heard her approaching because he turned, smiling. It looked about as genuine as the one she was trying to keep on her face. Until he reached out, pulled her to him and kissed her.

Then the smiles were real.

"How soon before you leave?" she asked.

"Soon."

That reminder made her smile waver. Anna wasn't sure how far to push this part of the conversation, but there was something she had to know. "Are you feeling any better about the instructor job?"

"I've accepted it. Sometimes, that's the best you can do with crappy lemonade. Sorry," Heath added when she frowned. "It was just something Riley said. An analogy of sorts."

Riley not only needed a new threat, he needed new analogies, as well.

Since their time together was about to end, Anna reached into her pocket and took out the "gift" she'd gotten him on her shopping trip the day before. She hadn't wanted it to be a big gift because that would have made this goodbye seem, well, big.

Which it was.

But she didn't want it to feel big to him.

She took his hand and dropped the smashed penny in it. "It reminded me of your dog tags, and it's supposed to be good luck."

He stared at it, gave a slight smile. "Thanks."

"I was going to give you the red panties," she added, "but I thought it would look strange if the TSA went through your luggage."

Now she got the reaction she wanted. A bigger smile. A bigger kiss, too.

"I have something for you," he said. He took out a silver heart locket. It was similar to the other one he'd given her nine and a half years ago. Very similar.

Right down to the Be My engraving.

Anna checked to make sure she had on the original one. She did. And she was shaking her head until Heath opened it, and she saw what was inside. Not pictures of him and her.

But of her parents. Her dad on one side of the heart. Her mother on the other.

"Della got the pictures for me," he explained. "You said sometimes you forget their faces, and this way you won't forget."

Oh, God.

She was going to cry.

No matter how hard she blinked, the tears came, and they just kept coming.

"I'm sorry." Heath pulled her back in his arms. "I didn't know it would upset you."

"It doesn't," she said, sobbing. "It's a good kind of upset." Still sobbing. "Thank you, Heath, thank you."

He held her while she sobbed, and it took Anna several long moments to stop.

"I got you something else," he added.

Anna couldn't imagine getting anything better than the second locket. It was even more precious to her than the first one. But Heath must have thought "the more the better" because he took out a wad of lockets from his coat pocket.

"I went to the jewelry store this morning and bought every locket they had."

She had no doubts about that—none. There was another silver one, one gold and another in the shape of a cat's head.

"They're, uh, beautiful." Though she couldn't imagine needing that many lockets. Or the ugly one with the cat's head.

"I had them engraved," he added, "and this time I watched to make sure they did it right. You can choose which one you want."

It took her a second to realize he'd finished his sentence. Not "which one you want *to wear*." Not "which one you want *to keep*." Not "which one you want *to remember me by*."

Heath turned over one of the silver ones, and she saw the engraving there. One word.

Lover.

He put the Be My locket next to it, and she got the message then. Be my lover.

She laughed. "Does this mean you want to see more of me?"

"Well, I've already seen more, but I'd like to see more of you more often."

That dried any remnants of her tears, and she blurted out an idea she'd been toying with for days. "I could look into transferring to a law school in Florida." And she held her breath.

No smile from him. "I don't want you to sacrifice going to a school that maybe doesn't have as good of a reputation as the one you're in now."

"No sacrifice. There are a couple of really good ones. And besides, I was transferring anyway. Might as well transfer so you can—" she held up the two lockets to finish that thought "—Be My Lover."

Anna tested his neck again with a kiss. And her tongue.

"Keep that up, and you'll be my lover again right now," he grumbled.

"If that's supposed to make me behave, then it won't work. Not with the hayloft so close. How much time do you have before you need to leave for your flight?"

"Not enough time for the hayloft."

She kissed him again, and he seemed to change his mind about that. He started leading her in that direction.

"Not enough time for the hayloft unless we hurry," Heath amended.

Good. The kisses were working.

Since she'd already put her heart on the line, Anna put the rest of herself out there, too. "I don't want a fling."

"Good. Flings are overrated." He kissed her again. "And temporary."

She released the breath she didn't even know she'd been holding. Heath didn't want temporary. Nor a fling. He wanted sex.

That was a solid start since she wanted that, too.

"I'm not done," he said. "Remember, you pick the locket you want." He held up the next one, the gold one, and it also had a single word engraved on it.

Woman.

As in Be My Woman.

Yes, they were so going to that hayloft, and then she was going to the university to start that transfer to Florida.

"Can I wear both the *Lover* and *Woman*?" she asked. Because she wanted both.

"You haven't seen the third one yet."

And she probably couldn't see it before the next kiss crossed her eyes. Along with singeing her eyelashes.

Still, he put the locket in her hand just as her butt landed against the ladder. Anna backed up one step at a time, which wasn't easy to do with Heath kissing her like that. And he kept on kissing her until they made it all the way to the top of the hayloft.

But Anna froze when she saw what was engraved on the tacky cat's head locket.

Love.

"Be My Love," she said, putting the words together.

Putting *everything* together.

"The *L* word?" she asked.

Heath nodded. "Sometimes it's the only word that works. What about you? Does the *L* word work for you?"

Anna had to catch her breath just so she could speak. "It works perfectly for me." She kissed him. "Does this mean we're going steady?"

"Oh, yeah," Heath confirmed. "That, and a whole lot more."

* * * * *

COMING NEXT MONTH FROM

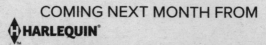

I N T R I G U E

Available March 22, 2016

#1629 TROUBLE WITH A BADGE
Appaloosa Pass Ranch • by Delores Fossen

Lawman Levi Crockett would never turn his back on PI Alexa Dearborn and the baby girl in her care. But as a serial killer stalks them, Levi must fight a powerful enemy—the desire between them.

#1630 DECEPTIONS
The Battling McGuire Boys • by Cynthia Eden

Secrets from their pasts threaten Elizabeth Snow and Mac McGuire—as much as the killer who seems to know their every move. Can they trust each other again? Or will a shocking truth prove fatal?

#1631 NAVY SEAL CAPTIVE
SEAL of My Own • by Elle James

Being abducted wasn't part of Sawyer Houston's R & R mission. Jenna Broyles claims she's rescuing the navy SEAL from unknown assailants. Only, it's her life on the line when the jilted bride becomes a target.

#1632 HEAVY ARTILLERY HUSBAND
Colby Agency: Family Secrets • by Debra Webb & Regan Black

When someone tries to kill security expert Sophia Leone, she's rescued by her husband, Frank—an army general she *thought* died a year ago. Now Sophia must trust her life to the man she married...the man she never stopped loving.

#1633 TEXAN'S BABY
Mason Ridge • by Barb Han

Bodyguard Dawson Hill is committed to protecting the woman who left him two years ago. Melanie Dixon has returned to Mason Ridge...with his son. Now a madman is threatening the family Dawson never dreamed he could have.

#1634 FULL FORCE FATHERHOOD
Orion Security • by Tyler Anne Snell

Fatherhood was never in the cards for Mark Tranton, until widow Kelli Crane and her daughter wrapped themselves around his heart. But digging into their past riles someone who won't rest until Kelli pays the ultimate price...

Levi eased into the shadows away from the pulsing neon
bar lights, and he listened. Waiting. It was hard, though,
to pick through the sounds of the crackling lights, the
wind and his own heartbeat drumming in his ears.

But somewhere there was the sound of an engine
running.

Because the driver had the headlights off, it took Levi
a moment to realize the car wasn't approaching from
the street but rather from the back of the bar. No road
there, just a parklike area that the local teenagers used for
making out. It could also be the very route a killer would
likely take.

Before the car eased to a stop, Levi whipped out his
gun and took aim. He froze. And not because of the
weather.

The person stepped out from the car, the watery lights
just enough for him to see her face. Not the Moonlight

Strangler but someone he did recognize. The pale blond hair. The willowy build.

Alexa.

Of all the people that Levi thought he might run into tonight, Alexa Dearborn wasn't anywhere on his radar. Heck, she shouldn't be anywhere near him, this bar or the town of Appaloosa Pass.

Because she had a bounty on her head.

Word on the street was that the hired guns who were after her had orders to shoot to kill.

It'd been five months since Levi had seen her, as the marshals had whisked her away into WITSEC to an unnamed place. A change of name, too. But five months wasn't nearly long enough for the memories to fade.

Don't miss
TROUBLE WITH A BADGE
by USA TODAY *bestselling author Delores Fossen,*
available in April 2016 wherever
Harlequin® Intrigue books and ebooks are sold.

www.Harlequin.com

EXCLUSIVE
Limited Time Offer

$1.⁰⁰ OFF

USA TODAY Bestselling Author
DELORES FOSSEN

The McCord Brothers are the most
eligible bachelors in Spring Hill, Texas.
But these cowboys are about to get
wrangled by the love of some very special
women—the kind who can melt hearts
and lay it all on the line.

TEXAS ON MY MIND

Available February 23, 2016.
Pick up your copy today!

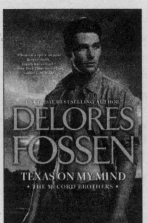

$7.99 U.S./$9.99 CAN.

HQN™

$1.⁰⁰ OFF
the purchase price of
TEXAS ON MY MIND by Delores Fossen.

Offer valid from February 23, 2016, to March 31, 2016.
Redeemable at participating retail outlets. Not redeemable at Barnes & Noble.
Limit one coupon per purchase. Valid in the U.S.A. and Canada only.